I083073

# PRICELESS WORDS

*A Collection of Short Stories* by Biff Price

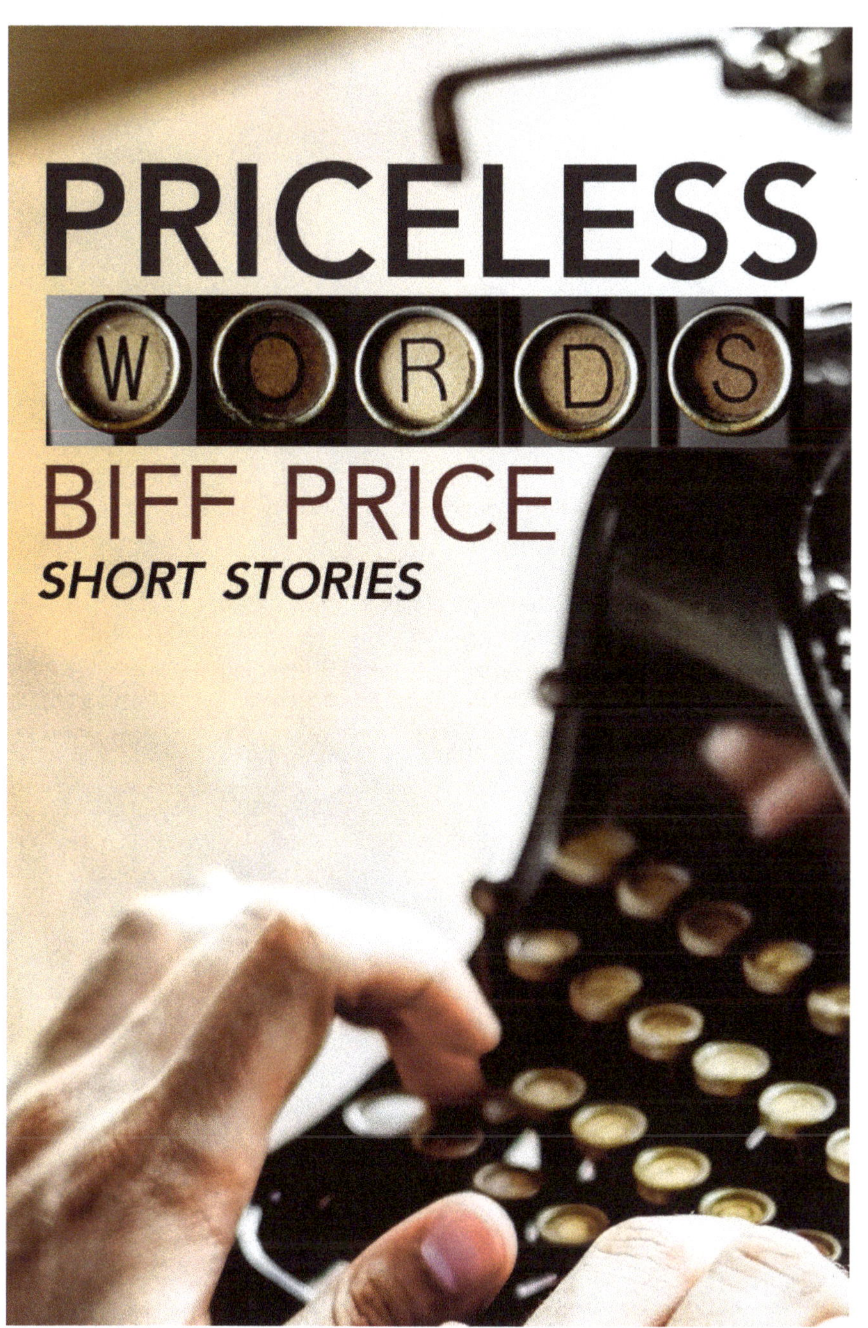

PRICELESS
WORDS
BIFF PRICE
SHORT STORIES

*Dedicated to those who know that sometimes the most powerful ideas are found in unexpected places. Therefore, reader, do not go forward in this book unless you are ready to go places you may never have been, see visions that may stir your soul, and risk realizing that there are far greater things in the universe than man alone.*

*Thank you,*
*—Biff*

# CONTENTS

Who Am I?

# Who Am I?

The doors were closed and locked at 10:00 a.m. I've been hiding in the maintenance closet since then. I look at my watch. It is 3:00 a.m. Time to move.

In the hours since I began my vigil, I've changed my clothes and placed them in a black gym bag. I am dressed all in black from my head to my feet in a tight-fitting black spandex top, matching pants, and black shoes with soft soles.

Finding the shoes was a problem. It took two months to locate them. I finally purchased them online.

My head is covered with a black ski mask, and I've blackened my face with camo. Only the whites of my eyes are visible.

The sword hangs at my side in its sheath. It is so sharp that I dare not touch the blade for fear of severing my fingers.

I pick up the gym bag, and quietly open the door, inch-by-inch until I see what lies before me in the darkened space. I don't dare forget the bag. It would be evidence.

I step into the space and stand silently. I listen carefully for a long moment and hear nothing. Like a shadow within a shadow, I move, ghost-like across the floor. They are there before me in their silence: unaware, unafraid and oblivious to my presence.

Slowly, as a lover would caress his beloved, I draw the sword from its sheath. The blade gleams in muted light as though lit from within. Holding the sword before me in the classic pose, I balance on the balls of my feet. My perfect stance comes from hours of practice. I am a warrior of the night. The time for retribution has come.

My feet are set, and with every ounce of power I possess, I thrust the sword through the middle of my first victim. The stroke is clean and sure. Hardly a noise is made.

I withdraw the blade and thrust again, and again. Suddenly, I am filled with rage, but I dare not give myself up to it.

I withdraw the blade and just as quickly thrust it through my next victim, and the next, and the next … I lose control, and malice rises up in me, like bile.

I thrust and slash, cutting them every which way. I hack, and stab, and rend with such fury that the scene before me is littered with parts. Some are cut in two, others grotesquely injured, gaping wounds spilling their insides all about me.

As suddenly as it began, the frenzy leaves me and sensibility returns.

Sweat pours inside my tight clothing. My head is drenched beneath my knitted wool ski mask.

I place the sword into its sheath, wipe my eyes with sweaty hands, pick up my bag and glide silently across the floor.

I turn and look at the carnage I've left behind. The damage appears to be incredible, even in the dim light, a testament to my skill and fury.

I spared no one. They are heaped in mounds upon the floor, one upon another. Daylight will reveal the horror of what I've done.

I smile in satisfaction. This will teach them to overcharge me.

Kellogg's, Post, Quaker Oats and all the rest lie hacked and dismembered in the aisle.

I push open the door and step into the night.

# THE GAME

# THE GAME

Poochie Chambers was a strange little man who lived off the grid. His father had left his mother before he was born, and his mother left him on the steps of St. Mary's convent near Matawan, New Jersey a week after his birth.

At the age of 18 he had to wear shoes with inch-thick soles to reach 5 feet in height, weighed 98 pounds soaking wet, and his blue eyes looked out of a face that only a mother could love. He was also deaf and dumb.

The good Sisters had taken him into their orphanage where he grew up. No one wanted to adopt him, so he lived there until he was 18. His favorite nun, Sister Madeline, took him under her wing as he grew, and she saw to it that he learned sign language,  and to read and write. She smiled at him every day and did her best to protect him from the other children who often made fun of him.

When he was eight he found a puppy on the grounds of the convent, and he secretly kept it in a small box hidden in a garden shed, sneaking food to it from the cafeteria, and watching over it until Sister Madeline had gone looking for him one day and discovered the child and the little dog together. She tried to explain that he could not keep the puppy, but her statement elicited a flood of tears, and, since he could not speak, a whoosh of air from his mouth.

Sister Madeline was overcome with remorse because he was in such a sad state, and she reassured him that he could keep the little animal until a good home was found for it.

The Sisters had to choose a name for the child when he had been left to their care, so they named him Oswald Chambers, after the early twentieth-century Scottish Baptist and Holiness Movement evangelist and teacher, best known for the devotional *My Utmost for His Highest*. One of the Sisters had been reading the book at the time, and it was she who'd suggested the name.

Oswald became Ozzie to the other children, and that was his

name, until the dog showed up. Fred Sampson, the orphanage bully, who was 13, declared that Ozzie would henceforth be known as Poochie when word of the little dog reached the rest of the convent community. The dog was a mixed breed, part terrier and part spaniel, and it was as nondescript as its young master.

The sisters allowed the boy to keep the dog only because of his physical infirmities, and it was the first and last dog to grace the institution. Unable to communicate aloud, "Poochie" Chambers wrote that he wanted Sister Madeline to name the pup, so she chose the name Spot because it was simple and easy to remember.

Poochie and Spot were inseparable. Spot slept in Poochie's bed and went everywhere with him except to the chapel, Poochie's favorite place. It was almost always quiet in the chapel except when the sisters gathered for vespers. This never bothered Poochie when the sisters were singing because he couldn't hear anything at all.

For their part, the sisters tolerated his presence because he might as well have been part of the furniture. When he was not reading books, or playing with Spot, he would make his way to the chapel and sit silently in the back row looking at the powerfully somber cross above the altar, and the form of the One who hung there.

Because he could not hear or speak, others assumed that Poochie was not very bright. Because he had no frame of reference, he did not know what it was to be either smart or dumb. He only knew that he liked to read books, and he loved to play with his dog. He was, for the most part, shunned by the other children and teens in residence at the orphanage. No one knew his secret.

The highest recorded I.Q. in human beings was estimated to be between 250 and 300 points on the measurable scale. The late William James Sidis held the title, but the man had died in anonymity and done nothing to merit adulation. Other less intelligent men, such as Albert Einstein, were well known as true geniuses all over the world.

Poochie Chamber's I.Q. could not be measured. No one would

have ever thought to test the intelligence of a deafmute living in a convent orphanage. The boy loved to read. Poochie had a photographic memory. By the age of nine, he had read the Bible from cover to cover. He remembered every word of it.

There was a small library at the orphanage. Poochie read every book in it. The sisters had their own library of sacred books, as well as recreational reading. Poochie devoured all of them.

Being so different from so-called normal people, Poochie sensed that if he revealed his ability, especially to the other kids, he would be ostracized, pummeled and beaten even more than he already was.

He had read enough to know that he had to keep his secret from the Sisters, as well. He was afraid that he would be regarded as a freak and locked up in some government institution to be evaluated and studied. He kept a low profile.

Sadly, Sister Madeline fell ill with cancer, and she died when Poochie was 13 years old. Spot was hit by a delivery truck in the convent parking lot two months later. Poochie cried for his dog and Sister Madeline every night, but no one heard his sobs.

He had lost his protector and pup. He was more alone than he had ever been. He spent hours sitting in the last pew in the chapel, staring silently at the Man on the cross.

The Sisters felt sorry for Poochie. Knowing that he would never amount to anything, the Reverend Mother Beatrix allowed Poochie to do small jobs around the convent. Poochie always followed orders perfectly. No one knew that this was because he never forgot anything. He had perfect recall.

She also allowed him to take the town bus to the local library, and he spent his Saturdays there reading every book in sight. The people at the library thought of him as a model visitor because he did not make noise.

Poochie found new things to occupy his mind. He fell in love with mathematics. He memorized every textbook on the subject. When a librarian showed him how to use a computer, he was off and running.

The young woman had explained to him that he had to be careful about what was true and not true on the Internet. She had given him a printed pamphlet that clearly outlined the pitfalls and the benefits of being online.

At 15, he had read every textbook on mathematics, physics and science, and the librarians had ordered in books for him not available in the town library. They thought that he was pretending to read such difficult subjects, and no one had any idea that the small, slight, silent boy with the homely face had any clear idea about anything.

When Poochie turned 18, the Reverend Mother asked the local chapter of the Association of Retarded Citizens (ARC) to find him a home with a family that would be willing to take him in. The thought was that a job could be found for him, perhaps at a Goodwill store, or maybe with some other organization that hired handicapped people.

To the surprise and dismay of the sisters, Poochie disappeared. The police were called, but no trace of him could be found. It was as if he had left the face of the Earth. Missing children often appear on milk cartons, but Poochie was anything but photogenic.

Poochie Chambers wore a disguise from that day forward. He made his way to Atlantic City, walked into a casino, and sat down at a blackjack table. The dealer, a middle-aged woman, looked at him and said, "You can't be old enough to be at this table. You'll have to leave!"

Poochie handed her a driver's license with his picture on it. It looked real, and it stated that he was 22 years old. He had a mustache, glasses, wore his hair long, and his clothing was neat and pressed.

"Why can't you speak to me? I want to hear your voice," the dealer said.

Poochie handed her a card that read, "I am mute and deaf. I read lips and use sign language. Please don't discriminate against me."

Her look softened. She said, "All right, but do you know how to play this game? If you do, I suggest that you find a less expensive table. This is a $25.00 minimum."

Poochie placed a hundred dollar bill on the table. The dealer gave him his chips. Thirty minutes later he smiled, got down from his stool, and took $500 in chips to cash them in.

The dealer watched him leave, smiling at his back. She was thinking how sad it would be not to be able to speak or hear.

In the next two hours Poochie won $500.00 at blackjack tables in four other casinos, then took his winnings to his car, a 10-year old Honda Civic parked in the Tropicana garage. He left the garage and took the Black Horse Pike out of the city to a motel a mile from town.

Being deaf, he was taking great risks to drive, but he did so by observing speed limits and his mirrors. He went to his room and counted his money. He had $2,500.00 in winnings. This would be his bankroll.

The motel was inexpensive compared to the hotels in A.C. He kept his living expenses low. For dinner he had a Big Mac, Coke and fries in the small refrigerator.

Poochie didn't bother to turn on the TV. He never looked at TV. Instead, he picked up a book on Quantum Physics with a bookmark near the middle.  He read more on the subject while he ate.

He was about to turn 19, and he was pretending that he was over 21. In that week he won over $10,000.00 at the casinos, in $500.00 increments. He was a master of numbers, a genius at odds, and having perfect recall didn't hurt.

From reading about the casino industry, he knew they watched for card counters and subterfuge. Maintaining a low profile was the only way to go. He gave himself three weeks in Atlantic City. He had no desire for confrontation.

Poochie played for another two weeks. He stuck with blackjack and avoided other games. Slots were of no interest to him. Neither was craps. He knew his diminutive size caused him to stick out like a sore thumb as he moved through crowds of normal-sized people, so he never walked through a casino in the same direction, and he never played at the same tables. He had no desire to become known.

Poochie wasn't greedy. At the end of three weeks he had won $53,000.00. It was time to head for Vegas. He had noticed a large Catholic church when he had come onto the southern end of Absecon Island and driven through Longport and Margate. He had already checked out of his motel. All his worldly possessions were in his car.

He stopped at the church and waited until an old woman had left the church. He moved swiftly down the aisle and placed a white envelope on the altar. In neat script on the outside of the envelope he had written, "For Him and His Great Work." Poochie left the church.

A half hour later Father John Kelly found the envelope, opened it, and discovered $10,000 inside. He went down on his knees and bowed his head.

"Thank you, Lord … thank you!" The unexpected gift would help the church meet its budget shortfall for the previous three months.

Poochie drove into Somers Point and began his journey westward. He preferred back roads and scenery whenever he could avoid busy highways. He did not need a GPS system. He had memorized all the maps from New Jersey to Nevada. It took him nine days to get to Vegas. He had stopped often to gaze at new sights.

*Chapter Two*

Atlantic City, New Jersey has a population of 39,551 people and eight casinos. Las Vegas, Nevada has a population of 603,488—a total metropolitan area population of 2,027,828 people—and 76 casinos.

Poochie had improved his odds, and he also now had the ability to amass a fortune and achieve his dream. Fifteen of the 25 largest hotels in the world are on or near the strip in Las Vegas, but these were too expensive, too flashy, and offered too much exposure to the likes of someone who looked like Poochie Chambers.

He had no credit cards, and he never intended to have one. He paid cash. Las Vegas is a city where cash, in proper amounts, would not run up a red flag. Poochie found lodging at a small, relatively cheap hotel at the edge of town. He planned his campaign, eating fast food and drawing a schedule on a business desk-sized calendar that he purchased at a Staples store.

He could win larger amounts at many Vegas casinos than he had in Atlantic City and still maintain a low profile. He had gotten a list of every Vegas club, and he carefully laid out a six-month course of action. He would run the list the way a high roller would run the table. He would devote Monday through Friday to his "work" as he thought of it. Saturdays he would be in the library; Sundays he would go to church.

Seven months in, Poochie made an offer on a house in Summerlin Village, west of Vegas. By this time he had a completely fabricated persona in the name of Walter J. Henderson. Digging in newspaper files, he had chosen the name of a man who had been dead for a hundred years. He was careful to find the right people to help him prepare the documentation. Cash was the grease that turned the wheel. He had a birth certificate, driver's license, and Social Security card, all of which looked authentic.

Poochie had a large safe installed in the wall of the wine cellar in the basement of his new house. He upgraded his car to a late-model, beige Buick. He had his house furnished and decorated by a small design firm in Summerlin, and then he began the third phase of his plan.

Poochie fed his mind by spending as much time as possible at two nearby libraries: Summerlin Library on Inner Circle and Rainbow Library on North Buffalo Drive. A year had passed and his fortune was growing.

In early June he was in the Summerlin Library on a Saturday when his life changed forever. Poochie was on a computer searching out places that he thought he might consider for his final move. He had always been fascinated by the Pacific Northwest, and he found a picture that was absolutely beautiful. It was a scene photographed along the Pacific coast highway. He looked at where the shot had been taken. It was in Oregon. The town was named Cannon Beach.

Poochie Chambers had found his destination. He knew that one day he would live in that town, but there was much to do before he could ever go there. He spent 45 minutes scrolling through pictures of the rocks, beaches and communities along the Oregon coast, but he always found himself drawn back to Cannon Beach.

He looked up and discovered that the hours had flown by too quickly. The library would be closing in fifteen minutes. He exited from the program, signed off, and stood up. As he turned around, he met the eyes of a young woman sitting at a table a few feet away. She was blond with warm brown eyes and an attractive face. She looked away, and Poochie looked down at the floor.

Women, old and young, had no time for Poochie. He was too small, and he was not attractive. He never expected to go on a date, much less have someone fall in love with him.

Poochie made his way to the door, went to his car, and drove home.

Months passed and Poochie steadily saved his winnings. The amount of money in his safe had passed the million dollar mark. His routine continued. He was still a long way from his goal. He did not have a bank account, and he did not want one. He wanted no parts of a world that would eat him alive, given the chance. Having so much money in cash was a problem, and he intended to get a lot more to build his dream. He tried not to worry about the logistics of it.

Six months later he was in the casino at the Monte Carlo in Vegas sitting at a blackjack table where two men opposite him were having a conversation. He had developed an incredibly adept ability to read lips, primarily because of his need for self-preservation, and he watched with interest what they were saying to each other.

"Did you hear about The Game?"

"What game? There are games everywhere. This whole city is one big game!" the man laughed.

"This is different. There is a supposed to be a blackjack game played in Vegas by the highest of high rollers. It's by invitation only. I heard that you have to put up five million to play, if you are even invited to the game. It's never held in the same place, and the man who runs it is so secretive that no one knows his name."

"Well, that's great! We don't have to worry about that, do we? Who cares? You got five million? I'm lucky if I got five hundred! Hey, it's a great story. Maybe they can make a movie about it! I'm cashing out. I've got to get home…"

Poochie played the hand, took his chips and walked to the window to get his money. All the while he was thinking, 'The Game? Maybe I could play it…if it's real.'

He celebrated his 22nd birthday, although the actual day was a mystery. His birthday was dated from the day the Sisters had found him, but the actual day of his birth was probably a week before that.

He had been spending the day at the Summerlin Library sitting at a table reading about a medical procedure to correct deafness when someone sat down opposite him. He looked up and warm brown eyes were looking back at him. He immediately looked back at the page he was reading.

He had recognized her face, although he had not seen her in months. After a few moments his eyes were drawn upward to hers. She was staring at him. No one even looked at him unless they had to. He looked back at the page, and then looked up again. She was still staring at him.

He reached into his jacket and took out the card and showed it to her.

She read it. Then, she signed to him, "I know. I am, too."

For a moment he didn't know how to react. Then, he signed, "You are what?"

"Deaf. I'm deaf. Like you." She smiled at Poochie, and it was as if the sun had come out.

He signed, "How can you be deaf? You don't look deaf!"

She signed, "You're silly. No one looks deaf."

He smiled. He signed, "I'm also mute. That makes me double dumb!"

Her smile changed to a frown. She signed, "Don't call yourself dumb. You're not dumb. You wouldn't be reading the things you read if you were dumb! I've seen you choose your books and magazines. You are probably the smartest man who comes into this library."

Poochie Chambers was stunned. No one, with the exception of the Sisters at the convent, had ever called him anything but an idiot or a retard when he was growing up. This beautiful creature had just said he was smart! He stared back at her.

She signed, "What's your name?"

For some reason he could not explain, he only wanted to tell her the truth. His note pad was next to his left hand, his writing hand. He picked up his pen and wrote, "My name is Oswald. It's not the name I use. I don't use my real name."

In Vegas, this wasn't unusual. That was one of the reasons why it's said that what happens in Vegas stays in Vegas.

She read what he had written. "What's your last name?"

He wrote, "Chambers. What's your name?"

She had a notepad with her. She took a pen out of a small brown purse and wrote, "My name is Eleanor Fields."

Poochie wrote, "I am very pleased to meet you, Eleanor Fields. You're the first person I've ever met who didn't look down on me. I know. I'm short. It's hard not to look down on me … that's a joke."

Eleanor wrote, "Ha ha! Very funny. You have a sense of humor, and you're good looking!"

He wrote back, "Now *you're* the one who is being funny. I've been called many things, but good looking has never been one of them!"

Poochie's life had changed again. The two became friends, and they agreed to meet at the library on Saturdays as often as possible.

Because they communicated in silence, they didn't not disturb other library patrons. Here, their handicaps were an asset.

Months passed. The two became best friends on their Saturday meetings at the library, so Poochie was disappointed when several weeks went by without Eleanor showing up. When she finally returned, he could hardly control himself enough to sign.

Instead, he wrote, "I haven't seen you in weeks. Where have you been?"

She wrote, "I went to visit my grandmother in Winslow, Arizona. She was very sick …"

Poochie wrote, "I'm sorry to hear that. Were you helping to take care of her?"

"Yes, but she passed away. I just got back from there."

He did not know what to write, and he sat silently for awhile.

Finally, he wrote, "I had someone in my life I loved very much. She died, too!"

Eleanor reached across the table and gently placed her hand on his. Her warm brown eyes had a gleam of tears in them, and Poochie Chambers fell in love in that moment.

Patrons saw Poochie and Eleanor together. Some made fun of them, but others thought it was an endearing sight: two deaf mutes spending time together.

Eleanor was deaf, but she was not mute. As a child she could hear and speak, but when she lost her hearing she gave up trying to speak because other children made fun of her. Her father had abandoned her mother and her when she became deaf. Her mother worked as a maid at the Bellagio, and they had an apartment at the edge of town.

Life was not easy. Eleanor had found work at a non-profit charity in Summerlin as a book-keeper. Because she worked in a back office away from people, she did not have to be an object of pity or ridicule.

She had attended a community college and managed to get a two-year degree. She loved to read good fiction, and her Saturday library visits focused on world history, accounting, economics and languages. She taught herself to read Spanish, but she would never be able to speak it, not being able to hear it spoken aloud.

Poochie did not read fiction, but she urged him to try it. He did, and he discovered that the imagination of writers wasn't a bad thing, but his preference for challenging non-fiction did not change.

He told her as much as he thought he should. He did not lie to her, but he avoided telling her his dreams and goals.

His fortune grew. A year passed, then two. Poochie had been reading everything he could on restoring hearing because he thought Eleanor might have a chance to hear again. He suspected he would not be able to because of his birth defects. He read about Stapedectomy, Transtympanic Injections, medications, hearing aids, the best centers for treatment, the names of physicians in the discipline, and much more.

Finally, he read about otosclerosis, the decreased movement of the stapes, or stirrup bone that causes conductive hearing loss. Being the next thing to dirt-poor, Eleanor would never have the money to find out if she could be helped. She and her mother lived hand-to-mouth so her prospects for ever being able to hear again were slim to none.

Poochie made up his mind. He settled on the University of California San Francisco Cochlear Implant Center. Poochie prepared and printed a three-page report from his computer at home. One Saturday he placed the report in a folder, and he handed it to Eleanor at the library.

She signed, "What's this?"

"Please read it," he signed. "I want to go on a journey so we can both find out if anything can be done to help us."

Eleanor took the folder and opened it. She read through it, then placed it on the table. She looked at it for a long moment. She raised her eyes and looked at him. She took her pad and wrote, "I can't afford this. I have no money for anything. It's a wonderful dream, but it's not possible."

Poochie reached across the table and handed her another piece of paper. He signed, "Please read this."

Eleanor took the page and read.

*Dearest Eleanor,*

*As my one and only friend in the world … it is time you knew more about me. I lack many things—hearing, speech, height, weight, and I don't look like Brad Pitt. I look more like Brad's brother that they don't talk about. His name is Arm. Get it? (It's O.K. to laugh!)*

*One thing I do not lack is money. This is not a problem for me. One day I will tell you everything there is to know about me. From this day forward you and your Mom will have no more money problems.*

*It is my intention to fly us to the city by the bay and see if these people can help us. Say the word, pick the date, and off we go. You are my friend. What good is money if we don't use it for the best purposes?"*

*Love, Ozzie*

Tears were streaming down Eleanor's face when she looked up.

Poochie reached across the table with his left hand and gently brushed them away. He mouthed the words, "It's all right. It's going to be all right from now on. I promise."

Poochie was true to his word. He arranged to buy a house for Eleanor and her mother in his neighborhood, furnished it, and helped them move in. Being used to Eleanor's handicap, her mother, Rachel, was not put off by Poochie's appearance or his handicaps.

Being incredibly smart, Poochie had arranged for a huge amount of cash to be transported through less-than-official means to a bank on an island where people looked the other way. Using the Henderson persona, he had opened accounts in a local bank, and a large money transfer was made from the island bank to the Henderson checking account and savings account.

The Henderson account was used to pay for the house in Rachel's and Eleanor's names, and a new white Acura TL was waiting in the garage when they arrived.

The celebration party was extremely happy even though only one of the participants could hear and speak! A quarter of a million dollars was transferred into a joint checking account in the names of Eleanor and Rachel. Funds from this account would be used to pay taxes, buy food, and live a normal life.

Rachel chose to keep her job at the Bellagio. Eleanor found a better paying job closer to home. When one is unable to speak or hear, communication must be by letter, written note, email and social media. It took six months of back and forth, but arrangements were finally made, and Rachel saw Eleanor and Ozzie, as she called him, off on their flight to San Francisco.

The medical evaluations were made, and, as Poochie suspected, he was not a good candidate. Eleanor, on the other hand, could benefit from cochlear implant surgery. The procedure was scheduled, a week passed, and Poochie was sitting by Eleanor when she heard her doctor pronounce his opinion that her operation would be successful.

Her tears flowed freely, and she tried to utter her first words in 15 years. Her effort was garbled, but time, patience, practice and desire would lead to the return of a normal voice, technologically-enabled hearing, and the end of the derision and pity of other people.

A few days later they spent three days touring San Francisco, riding cable cars, visiting Alcatraz prison, watching the sea lions, and enjoying Fisherman's Wharf.

Eleanor's doctor advised them to stay on the ground for their return trip as a precaution. Poochie rented a car and they drove north. They enjoyed Muir Woods, Napa, Sonoma and the redwood forests, and the coast of Oregon was spectacular. Driving north to south affords the best views driving on the Pacific side of the coastal highway, but they enjoyed the drive and finally arrived in the beautiful town of Cannon Beach, Oregon.

They found a parking spot, and Eleanor urged Poochie to go down to the beach by himself. She would follow a few minutes later. She gave him plenty of time.

As for Poochie, he felt like he never had before. Haystack Rock and the rocks adjacent to it were beautiful. He stared in wonder.

Eleanor found him sitting on a tree trunk looking at the ocean.

When she slid her arm around him she saw the tears running down his face. He was home. This was where he wanted to be.

They rented adjacent rooms at the lovely Tolovana Inn for three nights. They wandered through the town, looking at everything, and stopped at a real estate office and talked to Jane Emerson. It was awkward, at first, but through sign language, writing on notepads, and gestures, they managed to convince her that they were for real, and that they could afford anything she had for sale. It was an interesting meeting.

Poochie had a written three-page description of what he wanted, and advised Ms. Emerson that he hoped to be ready to move to Cannon Beach in three years. She said that was a long time, but he insisted that it was realistic. He also said that if she found the right property between now and then, he would make a good offer on it.

They parted company, and Eleanor and Poochie took an inland route back to Vegas. It was a long drive, but there were many wonderful things to see. Poochie took lots of pictures.

*Chapter Three*

Two years slipped by. Poochie was nearing his goal of $10 million dollars. He had corresponded with Jane Emerson in Cannon Beach regularly. Mid-way through the second year she had found what he thought of as the perfect place for his dream. The home was situated with a wonderful view of Haystack Rock. The price was 2.4 million. He made an offer of 2.1 million. The owner countered at 2.3, and they finally agreed at 2.25 million.

Eleanor did not know that this was only part of Poochie's dream. The closing was scheduled. Poochie and Eleanor flew to Oregon, rented a car, and made their way to Cannon Beach.

The owner was a bit shaken when he saw the couple who showed up to buy his property, but Eleanor's voice and diction had improved greatly, and when he saw the check he breathed a sigh of relief.

They did a walk through before the closing. Everything was satisfactory. In fact, it was splendid. Eleanor said that Ozzie had made a fantastic choice. Her tears flowed freely when she learned at the closing that Poochie had put her on the deed as an equal owner. She had fallen in love with Cannon Beach, as well, but she had not thought that it would be part of her life.

The trip home was interesting. She signed and he signed in return. They discussed the future. He told her that he wanted to spend two more years in Vegas and then move to Cannon Beach permanently. Then he explained the rest of his dream.

Eleanor was overwhelmed with his vision and ideas. She cried more tears of joy.

~ ~ ~

The Game had been going on for a long, long time. It even pre-dated Las Vegas. Its origins were in the dim past, so long ago that only one knew when it had begun, and that was the one who hosted The Game.

No one ever walked into The Game. Participation was by invitation only. It was held each year at a different location. No one ever knew where that location would be until the invitation arrived. Included in the invitation was an iron-clad agreement that had to be signed, and God help anyone who violated that agreement.

The Game was the stuff of urban legend. People had heard of it, but most people didn't believe it was real. Those who had participated in The Game over the years were sworn to silence. The truth was that those who had played The Game had been so shaken by the experience that they had no desire to elaborate about it to anyone.

There were three criteria for being invited to The Game. First, the individual had to be extremely wealthy and able to pay the $5 million dollar entrance fee. Second, that person had to sign the agreement and state, on pain-of-death, that he or she would never reveal information about The Game or its host, and third, the player must be among the best high rollers in the world.

The host of The Game was very tall, at least six foot six. He was powerfully built, with huge hands. His skin was pale, and his hair was black, as were his eyes. He always dressed in black from head to foot: black trousers, shirt, tie, shoes, belt, etc. He wore no ring, watch or other jewelry. Strangely, no one could remember his face after they played The Game. No one could describe his features. No one knew his name. He did not provide it.

Only the wealthiest high rollers in the world were summoned to The Game. They were people who had vast fortunes, and who loved blackjack. No one was ever invited back to The Game a second time.

Unknown to the players, no one had ever beaten the Dealer in the long history of The Game. The Game might be held high atop a beautiful hotel in a kingly suite, in a back room off a seedy street, or at a palatial estate with gates, guards and tight security. The host of The Game always picked the location.

The thrill of The Game was the chance to play blackjack against the best players in the world, for the highest stakes. The number of players was always limited to six: five players plus the host, who was incredibly smart. He kept tabs on world blackjack players, and was worth so much money himself that the world would have been incredulous at the amount of his fortune.

The host did not lose. He had started The Game, and he would never be beaten. This was the way it was. Those who were invited to play against him did not know that they could not beat him. They were people of intelligence, great accomplishment, extreme wealth, and used to the best that life could provide. They waged sums of money that ordinary people could not imagine.

The thrill of the cards on a blackjack table was like an opiate to them. Whether they won or lost millions was of no consequence. Money did not matter. Winning was all that mattered.

The host had been perplexed for some time. Nothing ever got by him, but something had been going on in his city for several years now, and it was nagging at the edge of his awareness. Somewhere out there, a player of unparalleled ability had appeared in Vegas. The player was careful, steady, unwavering, and brilliant. He or she had won millions in the last few years. The Dealer and host of The Game had become aware of the activity when it began, but because of the small amounts that were being won he had not paid attention. Until, one day, he realized that someone was playing brilliantly and winning steadily. He was intrigued.

He had to find out who the player was. It required two years, but he finally uncovered a name: Henderson. Whoever Henderson was, he was not a captain of industry or a billionaire, but he was a player of incredible skill. Apparently, this Henderson did not lose!

The Dealer had beaten the best players in history. All of them. The temptation was too great. He had to track down Henderson and play him. He had to show the man that no one could possibly win against him.

~ ~ ~

The invitation to The Game did not come by mail. It was handed to Poochie as he sat at a blackjack table in The Venetian. When he got home he opened the manila folder and looked through the documents. He sat for two hours thinking about what he should do.

He wasn't sure how anyone could have identified him.

He left his home and drove down the street. He saw a church ahead, pulled to the curb, parked, and went inside. He sat in the back pew looking at the cross above the altar. He didn't know what kind of church it was, and he didn't care. It wasn't important.

When he got back home, he signed the documents and placed them in an envelope. He drove to the local post office and mailed it. He kept the card containing the address, time and date of The Game, but did not say anything to Eleanor. He did not want her to be involved, or to worry about him.

On the specified date, Poochie arrived at the massive, gated estate.

Security guards posted outside looked at the little man in his Buick in wonder. The others who had already arrived at the estate had come in the backs of limos, but this little man had driven himself. Nevertheless, he had an invitation in his possession, so they admitted him.

Poochie parked his car and walked up the steps and through the front door.

A butler met him and led him across a huge foyer to a set of high, polished mahogany doors that opened onto a magnificent paneled room. A table was waiting, and five men were seated at it. A Saudi Arabian prince, a shipping magnate from the Baltic nations, a Texas oil tycoon, a diamond baron from South Africa, and the Dealer waited at the table.

When Poochie entered the room, the oil tycoon started to laugh. He was joined by the others.

The tycoon finally managed to control himself and said, "What is this? Are we going to play against a midget? Look at him! This is hysterical!"

The others agreed with his analysis, offering their laughter and comments, until the silence of their host stopped their outburst. The Dealer was staring in wonder at Poochie, his black eyes glittering in the light.

"Mr. Henderson, welcome to The Game. Come, join us. Please take a seat," he said.

Poochie walked to the chair indicated and sat down.

"You have proof of fortune, do you not?" the Dealer continued.

Poochie placed the requested information on the table in front of the Dealer, who examined it with keen interest. When he was satisfied that it was genuine, he said, "Why are you silent? Are you afraid? Has an error been made in inviting you here? If so, it is the first error I have ever made! Should you be allowed to play with such opponents? Tell me! Speak!"

Poochie took out his card and handed it to the man who stared at him.

The Dealer read the card and a look of disbelief came over his features. He finally managed to say, "Gentlemen ... not only is Mr. Henderson tiny, he is also deaf and dumb! This is extraordinary! I will allow him to play only if you will allow it. What say you?"

The men broke out in consternation with complaints about Poochie's condition. One man referred to him as an idiot. How dare he even come to The Game!

The bickering had gone on for a few minutes when the Dealer raised his hand and said, "Please, let's settle this. Mr. Henderson was invited just like you because he has the money to play, and he is also a player of consummate skill. Time slips away. It is 6:00 p.m. It is going to be a long night. Let's get on with it. He will either stay or leave. Decide!"

The latter was said with such force that the men quieted their complaints. The South African spoke up first.

"All right. Let him stay. At least he won't be able to bother us with any whining or compaining when we clean him out."

The others laughed heartily. The Game began.

By midnight the oil tycoon and the Saudi prince were gone. The shipping magnate and the diamond baron were barely holding on, and roughly equal stacks of chips stood in front of the Dealer and little Mr. Henderson.

The Dealer had never seen anyone like the small man in all his years of playing The Game. He was enthralled and a little concerned.

The diamond baron left the game an hour later. Just three players remained. The shipping magnate had rallied somewhat. The pile of chips in front of the little man rose slightly higher than the stacks in front of the Dealer.

The magnate finally gave up a few minutes before 2:00 a.m. and left to go back to his hotel.

Now, the Dealer faced Poochie alone.

At 4:15 a.m. the Dealer had been reduced to a tiny stack of chips; while a vast mound rested in front of the little man. It was so high that Poochie could barely see over it.

"Who the hell are you?" the Dealer shouted in consternation.

Poochie wrote on his notepad and held it up. It read, "My name is Henderson."

"That's not what I need to know. No one has ever done what you have done! No one! Damn it, who are you? What are you?"

Poochie wrote, "That doesn't matter. I came to play blackjack. I read the rules. I obey them. I am here to play. That's all. Shall we finish The Game?"

The Dealer looked at him. He picked up the cards and dealt them. A few moments later all the chips on the table were in front of Poochie.

Poochie wrote, "Good game. You are a fantastic player! How much have I won?"

The Dealer stood up from his chair and stared angrily down at the little man before him.

"How much? You can't count that high. How much, indeed! This is unacceptable! I cannot lose! Damn you! Do you know who I am?"

Poochie wrote, "I think I know who you are, but that means nothing here. The Game is over. Even you must abide by the rules, because you wrote them. I won, fair and square. I'm tired. I need to get some sleep."

The Dealer said, "No, wait! One more hand—winner take all. Give me one more chance. It's not fair!"

Poochie looked up. The Dealer towered over him. After a long moment he wrote, "Fair? All right, I will play one more hand. It has been great fun. If you win you have all your money. But, if I win, I get the money, and there is one more condition."

The Dealer smiled a chilling smile. "Thank you for giving me another chance. You are most gracious, but what is your condition? What else do you want?"

Poochie wrote, "If I win, you must become like me."

The powerful figure of the Dealer loomed over him. "Like you? How?"

The little man wrote, "You must agree to become deaf and mute like me, so you will appreciate the plight of those of us who face such challenges."

"You can't be serious. Do you know who I am?"

"Yes, I know."

"And you are not afraid?"

Poochie wrote, "I am intimately acquainted with pain, fear, abuse, sarcasm, misunderstanding, punishment and rejection. I know as much about hatred as anyone who has ever lived as a human being. Am I afraid of you? No. There is One far greater than you who holds my heart. He is my Champion. It is you who are afraid … not of me, but of Him. Accept my challenge, or let's end this now."

The Dealer might as well have been slapped across his face. He sat down heavily in his chair.

"You have identified my Enemy. So be it. I accept your challenge, but I will not be deaf or mute forever. Set a limit. If you win I will honor it for that time. I will not promise more."

The small man wrote, "A year, one year, so you will know what it is like to be me."

"Agreed. Let's play."

Poochie wrote, "One more thing—"

"What?" roared the Dealer, "I have agreed to your condition. What do you want now?"

Poochie wrote, "This time, I deal."

For what seemed an eternity, the Dealer stared at him. Then, he smiled and handed Poochie the cards.

*Chapter Four*

Poochie walked along the shore looking out at the rocks. It was early in the morning. He smiled and waved his hand. Down the beach running full out came two dogs. When they reached him they danced around him in happiness, a matched pair of golden retrievers named Madeline and Spot.

Poochie hunkered down, and the beautiful animals covered his face with kisses. He was filled with joy. There was no more beautiful place in the whole world. He thought he would burst with happiness. Poochie had all he had ever hoped to achieve, but he was only just beginning.

~ ~ ~

Ground had been broken to begin construction of the Eleanor Fields School for the Deaf and Disabled just outside Cannon Beach. The setting was beautiful, and when the complex was finished it would be a world-class school staffed by the best physicians, nurses, teachers, and specialists in the nation. Eleanor Fields was its Director, and the school would never run out of funding to do the good work. The research wing would contain the finest facilities that money could buy. Eleanor and Poochie intended to change the world for the better.

~ ~ ~

St. Mary's convent and orphanage had fallen on hard times. There had been the very real danger that they would have to close, but a miracle had occurred. Sister Ann and Sister Dominique entered the office on a Thursday morning to find the Reverend Mother Beatrix in tears. The woman was weeping so hard that it took 10 minutes of reassurance on the part of the nuns to quiet her and find out what had caused such an outburst.

She pointed to a letter on her desk. There was a piece of paper with a message typed on it. It read:

*Silence is not golden where there is misunderstanding.*
*Judgment is flawed when the one ridiculed*
*is imprisoned within his own mind.*
*The Master said, "Do not judge that ye be not judged!*

There was a check in the envelope for $20 million dollars. The money was being given in memory of Sister Madeline and a dog named Spot. There was no way to prove where the letter had come from, but the Reverend Mother did not need an explanation.

Reverend Mother Beatrix began weeping again.

~ ~ ~

Shriners Hospitals and St. Jude's received checks from an unknown, untraceable benefactor for $100 million dollars each! Other institutions that served handicapped children and adults also mysteriously received huge amounts of money.

A writer at the Washington Times wrote a story about how unusual the year was. It was the most peaceful year the world had seen in decades, perhaps ever. The usual conflicts, wars, and angry outbursts between nations and neighbors were at an all time low. The story was picked up by the media and made the headlines almost daily. Journalists everywhere noted that crime levels had fallen to almost nothing around the world. No one could figure out why.

~ ~ ~

In darkness and silence, the Dealer played solitaire. He had agreed to remain deaf and mute for one year, and the lack of his activity had been noticeable in the world.

When Poochie had turned over the last card, he had wanted to reach out and crush the little man to a bloody pulp. But then, he saw the One standing behind him. Everyone had fears, but it had been millennia since the Dealer had faced his. He dared not touch the little man.

It was a quiet year, indeed.

# Don't Eat
# What You Can't
# Pronounce

# Don't Eat What You Can't Pronounce

Sandy Spalding was a very good cook. Everyone said so. When the holidays came and her extended family joined her for meals, they "ooohed" and a"aahed" over her culinary creations, exclaiming in delight about the deliciousness of her turkey and ham, the magnificence of her mashed potatoes, the sumptuousness of her green beans, and the epicurean wondrousness of her pastries!

Her sister Helen said that she should become a professional chef. Brother Dan thought she ought to sell her baked goods through local supermarkets. Nieces and nephews pounced upon her desserts like lions on a gazelle. Almost everyone was enthralled with her palate-pleasing concoctions—everyone with the exception of Matilda Madison, her neighbor four doors down.

Matilda envied Sandy because Sandy's meatloaf always won first place in the annual Founder's Picnic in July. Sandy's pie always won the gold at the August bazaar held by the parish to raise money for St. Stephan's. Sandy's chocolate-chip cookies were the star of the annual rotary picnic in September. Sandy's cornbread was now being sold by Kline's Bakery on Main Street. It was enough to make Matilda apoplectic!

Year-after-year, no matter how hard Matilda tried, she could never beat Sandy. Never! Matilda had hundreds of cookbooks. She followed directions. She embraced the beautiful creations in magazines. She copied world-class chefs when she made her contest entries. Nothing worked. She labored. She labored even more. She traveled near and far seeking the Holy Grail—the recipe that would sweep the events and cast Sandy Spalding into the dust as an also-ran!

Sandy had no idea that Matilda was filled with such rage because, strangely, Matilda pretended to be Sandy's best friend!

Outwardly, Matilda was a poster woman for friendliness. She exuded warmth and well-being. She smiled, said nice things, and she was helpful, kind and considerate.

What no one knew was that Sandy had a secret ingredient that she used in almost everything she cooked, sautéed, baked, broiled or fried. She had never told anyone. Her grandmother had shared the secret with Sandy when she was 12 years old, during a visit to her home.

Sandy and Matilda lived in the town of Lock Haven, Pennsylvania. They had grown up together, graduated together, and Sandy had attended the local university, while Matilda had gone to Penn State. Sandy had become an elementary school teacher, and Matilda had become an accountant.

Their husbands were also best friends and golfing buddies. The ties that bound them were strong, but Matilda's jealousy was as secret as Sandy's magic ingredient.

Matilda and her husband, Mike, had one child, a daughter, Melanie. She was a sophomore at the local high school. Sandy and her husband Fred did not have children.

The couples vacationed together, went hiking and camping, and spent many evenings at each other's houses. No one would ever suspect Matilda's state-of-mind regarding her friend.

The tipping point came when Sandy's husband secretly sent a copy of Sandy's apple pie recipe to a contest he saw in Martha Stewart's magazine. The Diva of Domesticity was writing a new cookbook called *Great American Recipes*.

Sandy's recipe had won a place in the new book. In a two-page spread at the beginning of the section on desserts, Ms. Stewart posed with Sandy in a beautiful photograph. The icon was smiling broadly and holding a plate containing a piece of pie. Sandy posed holding a knife, having just cut the pie.

Sandy was not paid for the recipe, but the notoriety she had received from the photo shoot ended up being covered in a full-page story in the Lock Haven Express newspaper. She was interviewed on the local radio station, and she was also named in Who's Who in Central Pennsylvania!

When Matilda opened her copy of the new Stewart cookbook and saw Sandy in its pages, she lost it!

She jumped into her Ford Explorer and drove through four stop signs before she managed to regain some semblance of control.

*Martha Stewart!* Was there no justice in the universe? Her head was going to explode! There would be ganglia everywhere! When they found her they would wonder how a woman's head could go nuclear!

Where could she find relief? She didn't drink, so that was out of the question. She didn't do drugs. She didn't even know to go to buy drugs in Lock Haven! What could she do?

This was a personality-altering moment in her life. No more Mrs. Nice Person! She thought about going to see Father Ambrose, but how did one go about confessing such envy? She hadn't just broken the 10th Commandment. She was way beyond coveting! She had destroyed the commandment over and over again! She could not possibly say enough Hail Mary's in a month-of-Sundays to wash away her envy!

*Martha Stewart*! Dammit! She had to do something! It felt like someone had poured acid on her brain! She wanted to scream!

Reason had fled. Insanity had arrived. This could not go on! She had to do something! This was the end. They were going to remember Matilda Madison for a long, long time!

Matilda realized that she had taken a wrong turn somewhere. She was so angry that she was not paying attention. She was on a country road that twisted and turned this way and that, and she had no idea where she was. She saw nothing but woods on both sides of the road.

She started into a turn too fast and thought her car was going to slide off the road. She managed to slow enough to prevent disaster, and she pulled to the side of the highway. She was gasping for breath. Matilda Madison was over the edge—of the road and of her mind, too!

It took her five minutes to gain control of her beating heart and racing mind. When she had achieved a small degree of normalcy she pulled back on the road and drove along looking for a place to turn around. She didn't find one. The woods remained unbroken on both sides of the road. She had lived in this area all her life. How was it that she had never been on this road before?

Then she saw an opening on her left and she turned into it. It was a dirt road leading back into the forest. There was no mailbox or sign along the road, but she thought it might lead to a house anyway, so she decided to try it. She had driven at least half a mile and was becoming desperate. The trees were close together and there was no place to turn around. The dirt road had turned and twisted so much that backing up for a half mile would take forever!

She drove a little further and was relieved to see a clearing ahead. When she reached it she saw a house in the middle of the open area. It was not like any house she had ever seen before. It looked like a Walt Disney idea of a cottage. In fact, it was exactly like that—a movie cottage. She would not have been surprised if one of the Seven Dwarfs stepped through the front door to greet her.

There was enough space for Sandy to turn the Explorer around, and she did so. She sat thinking for a moment. She decided to get out of her car and knock on the door. She left the motor running.

As she approached the cottage she thought she saw someone looking at her from behind a curtain in the window to the right of the door, but whoever it might have been disappeared so quickly that she thought she had imagined it!

Whoever had built this place had been filled with whimsy on steroids! It was so over-the-top that she had a vision of Alice falling down the hole into another world. It was then she noticed the sign above the door. It was bright blue, and painted in delightfully cartoonish letters in white ink were the words, *Potions for All Needs!*

There was a small bell hanging from the sign on a golden cord at shoulder height. Matilda reached out and tugged on the string. What happened next was so unexpected that she found herself jumping into her vehicle ready to race down the dirt road.

The little bell should have tinkled. Instead, when she pulled the cord a horn that sounded exactly like an approaching train that was right on top of her blew deafeningly, and the woods around the house erupted in hysterical laughter!

This was madness! Matilda was in no mood for nonsense. She had to focus! She was going to give a piece of her mind to whoever lived in this silly place about scaring her! She jumped out of her car and walked up to the front door and rapped as hard as she could.

No one responded. She rapped even harder. There was still no response. She was ready to turn and leave when she saw words appear on one of the panes of glass in the door as if by magic.

She read, "Try the bell again!"

Matilda screwed up her courage and tugged on the golden cord. This time, the little bell sounded like a little bell and the front door opened by itself. Someone had a demented idea about having fun with people!

She stepped into the cottage and was greeted with the sight of what one would expect. The inside of the cottage continued the whimsical theme. It was crammed with shelves that looked like what one would see in a Disney film.

There were antique glass jars carefully arranged on the shelves, and each was sealed. She could not make out what was in them, but there were labels on each jar.

One read, "*Curmudgeon Juice.* "The one to its left said, "*Chortle Cure.*" To its left, the legend read, "*Chin Lengthener.*"

*What nonsense was this?* Matilda thought. She looked around some more. She was certain that if she looked harder, she would find Eye of Newt and Tongue of Toad!

No one had yet greeted her. She walked through the room, reading the labels on jars. There were hundreds of them, all arranged in alphabetical order. She noticed a counter at the rear of the store and approached it. As she did, a woman suddenly appeared from a doorway. Matilda was so startled, she let out a little yip of fright.

In a voice that sounded like that of a Disney cartoon witch, the woman said, "What's the matter, dearie? Did I scare you? Heh, heh, heh!"

The woman laughed, sounding like she was enjoying herself immensely.

To add to the surreal scene, the woman was dressed all in black, like a witch. She even wore a pointed hat and held a broom in her hand. The broom was not a modern creation, but an object that looked like a drawing of a broom in a cartoon. She had white hair and a pleasant face, with red apple cheeks and a friendly smile. At least she didn't look evil.

Matilda vacillated between anger and amusement.

"What is this place?" she asked.

"Didn't you read the sign our front, dearie?" the woman said.

"Yes, and your doorbell nearly gave me a heart attack!"

The old woman started cackling so hard that her face grew redder and redder. Finally, she managed to get some control of herself.

"Yes, yes. Isn't it a hoot, dearie?" she asked. Then, she was off and cackling again.

Matilda couldn't help herself. She started laughing, too. The madness was bubbling just beneath her surface. She laughed as hard as the witch until finally, they both stopped.

The old woman asked, "How may I help you, Matilda?"

"You know my name? How is that possible? I've never seen you before in my life! I would have certainly remembered you!" Matilda said.

The witch said, "It's my business to know things. Look around you. What do you see?"

"It looks like something out of a fairy tale," Matilda said.

"Precisely, dearie. I specialize in very special things. Now, I believe you are looking for something in the cooking area, are you not?"

Matilda stared in wonder at the woman. "How could you possibly know what I want?"

"I know your name, and I know what you want—a very special ingredient, indeed. I have it right here."

The woman pointed to a small package wrapped in plain brown paper on the counter.

"What is it?" Matilda asked.

"You mix it with a recipe. It is especially wonderful in baked goods. The result is, may I say, catastrophic! It's stupendous! It's beyond belief!"

Matilda smiled. A plan had formed in her mind. "I'll take it!" she said. "How much do you want for it?"

"That would depend on how badly you need it, dearie," the old woman said. Now she was smiling with a smug look on her face.

Matilda was flustered and angry! She exclaimed, "*I need it! Now!* I'll pay anything. Do you understand, old woman? I have to have it, *now!*"

The old woman said, "Take it. Consider it a gift. I don't want money. The result will be enough payment."

Matilda swooped up the package, turned on her heel, and pushed through the front door. She jumped into the Explorer, which was still running, and drove off.

The sound of cackling was heard in the whimsical cottage.

St. Stephan's Bazaar and Festival was approaching, and there was lots of planning to do. Matilda set to work. Her cornbread muffins were the only thing that she had ever entered in any contest that had finished in the running against Sandy. She had garnered third place the year before.

Matilda went through all her cookbooks examining any other possibilities, but the witch had said the special ingredient was best in baked goods. She thought about breads, pastries, pies, croissants, etc. She kept coming back to her first choice: cornbread muffins.

They were very good. Her husband, Mike, thought so. Her daughter, Melanie, could not get enough of them. Even the divine Sandy liked them, and Fred, Sandy's husband, had declared them his favorite when they had dinner at the Madison house!

It would be her cornbread muffins.

The night before the festival she carefully prepared her muffins for baking. When she had her mixture ready she opened the package the witch had given her and added the contents. She mixed everything thoroughly, put the muffins in her tins, and put them in the oven.

The odor filled the house and her husband and daughter came into the kitchen, eager for a sample.

"I'm sorry," Matilda said, "but I need all of them for the Festival this year."

Mike and Melanie looked mournful.

"I promise that I will make another batch just for you, after the Festival is over."

St. Stephan's Festival was held on a super day. The weather was perfect, the sky was blue, the sun was shining. The whole town was there. The tasting and judging would be held at noon, and the winner and runners-up would be announced at 2:00 p.m.

Craft and food booths were doing brisk business, a local rock band was playing at one side of the festival grounds, a country group at the other side, and the local radio station was broadcasting from the event. People from out of town were coming to enjoy the day.

The people who had entered the baked goods competition all shared long tables that had been set up under a tent. They would not be available to the public until after the judging.

At noon the judges came into the tent and began tasting and judging. There were sixteen entries, the largest field of competitors in recent memory. Cakes, pies, croissants, donuts, and assorted cookies were all tastefully displayed. The reigning Queen of Cooking, Sandy Spalding, would have her apple pie judged last.

Everyone knew that Sandy would probably win, but no one was kept from entering. After all, the festival raised money for a very good cause, and everyone was there to have fun —except for Matilda Madison!

There were five judges this year. Three of the five had to agree that one of the entries was better than all the others. Deputy Mayor Frank Blake, Postmaster Helen Crawford, School Superintendent Albert Holloway, police sergeant Stan Fredericks and Sharon Seevers, the Queen of the Festival, had been appointed to judge the event this year.

Each judge had a printed form with the names of each entrant and a grading scale of 1-to-5, with 5 being the best. They made their way slowly from entry to entry.

There were exclamations of, "Wow, that's good!" and "This is delicious!" along with, "Oh my, I need to take some home!" and other warm statements from the judges as they made their way through the tent.

Matilda stood by her entry in nervous anticipation near the rear of the tent. Her muffins would be fifth from the end to be judged.

The judges arrived at her station, and Deputy Mayor Frank Blake declared, "Matilda, I hoped you'd bring these this year!"

Because of the amount of food they needed to taste, small samples were provided to each judge. Matilda had cut one of her muffins into five pieces, which she carefully placed on a lovely plate.

Each judge took a piece and placed it in his or her mouth as they ate their samples together.

In the next moment, there was a look of distaste on each face.

Helen Crawford started to gag. Albert Holloway's face turned bright red. The Festival Queen spit out her sample on the ground, followed by Sergeant Fredericks.

Deputy Mayor Frank Blake loudly exclaimed, "My God, Matilda, are you trying to poison us?"

The judges left the tent in search of water.

Everyone was looking at Matilda, and Matilda was staring in horror at her muffins. What the hell had the witch given her? She was embarrassed beyond words.

She ran from the tent in shame and hid in a Porta-Potty. Her husband, Mike, tried to reason with her, but she would not come out and face anyone.

The judges returned, a bit discomfited, but determined to finish their duty. They tasted the rest of the entries, did their scoring, and left the tent.

Mike Madison went to the baking tent, swept Matilda's muffins into a garbage bag, and left the scene.

Sandy Spalding, was, as usual, judged the winner. When the moment came for one of the radio deejays to announce the winners, Matilda lurked behind the bandstand, looking at the crowd. She saw a familiar face. However, the old woman was not dressed as a witch this time. She sat in the first row of the crowd, smiling as the winners were announced.

Matilda followed when she moved away from the bandstand. She tapped on her shoulder, and the woman turned around.

When the woman saw who it was, she smiled, brightly.

Matilda, filled with hatred, spat out her words.

"What the hell did you give me?"

Instead of answering, the old woman said, "Tell me, Matilda, how old are you?"

"What does that have to do with what you gave me?"

"Everything. How old are you?"

"I'm 43. What?"

"And you still believe in witches? That's delightful!" The old woman laughed at her.

Matilda was so stunned, she couldn't articulate her words clearly.

People were gathering around them, staring and pointing.

"Uhhh, uhhh, uhhh …" Matilda grunted, her face contorting. Finally, she managed to yell, "Who the hell are you?"

"I'm Sandy's grandmother, dearie," the old woman said, adopting the voice of the witch.

The veins were sticking out of Matilda's throat.

"What did you give me to put in my muffins?" she croaked.

The old woman smiled and said, "The scientific names are phenylthiocaramide and 6-n-propylthiouraicil, more commonly known as PTC and PROP. You see, dearie, I am a retired chemical engineer! The best witch in the business couldn't get close to all the things I know."

"*Uhhh! Uhhh, uhhh.* I can't pronounce what you said! What did it do?"

"It makes everything very bitter!" the old woman said, smiling sweetly.

"What the hell is her secret ingredient? Tell me!" Matilda said. "She must have one, dammit! What is it?"

"It is an emulsion of natural ingredients, dearie."

"What is that?

"It's called butter, dearie."

Matilda could not get her mind to work. She was stupefied. Finally, she screamed, *"Why did you do this to me?"*

The look on the old woman's face had changed. There was no sweet smile and no warmth in her voice when she leaned in and whispered, "Because, Matilda, dear, the women in our family don't lose. We never lose at anything! I guarantee it!"

With these words, the old woman turned and began walking away.

Onlookers heard the blood-curdling scream and watched in horror as Matilda lunged forward.

Before she could sink the cake knife into the old woman's back, Matilda was tackled and brought down by police sergeant Stan Fredericks. However, Fredericks, even at 6'4" and 230 pounds of muscle, had not bargained for what happened next.

In her rage, Matilda Madison, at just 5'3' and 130 pounds, threw off the officer like he was a mere child, and lunged again for the woman. She had nearly reached her when five men from the crowd brought her down a second time. It was all they could do to hold Matilda until the sergeant was able to cuff her and lead her away.

Sandy Spalding, who had heard the commotion, stood watching with a smile on her face. It was wonderful to win—again.

Matilda Madison was kept heavily sedated in solitary confinement for five months before she was deemed safe enough to mix with the general population at Piersall Psychiatric Hospital near Harrisburg.

No one on the staff could get her to eat desserts of any kind. One day, when they served cornbread muffins, she went berserk, stuck a butter knife in a guard's arm, and had to be restrained again for six months.

The Madison family left town. Sandy Spalding got her own TV cooking show. Life was very good!

# THE SONG OF BENJAMIN

# THE SONG OF BENJAMIN

Doctor Wiseman told Ann Reynolds that she had to be careful. Three miscarriages in four years had left her reproductive system weakened. The fourth pregnancy had made it to the third trimester without any problems, but he would prefer that she spent the last months at home. No traveling. She was not to do anything strenuous. There was also the factor of her age. Being 40 was not the end of the world, but the risks involved were multiplied.

Jason Reynolds, her husband, was little help because he was never around. Working in the oil industry had him on the road most weeks of the year. He spent more time in the air than many birds, coming down to do business, make deals, solve problems, and act as front man for his company, Ellison Industries.

The task of taking care of Ann fell upon her mother, Agnes Cathcart, age 63. The problem was that the Reynolds family lived in an upscale subdivision just outside Dallas, Texas, while Ann's mother lived in the small town of Greentree, Indiana. Something had to give.

The decision was made for Agnes to come to Ann. She arranged for her home to be watched over while she was gone. This was, fortunately not a problem since Agnes's brother, Ralph, and sister, June and their families still lived in Greentree. There were plenty of people around to keep an eye on the place. Besides, Ann it was of paramount importance that that Ann have access to her doctor and the hospital in Dallas.

The first child of Jason and Ann Reynolds arrived in the world on June 10th, six weeks premature. Tragically, Ann did not survive the birth. Doctors did all they could to save her, but could not.

Their concern then turned to the 4 pound, 10 ounce boy and his needs.

Jason Reynolds was in Dubai when the birth occurred. He returned home four days later. The funeral was held the next day.

Dr. Jacob Wiseman sat down with Jason and explained the status of his son. He appeared to be normal, but his birth weight and slightly jaundiced condition, weakened lung capacity, and other problems were going to require three to four weeks of hospitalization.

"Will you be able to remain at home during that time?" the doctor asked.

Without batting an eye, Jason said, "No. Other arrangements will have to be made."

He could not possibly remain at home. His job depended on him being in the field. If he elected to stay home he would lose his job. There were deals that had to be made. In fact, he should be on a plane that evening!

Jacob Wiseman stared at the man. Was the man in shock … denial? His wife was dead. His child might be in danger. Yet, he sat there saying that it would be business as usual.

"Do you love your son, Mr. Reynolds?

"What? What's love have to do with this? What kind of question is that? Without a job…without money, what good is love? I have to work, just like you do! Do you understand that?"

For a moment Dr. Wiseman looked at Jason Reynolds as if he was some kind of strange creature that he had never seen before, and wondered what to say next.

Finally, he managed, "Well, what kind of arrangements can you make? Who will care for your son? The child will eventually come home. Who will be there to receive him?"

"That's not my problem!"

"Yes, Sir, it *is* your problem. He's *your* son, *your* flesh and blood! For the love of God, Mr. Reynolds, how can you sit there at this moment and deny him?"

"There is no God, Doctor Wiseman, no such thing! You want me to sit here in remorse agonizing over my dead wife and my son. Sorry, I'm not buying it. Frankly, I never wanted a child. Ann did. It was her deal. I was along for the ride. I thought she'd have someone to be with. I have my work. She could have her child. That would be fair.

"Life isn't fair to most people because most people don't see life the way I do. Opportunity doesn't fall from trees. If you want success you have to chase it. My dream is wealth and all that comes with it. I'm 42 years old. I plan to be able to retire at 50 to do whatever I want. My stock options and savings will take care of me forever."

If Jason had punched the doctor in the face he would not have been more stunned. He was filled with such anger in that moment that he could barely speak. Finally, he got control of himself and said, "Mr. Reynolds, what are you going to do with the child?"

"Well, I'm certainly not going to take him on the plane with me! It's your problem. You take care of it," Jason said.

"I can't take care of it. I'm not his father. You are!"

"I told you it was Ann's deal. Give him away. I don't care!"

"Where in God's world did you come from, Mr. Reynolds? I've never met anyone like you in all my years. It's the law, man! He's your son, your responsibility! You can't just give him away, like a puppy! He's your flesh and blood!"

"You mention God again and I'm leaving here now! I don't believe in that crap! I never have. Besides, I thought you doctors didn't believe it either. Aren't you supposed to be men of science?" Jason said.

Dr. Jacob Wiseman felt his heart lurch within his chest. This was a nightmare. Jason Reynolds was, without a doubt, the most selfish person he had ever met, or hoped to meet, in his 56 years of life. Jacob was a believer. He could not get through the week without going to Temple Beth El.

He ran his hand through his hair and said, "What about your mother-in-law and her family, or your own family? Could someone be there for the child while you are away?"

"My parents are dead. I don't have any relatives I bother to speak to. As far as my mother-in-law is concerned, ask her yourself. If she's willing to take him, let her. I will allow her to stay at my home until the kid gets out of the hospital, but I want her out of my house when the child is released. She can take it back to Indiana for all I care."

The following day Dr. Wiseman met Agnes Cathcart in his office at the hospital and they discussed the baby's prognosis. He was identified only as "Male Reynolds" at that moment. No name had been given yet.

"What will his name be?" Dr. Wiseman asked gently.

"That would be up to Ann …," Agnes began to cry. "Or his father. She talked to me about three possible names. James, Benjamin and William. I can't choose the name for him. I'm only his grandmother."

Dr. Wiseman got up from behind his desk, walked around it and pulled a chair closer to Agnes. He sat down and took her hands in his.

He explained about Jason Reynolds, about what kind of man he was, and about the fact that he did not want his son. He told Agnes she could take the boy when he was well enough to travel, if she wanted to. The only other option would be to contact Social Services.

Of course, Jason Reynolds could not escape financial responsibility for the child that easily. This was going to be a complicated situation, and he needed her input. She was the boy's maternal grandmother. What did she think Ann would have wanted her to do?

"He should have a name. He's Ann's son!" Agnes said with anger.

"What name would you choose, Mrs. Cathcart?"

"I like James and Benjamin both …"

The doctor smiled. "They're both good Jewish names," he said.

Through her tears, Agnes managed a smile.

"Dr. Wiseman, you have a wonderful name. You are, indeed, a wise man. Let's name him, then. We can use both. My vote is for Benjamin James. What do you think?"

"And I think you are a wise woman, Mrs. Cathcart. He is Benjamin James forever. That would make him Benjamin James Reynolds. Do you like the sound of that?" Dr. Wiseman asked.

"No, it will be Benjamin James Cathcart. If his father wants nothing to do with him, so be it. I won't have him growing up in my house with that name. The man gave up more than his son! He gave up the right to be part of his life!" Agnes said.

"Do you have the resources to care for him and the help you'll need?" Wiseman asked.

"I'm not a wealthy woman, but I own my home, and Greentree is a lovely town, a wonderful place to grow up. My family is large and supportive. There will be no problems making sure he's cared for. I will treat him like the son I never had. If this can be done, let's do it. I'll contact my family and let them know what is going on."

What followed was complicated, but the authorities heard the situation presented, and with the support of Dr. Jacob Wiseman, Agnes Cathcart was given permission to take Benjamin James to Greentree, Indiana when he was released from the hospital. Agnes's niece, Rachel Cathcart, who was a nurse-in-training, flew to Dallas and helped bring the boy home.

## Chapter Two

B.J. was a quiet boy. He loved books. Agnes read to him almost every day from the time he was six months old. He was reading by the time he began pre-school, and by kindergarten he was a star student, even for such a small town. Greentree Elementary had about 500 students in grades pre-K through 4th. The middle school had roughly the same amount, and Greentree High was a regional school with kids bussed in from the surrounding area.

Greentree was a lovely town of about 8,000 people. Agnes had been right about that. Its quiet tree-lined streets, cozy town center, shops, restaurants, churches, businesses and economy were kept healthy by a prosperity based on a strong work ethic. Its hamlets, villages and smaller towns spread throughout the county. Farming was king in the region. Greentree's farms helped feed the state and the nation with their produce.

Agnes, now 72, was in reasonably good health. She was the youngest among her siblings. Ralph was 74, and June was 77. Their children were in their 50's, and their grandchildren ranged from the oldest at 22, down to B.J., now 9.

B.J. was tall for his age and thin, with dark brown hair and eyes. He preferred dungarees and tee-shirts as the uniform of the day when he wasn't in school. Agnes always saw that he was dressed in clean, pressed khakis and polo shirts when school was in session. Kids were wild for designer clothes, and tee-shirts with strange images on them, but he liked plain shirts without rock 'n roll or other such emblems. Scuffed sneakers, a worn brown leather belt, white socks, and a baseball cap completed his appearance.

He was strong for his age, and well-coordinated. He played pick-up baseball and softball, and handled a basketball well enough, but he spent most of his time in the tree house in the large maple at the rear of the yard.

His relatives had built the thing when B.J.'s mother had been 10, and the structure had nearly fallen down by the time older cousins decided to re-build it for B.J. for his 6th birthday. It had been a fantastic present for a little boy. He loved it there. They had made sure it was sturdy. It wasn't overly high up in the tree, but high enough that he could sit in the tiny room and look out the door, or read a book in the sunlight that streamed through its only window.

The Cathcart home was lovely, as well. Built in the Victorian style in 1895, the house boasted plenty of exterior gingerbread, a raised deep, wide front porch suitable for rocking chairs, chaise lounges, and side tables. It boasted a living room, parlor, formal dining room, and a big country kitchen with table and chairs that opened onto the back porch. A powder room completed the layout of the first floor.

Upstairs, the second floor consisted of three bedrooms and one large bathroom. The attic had been finished with a playroom and a fourth bedroom.

The back porch faced the rear yard with a garage and lots of grass. The garage was only big enough for one car, but there was also room for the lawnmower, gardening tools, shovels, and a wheelbarrow.

The house was set back from the street in roughly the middle of the 150-by-200-foot lot.

A slate sidewalk extended from the wrought iron fence and gate at the front of the property to the house. There were big trees and flower beds everywhere. The slate gray siding and accent colors gave it a near perfect Victorian finish. It was one of the prettiest houses on a street filled with them.

At age 9, B.J. did well in school. He was well-mannered and kind. He was soft-spoken and treated people with respect. He got along with most everyone. Having neither father nor mother was unusual as far as some kids were concerned, but his grandmother was a well-respected woman in the town. When she was asked about B.J.'s parents she always said that they has passed away. People did not pursue the topic out of courtesy.

B.J. rarely got angry or lost his temper. When he played sports he played to win. Because he did not brag or act like he was a big deal, a couple boys in the neighborhood made the mistake of trying to push him around one day at a baseball game behind the school.

Alan Bailey was a bit of a bully at times, and his friend Stephen Kroll would help him intimidate kids. Alan was a little bigger than the other kids, but Stephen was short. They played a game in which Alan would get in someone's face, and Stephen would jump on the kid's back and wrap his arms around the victim's neck. The kid would be so distracted that Alan could sucker punch him and he wouldn't be able to defend himself.

B.J. had seen them do this a couple of times. He had thought about what he would do if it happened to him.

When he felt Stephen on his back, he whipped around so that Alan punched Stephen in the back. As Stephen yelled, released his grip and fell to the ground in pain, B.J. turned around as fast as he could move. He knocked Alan to the ground with a right cross to his chin.

All the other boys stood there in amazement. The last person they had ever expected to punch out Alan Bailey was quiet B.J. Cathcart. Everyone, including Alan and Stephen, gave B.J. a wide berth from then on. No one ever messed with him again.

His grandmother heard about it and she asked B.J. if he thought what he had done was right. He said yes, and that was the end of it. He did not feel the need to elaborate, and she accepted his statement. She knew his character better than anyone, and if B.J. said something, it was true. He never felt the need to exaggerate.

When B.J. turned 11, summer began and school closed for vacation. It was a warm summer that year, and when the end of July rolled around a series of near perfect days arrived. Some years were too hot, but one week the temperatures dropped into the middle 70's. There was a soft breeze, and the sky was either totally clear, or white, puffy clouds passed slowly overhead with lots of sunshine.

The hallway of the Cathcart house was wide with a high ceiling. Double pocket doors were on the left and the right. As one came into the house the doors to the left were kept open onto the parlor; the doors to the right opened on what was called the living room. The front door was open, and the screen door was closed.

Agnes was in the kitchen baking bread. She had the reputation as the best maker of bread in the neighborhood. The only thing better than a piece of her bread warm from the oven with butter spread on it was a second piece!

She had two loaves in the oven, and two more loaves were rising on top of the stove.

She looked down the hallway. What a beautiful day it was. It almost looked like something from a movie. She had the kitchen timer running, and it would let her know when it was time to remove the bread from the stove. She decided to go out on the front porch to her rocker. She started quietly down the hall, but when she approached the screen door she saw something so beautiful –and so strange– that it took her breath away. She stopped cold.

B.J. was sitting on the steps with his back to her. The angle of the sunlight created a halo around his head. It was almost ethereal. Resting on his shoulders were three butterflies, two on his right shoulder and one on his left. One was a monarch, but the other two were of different varieties. As she stood there, another butterfly landed on his head, and then another on his left shoulder.

Time stopped. As she stood there she saw butterflies flitting about and coming from every direction in the yard. Soon, there were a dozen on B.J.'s head and shoulders. The number increased to at least 20, then 30, and then she lost count. Some sat with wings folded and perfectly still, while others gently opened and closed their wings. His shoulders and head were completely covered now.

Agnes did not know what was happening. She felt tears running down her cheeks. During this time B.J. did not move. Then, slowly, steadily, he lifted his right arm and extended it outward, palm up. More butterflies came and landed on his arm and hand. He extended his left arm and the same thing happened.

Now, he was like a tree with branches reaching outward, and there were hundreds of butterflies resting upon him.

Agnes felt as though she were seeing something that no mortal should see. It was—there was no other word she could think of—a holy moment. There was something so pure and unspoiled here that she wanted to weep.

It was magnificent.

The kitchen timer sounded in that moment, startling her, and the great cloud of butterflies lifted from B.J. They flew gently into the air, spreading outward as they moved away into the yard and beyond. B.J. lowered his arms slowly.

It was then she heard the sound. The boy was humming softly to himself. It was a tune she thought she recognized. She did not want him to think she was spying on him. She quietly backed away from the screen door and went down the hall to the kitchen. She reset the timer. The bread was ready and she took it from the oven and placed the bread pans to cool on the sideboard.

Whatever had taken place on the front porch was swirling in her mind. What was it that had happened? What did it mean? She felt the tears on her face again.

At dinner she fought the urge to question B.J. He appeared quite normal, simply an 11-year-old boy who was hungry. They laughed and talked and enjoyed each other's company. She was a reader like B.J. They rarely turned on the T.V. That evening they sat reading good books quietly in the parlor. The only sound was the ticking of the grandfather clock in the living room, and its chime on the quarter hours.

At 9:30, B.J. gave her a kiss on the cheek, said goodnight, and mounted the stairs to his bedroom.

Agnes turned off the lights, closed the front door, and got the house ready for sleep. She mounted the stairs softly so as not to wake him.

In her room she lay under moonlight streaming from her windows and thought about what had happened on the porch. She could not get it out of her mind. It had been utterly beautiful.

What had happened to B.J.? What song had he been humming? Then, it hit her. She knew the song. When he had turned 5, she had taken him to Sunday school at Trinity Church. They went to Sunday school and church every week. It was part of the fabric of their lives. The only time either of them missed was because of illness, or being away camping or traveling with other family members.

It was B.J.'s favorite song at church. She felt the tears on her face again. He had been humming the tune to *Amazing Grace*.

### Chapter Three

Four years slipped by. Agnes celebrated her 76th birthday. Her sister June had passed away the year before. She did not feel much like celebrating anything. Growing old is not for the timid. Some days she thought she'd like to find whoever said these were the "Golden Years" and give him a piece of her mind!

B.J. had shot up. At 15 years old he was just over six feet tall. He was still on the thin side, but he had become a good-looking boy. This was when the trouble started. Teens seem to become deranged when they turn 13 or 14. Hormones rage and kids who used to be agreeable become disagreeable. They say things that shock their parents. Sometimes grades suffer. Preoccupation with how they look becomes paramount, especially among girls.

Kids start dating and doing things parents don't approve of, and parents conveniently forget that they drove their mothers and fathers nuts at this age, too. However, the trouble that kids could get into today was often far worse than generations before because of the prevalence of illegal drugs, prescription drugs, and the absence of religious influence.

Thankfully, B.J. had not turned into a monster. He seemed forever grateful towards his grandmother. He was civil and open, and talked to her all the time about everything. Perhaps it was because there were only two of them, or maybe he recognized that she was slowing down and needed more care and consideration. He now did the laborious tasks involved in cooking, such as peeling potatoes and other vegetables, as well as other preparatory cooking tasks so that she did not have to do them. Her arthritis was taking its toll, and he did not want her to suffer pain.

B.J. helped his grandmother with laundry, cleaning, vacuuming, and other necessary but mundane jobs. He was helping to carry the load.

He had become a handsome boy, and girls were paying him a lot of attention. Still, he went home right after school to help Agnes. He didn't hang around downtown with the other kids who were becoming more and more social as the days slipped by.

There was a fine old home next to theirs that was occupied by Agnes' dear friend, Helga Sterling. She was two years older than Agnes, and her daughter, Mary, the Greentree librarian, lived with her. Mary was unmarried. She had left home long enough to get her degree in library science and then returned. Her father served as mayor of Greentree in the 1980's. He had passed away with a heart attack in 1994.

Town folk had thought highly of Everett Sterling, and when the head librarian had retired, Mary seemed like the logical choice to take her place. The town council had voted for her on the first ballot.

Mary Sterling was something of a stereotype. She looked like a librarian. She rarely smiled, and she wore her hair in a tight bun. She dressed in dark suits that were professional looking, wore sensible shoes, and used little makeup. She was soft spoken, but firm. Little kids liked her because she was an excellent reader during story hour, although she usually assigned the task to volunteers.

Ms. Sterling ran a tight ship at the library. The council never had anything to complain about. She stayed within her budget, avoided asking for things that were flamboyant or expensive, and did her best to make the patrons and her workers happy.

Sadly, more and more libraries were falling on hard times. The ones that did survive had to become media centers with computers, special classes and events, and things to attract people and make them want to visit. Greentree Library was somewhat unusual because it was the largest library in the county, and the desire to read in mid-America was still strong, particularly in more rural areas where the Internet, laptops and cell phones did not yet dominate every waking moment.

B.J. worked at the library as a volunteer three afternoons a week after school on Mondays, Wednesdays, and Fridays from 3:30 until 6:30. He restocked shelves, helped at the counter, and did odd jobs to help Ms. Sterling and the other adults.

There was a large meeting room near the entrance to the front of the library where civic groups and other organizations held meetings. Two smaller rooms were located in the rear of the building. One was a study room where people could plug in laptops and use the library's WiFi. It was the way of the world.

The second room had high shelves in it that contained old and rare books, first editions, some reference books, and storage files for papers, periodicals, and other stuff. It was usually empty, patrons most often choosing to use the study room.

B.J. was returning a book to the second room when he heard sobbing coming from the area behind the shelves that ran through the middle of the room. There was a single window, high up, that faced the parking lot at the rear of the building. It was a cloudy day, and the light in the room was dim. The overhead fluorescent lights were not turned on.

"Hello?" B.J. said. The sobbing stopped. B.J. walked to the rear of the room and saw Mary Sterling sitting in a chair holding tissues in her right hand.

When he was home and visiting next door he always called her Mary. In public, he addressed her formally as Ms. Sterling. He said, "Ms. Sterling, it's B.J. Are you all right? Can I help you?"

At this statement, Mary started sobbing heavily, saying between sobs, "Oh, B.J., I wish…wish you could help me. No one can help me…no one. I-I'm so scared. So frightened…"

B.J. didn't know what to say. There had been very few times that he had seen an adult cry, and he felt totally awkward. Besides, she was a neighbor and a friend of the family, not to mention his boss.

Finally, he managed, "Ms. Sterling…Mary, you can talk to me. It's B.J. You've known me since I was born. How can I help?"

Mary Sterling finally got control and stopped sobbing. She looked up at B.J.

"You're getting very tall, you know that? I'm so sorry. I came in here to get away from everyone. I have to get back to work. Please, B.J., keep this to yourself. It will pass. I'll be all right. You can go back to your duties."

"Is there anything you want to talk about? I'm a good listener."

"No, it's fine. You get back to work."

B.J. was about to insist that he stay with her, but he saw the look

on her face, the determined look that said, "Don't bother me now."
Those who knew the look had been warned.

He turned and left the room and went back to his work.

When B.J. got home he found his grandmother sitting in the parlor staring silently in the quiet room. She looked up and B.J. saw she had been crying. He went to her and said, "Grandma, what's wrong?"

"Helga came over for tea this afternoon, and, and she told me Mary is sick. Very sick."

B.J. took her hand in his and said, "How sick? What's the matter?"

"Please sit down B.J. I'll explain."

B.J. went to a nearby chair and sat down.

"Mary has cancer, breast cancer, stage four. There is no hope. They just got the report last night. It's too advanced to stop it. Radiation and chemo therapy won't fix anything. Just make her so sick she'll wish she was…gone. I didn't know what to say to Helga. She has been my friend forever. She comforted me when I lost your grandfather, and I comforted her when Everett died. Mary is her whole life. They have very few relatives, and no one close."

B.J. was silent for a long minute. Then, he said, "I found her crying at the library this afternoon and she wouldn't tell me why, Grandma. I tried to talk to her, but she turned me away. I don't understand why."

"Dear B.J., she didn't know how to tell you something so terrible. She has known you since you were a baby. She thinks the world of you. It's all right. As a woman, she simply didn't know how she could say something like that to a young man, even one she has known for so long. Mary is a very private person. Everyone has always seen her as so sure, so capable. I…"

Agnes began to cry softly, and B.J. felt tears on his face. They sat together for an hour, neither of them speaking.

Dinner had been forgotten.

Days slipped by and it became obvious to everyone that Mary Sterling was not well. Finally, the day came when she did not come to work. Her assistant, Rhonda Baretti, called everyone into the meeting room that afternoon and closed the door.

"Ms. Sterling is very ill." There were tears in her eyes. All of the staff looked distressed.

"I'm afraid she is not expected to recover. If you wish to send her cards you can bring them here and I'll see to it that she gets them. We will respect her privacy. I know that many of you like her and think very highly of her. This is going to be very difficult for all of us. We can all show her how we feel about her by…by doing our jobs well. I-I can't…" She could not finish her sentence and began to cry.

The girls and women rushed to comfort her.  B.J. and two other boys who volunteered at the library stood helplessly looking at them.

When the meeting ended everyone went back to work.

June arrived and school vacation began.

Mary Sterling was near the end. Hospice had been called. She wanted to leave the world in her own home, in her own bedroom.

B.J. was in his tree house. He had outgrown it now, but he still climbed up and sat with his long legs dangling down, book in hand, to spend a half hour reading in one of his most favorite places in the world.

Agnes was looking out the kitchen window at B.J. There was no book in his hand today. Even from this distance, she could see his face was sad. Then, as she watched him, he seemed to have arrived at some decision. He climbed down from the tree and walked across the yard and out of her view.

B.J. walked over into the Sterling's yard. He went up the steps to the porch and knocked gently on the door.

A woman in a nurse's uniform answered the door.

"Yes? May I help you?" she asked.

"I want to see Mary," B.J. said.

"I'm afraid that's impossible. You see—"

"Is that you, B.J.?" Helga Sterling had come from the kitchen.

"It's all right, Mrs. Drew. It's B.J. He's our neighbor. Come in, B.J.," Helga said.

B.J. stepped into the hallway. "I've come to see Mary, Mrs. Sterling. Would that be okay?"

"Oh, B.J., I don't think it's a good idea. She's, she's not like you remember her. No, I'm afraid my Mary is, is nearly, nearly gone." With these words, Mrs. Sterling's tears began.

B.J. stood helplessly by for a moment. Then he said, "I want to see her, please. She has been my friend since I was born. I want to see her, just for a moment."

Helga Sterling's tears slowed. "All right, but don't expect her to be as you might hope. She is unconscious. She has a morphine drip. It won't be long now. You know her room is at the top of the stairs. Go ahead, B.J. Say goodbye."

B.J. walked to the stairs and mounted them slowly.

He opened the door to the bedroom and stepped into the room, closing the door quietly behind him.

The woman in the bed bore no resemblance to the woman he remembered. Medical monitors beeped softly, and a metal rack held a bag of morphine.

B.J.'s face glowed in the dim light. He stepped closer to the bed and gently sat on the edge to avoid hurting her.

Then, he began speaking in his young man's voice. "Mary, when I was little you read to me on our porch. You always loved to read. You're such a good reader. You taught me to love reading as much as you do. Books take us away wherever we want to go. They bring us wonderful things. I am going to tell you a story now.

"Once upon a time there was a place where everything was perfect. There was no sickness, no one ever hurt, and no one ever even caught a cold. It was a beautiful place, so beautiful …"

There was a strange heat in B.J.'s hands. He placed them gently on Mary's right hand, so thin, lying on the sheet.

"In this place there lived the Master, the Master of all things …"

B.J. softly continued his story. When he finished, he stood up, bent over, and gently kissed her forehead.

He turned, opened the door, and went down the stairs to the foyer.

Mrs. Sterling and the nurse were in the living room.

Helga looked up. "Did she speak to you, B.J.?"

"No ma'am. I spoke to her, though."

"Did you tell her goodbye?"

"No. I didn't say goodbye. I told her a story, like she did with me when I was little."

"Dear B.J. That was sweet of you. Thank you for coming to see her. It means so much to me. Please ask Agnes to come over soon. There's not much time."

"I will, Mrs. Sterling."

B.J. went through the front door and down the steps. When he entered the house he found his grandmother in the kitchen.

Agnes looked at him. "Did you see her?"

"Yes. Mrs. Sterling wants you to come over. She says there's not much time."

"Were you able to speak to Mary? Can she talk?" Agnes asked.

B.J. looked at his grandmother for a moment and then said, "I told Mary a story like she used to tell me when was little. "

Agnes said, "What kind of story?"

"I told her a good story. When she told me what she thought was a really good story, she used to call it a 'keeper.' Remember?"

Agnes smiled. "I'd forgotten Mary said that,like catching a big fish and keeping it. What was your keeper about, B.J.?"

B.J. had started to turn away to go down the hall toward the stairs and up to his room. He turned back and said, "It was about keeping Mary."

"What do you mean? I don't understand."

B.J. said, "Maybe you'd better get over there. Mrs. Sterling said there's not much time. She might be right."

"Yes, yes, I'd better hurry," Agnes said, distracted by the thought.

"I'll set the table when you get back," B.J. added. He made his way to his room. He heard his grandmother go out the front door and down the steps.

B.J. lay down on his bed and stared at the ceiling. He felt very sleepy. He fell asleep.

Three hours later, Agnes returned to her house. She mounted the stairs and softly opened the door to B.J.'s room. He was fast asleep. She stepped lightly over to the bed and covered him with a blanket.

She went to her room and got ready for bed. Agnes lay in the darkness. There was not much time left for Mary. She expected the phone to ring at any moment. She fell asleep.

In the morning the phone rang at a few minutes after 8:00. It was Helga.

"They've taken Mary."

"Oh, I'm so sorry. She's gone, then?" Agnes said gently.

"No, something has happened …"

"Oh Helga, what?"

"Mary is better …"

"How could that be? Last night she was as close to the end as I've ever seen anyone!"

"No, she's better. She woke up this morning. She had color in her cheeks. She has no strength, but she was hungry! I called Doctor Wilson. He ordered an ambulance to come for her. They want to find out what's going on. I will talk to you later. I've got to get to the hospital. The nurse is driving me. I'll phone you when I find out more."

Agnes sat down in a kitchen chair. How could Mary be better? It made no sense at all. Hopefully, Helga wasn't in for a terrible disappointment.

One week later, Mary Sterling was declared free of cancer. A miracle had occurred. The impossible had happened.

When the news was announced B.J. was playing basketball behind the high school. When he got home supper was on the table.

He said, "I wasn't here to help you. I wish you had waited 'til I got home, Grandma."

"This is a celebration dinner. We're celebrating the great news!"

"What news?"

"Mary is cured! They've never seen anything like it. They're building her back up with good food and rehabilitating her muscles. She should be home soon. So, I cooked your favorites tonight!"

B.J. smiled at her. "Fantastic!"

"You mean my meatloaf, mashed potatoes and green beans?"

"No, they're awesome, but I mean about Mary!"

"Yes, isn't it? Go wash up. We'll eat in a few minutes."

When B.J. left the room Agnes had a flashback. She remembered the day of the butterflies. She had not thought about that incredible moment for a long time. Apparently, B.J.'s story had been a real keeper after all. She would keep it to herself. Some things were best left unsaid.

*Chapter Four*

Greentree High's graduation ceremony was held at 7:00 p.m. on May 27th. B.J. looked handsome in his cap and gown. Agnes Cathcart had to use her walker to attend. At 79, Agnes was plagued with the ailments of the elderly, but she vowed that she would be there. Her brother Ralph was gone, and she was the last of the older generation.

The Cathcarts and related families were very well represented. Agnes was surrounded by cousins, nieces, nephews and their children. The day was bright. They had feared that rain would drive the people into the auditorium, but the sun had come out and the event was held at the football stadium. When B.J. walked across the stage to receive his diploma everyone cheered and clapped their hands.

Thanks to Pastor Don Fitzsimmons at Trinity Church, and the influence he had in B.J.'s life, B.J. had applied and was accepted to Indiana Wesleyan University in Marion, Indiana. As an in-state student, it would be more affordable. He had applied for scholarships and received a partial one that would help him go through the program, but he would also work on campus part-time to help pay his way. He planned to complete a bachelor's degree in Biblical Studies. He wanted to be a minister.

In the summer of his junior year he came home from college, and brought Elizabeth Ann Atkinson with him to meet Agnes and share a special announcement. They had already told Elizabeth's parents.

His bride-to-be was tall at 5'9", and her long black hair framed a face with warm brown eyes, dimpled cheeks, and a smile that could stop a train. Elizabeth was gorgeous and very much in love with Ben. Everyone else might think of him as B.J., but he had become Ben to his future wife.

B.J. and Elizabeth would be married in mid-June after graduation next year. Elizabeth played the piano, flute, clarinet and a passable violin. She planned a career as a school music teacher.

B.J. would begin seminary at Trinity Evangelical Divinity School in Deerfield, Illinois. He had received an early scholarship notification. The award would go a long way towards helping him complete his dream.

Agnes was overwhelmed with such good news. She chose to with-hold her own news. Agnes liked Elizabeth the moment she saw her. After they spent the day together, she knew she could love this young woman. The good Lord had brought another wonderful person into her life. Agnes's one regret was that she might not have much time to spend getting to know Elizabeth.

Elizabeth had grown up helping her mother in the kitchen, just as B.J. had helped Agnes when he was at home. They put together a meal of chicken, salad, peas, and a delicious loaf of Italian bread that they had brought. They insisted that Agnes sit and talk to them while they worked. Then the three of them enjoyed dinner together.

That evening, Elizabeth had the guest room while B.J. enjoyed being back in his old room.

The following day B.J. took Elizabeth to the bus station where she took a bus home to Champagne, Illinois. She had a summer job waiting at her father's restaurant. She would wait tables, fill in at the register, and wash dishes when necessary.

B.J. had a summer job at Hanson's Lumber Yard and Hardware stocking shelves, making deliveries, and filling in for full-time employees during vacations. He had also been invited to do some lay preaching at Trinity Church, and that would give him some valuable preparation for his future career. He proved to be an excellent speaker, and Agnes beamed at the nice comments folks made about his messages.

Summer slipped by all too quickly, and B.J. said his goodbyes to his grandmother. She was sad to see him leave, and her illness felt like it had progressed to another level two weeks after he left for college.

The phone rang at the off-campus apartment B.J. shared with three other seniors. It was Rachel Cathcart, the cousin who had come to Agnes's aid when B.J. had come home from the hospital. The news was not good.

An hour later he was heading home in the 8-year-old Buick that he had purchased two months before.

When B.J. got to the house there were cars in the driveway and parked along the road. He parked quickly, jumped out of the car and ran up the steps into the house.

The parlor and living room were filled with relatives. Rachel came forward immediately and hugged him.

"She's asking for you, B.J. There may not be too much more time. Please go to her right now."

As he mounted the stairs he felt tears on his cheeks.

When he opened the door to her bedroom, Agnes was alone. She looked very small and shrunken beneath her blankets. Her eyes were closed when he entered the room, but she opened them when she heard his step.

"B.J., child, please come here."

It was all he could do to keep from sobbing. He went to her and gently kissed her on the forehead.

"Grandma, what happened? Why didn't you tell me what was going on? I would have stayed with you to help you."

"Don't be angry, B.J. You have so much goodness in your life that I didn't want to spoil it. I love you child. You know I do. You've been my son for 21 years. My only son. Now, you have Elizabeth to make your life complete. The two of you will have a wonderful marriage. You may have sons and daughters of your own. I'm content about your future. It looks like a blessed one."

B.J. sat on the edge of her bed and took her hands in his. Her hands were cold because her circulation was poor, and Agnes felt the heat in his hands. Arthritis had been raging for months in her body, and the doctor said that she was suffering from congestive heart failure. She had been racked with pain for so long that she could not remember when she was last free of it. Now, her pain disappeared as B.J. held her hands, and the blessed relief she felt made her feel at peace.

Agnes smiled up at this fine, handsome young man. She was so proud of him.

"You took away my pain, B.J. It's gone."

B.J. said, "I didn't know you were in pain. I love you grandma, so much!"

"That's all right child. There are things none of us knows, and it's time for me to tell you something I've never told you. I've kept it from you for selfish reasons. I did not want to see you hurt.

"I avoided the truth because I didn't want to face it. I told you both your parents were dead. That is half true. Your mother, my dear daughter Ann, is dead. However, your father may still be alive. I have kept you from knowing that he even existed. Let me explain …"

Agnes told B.J. the circumstances of his birth. When she finished
her tale he sat for a long time looking at her in silence. Then, he took
her hands in his once more and said, "You did the right thing. You are
my mother in every way. No one could ask for more than what you
have done for me. You have blessed me beyond words. I love you with
all my heart."

"Then you forgive me, B.J.?"

"How could I not forgive you, Grandma? Had my mother lived,
she would have loved me and taken care of me, but you chose to
act in her place. This house is my most favorite place in the world
because you are here. You are the light in this home, and its love and
joy. When I am at home nothing else in the world matters. It has
always been my home, and it always will be."

Agnes looked at him with love. Then, she said, "Do you remember
the day when the butterflies came, when you were 11 years old?"

"No, I don't remember. What happened?"

"I guess it doesn't matter. What about the story you told Mary
Sterling? Do you remember what it was about?"

"No, grandma, I'm sorry. I can't recall anything about it."

Agnes looked at him in wonder.

"You are special, B.J. Different. You have a gift, a strange gift that
heals others. You took away my pain."

The look on B.J.'s face was very serious.

"Grandma, I am not special. Our Master is the special One. If
anyone is healed it is because of Him."

Agnes smiled. "You are becoming a minister to serve Him, and
others, too."

"Yes, I feel called to do so. The pain in this world is frightening.
He's the only One who can relieve it. I will serve Him as long as I
have breath. I love you so much!" Tears were on his cheeks. "I'm
certain of His love, just as I am certain of yours. He has prepared
a place for us, you and I, and I wonder if it will look like this? I
think He might give us our heart's desire when it is good and pure.

Whatever it looks like, it will be perfect. I know this in my spirit. I will see you there. I-I ..."

B.J. began to cry, and Agnes comforted him. After a few moments, he left her to rest. He descended to the first floor and joined his relatives.

The grandfather clock rang the noon hour. The nurse went up the stairs to check on her. Agnes was gone. There was a smile on her face.

The funeral of Agnes Cathcart saw standing room only at Trinity Church. She had made a tremendous impact on the community. Her church and charity work were legendary. She had given of herself all the days of her life, and the message given by B.J. Cathcart on that day had everyone crying and laughing. It was something no one would forget.

John Cathcart, a member of the family and an attorney, met with Rachael Cathcart Pierce, who served as Agnes's estate executor, and B.J. three days after the funeral.

John said, "B.J., your grandmother loved you very much. The home is now yours. She lived wisely, and frugally, and she managed to save just over a hundred thousand dollars during her lifetime. That is yours, as well."

B.J. was stunned. "But, Mr. Cathcart—"

"Call me John, please. I've known you all your life. There's no need to be formal with me."

"Yes sir. How can I maintain the house? I'll be at school for a long time yet. I want to come back to Greentree one day if I can, but ministers are assigned to go where they are placed. I can't possibly come home every week to check on things. The money is needed, and I have no intention of spending it foolishly. It will be used sparingly—"

Rachael spoke up at that moment. "B.J., I have a solution to the house situation, if you agree. My daughter Ruth and her new husband Eric need a place to live. They want to save money to buy a house, or even build one. They could live in the house and rent it from you. You know that Ruth and Eric would take good care of it. The house should be part of the family for as long as you want it. What do you think? Would you be willing to rent it to them until you are ready to come home?"

B.J. smiled. "That's a wonderful idea, but let me go one better. I will let them live in the house rent free. That way they can save even more money. All I ask is that they pay for the taxes and utilities. If I decide that I won't be coming back to Greentree, I will let them be the first to offer me a fair market price for the house at that time. If I am going to come back here, I will provide plenty of time for them to move on to a new home. It is a wonderful house. It needs good people in it. Does that sound like something they would agree to?"

Rachael's tears and smiles were the answer B.J. needed. It was time for him to return to school.

*Chapter Five*

B.J. and Elizabeth were married. They rented an apartment in Deerfield, Illinois, where B.J. would attend seminary. Elizabeth secured a position as a kindergarten teacher at an elementary school near enough to where they lived that she could walk to work.

The years that followed were good ones. The money that Agnes had left to B.J. was used carefully. In the third year of seminary the old Buick died and they purchased a four-year-old Ford Explorer so they would have more room to carry things when necessary.

When B.J. was ordained, he was assigned to a position with a group of three small, rural churches near Deerfield. He preached three times on Sunday mornings at 8:00, 9:30 and 11:00 a.m., traveling between the three churches. It was good training, but exhausting. The Illinois winters also made it perilous to travel at times, but the Explorer did its duty, and B.J. rarely missed his sermons.

Two years slipped by. B.J. and Elizabeth wanted to have children, but their busy lives were such that it would have been difficult to take care of babies at that time.

However, people in the three churches were on fire with their pastor. The churches were growing rapidly.  B.J.'s salary had been miniscule when he began. The people had little money to pay a full-time preacher. Now, because the Lord was blessing them profoundly, all three congregations were bursting at the seams. They each had to expand their buildings, which would be a prohibitive expense, or all three congregations could come together and build one large church in order to save money.

The decision was put to a vote. The people elected to build one large church in the center of the district to be fair to all concerned.

Ground was broken, and the new church, called Grace Community, was built on a 10-acre plot of farmland donated by a church member. No one had the faintest premonition of what was coming.

B.J. Cathcart's messages stirred souls with faith. The power of his sermons was such that they reminded people of another young evangelist from generations before: Billy Graham. Things were happening. The new church was up and operating for two years when the decision was made to expand the sanctuary's size. Fortunately, the necessary space existed because of the size of the plot. The expansion took a year, and when finished the new sanctuary could hold 1,500 people.

The congregation grew. Three services were held on Sunday mornings. The church had over 4,000 members.

A ministry had begun involving outreach in every direction. The staff at the church grew to 22 people, including two associate pastors serving as children and youth ministers. Grace Community had a fulltime music director. Elizabeth served as a back-up piano player when the primary player went on vacation, or was ill.

Then, the television ministry began. The world changed again. B.J. the hard decision to sell the house in Greentree to the couple who lived there. Ruth and Eric had two children now, Jennifer and Alan. Jennifer was three years old and Alan was six months old. They loved the house and promised to care for it the way B.J. expected.

In turn, he promised to come visit once a year and sleep in the third floor bedroom. He asked if he could use the treehouse, too. They laughed at his request, but understood why he had made it. It would be Jennifer and Alan's treehouse when they could safely climb up to it. They would maintain it, as well, in Agnes's memory.

The world was taking notice of B.J. Cathcart. Television exposure, in turn, led to crusades, and crusades led to decisions for Christ. Like Billy Graham, B.J. decided to set a fixed income for himself. With his board of directors, he insisted that reasonable cost-of-living increases could be made when necessary, but the money that came in from tithes, regular giving and gifts would go to charity and good works. There was no place for temptation in the Body of Christ. It would not be allowed.

Elizabeth could not have children, so B.J. and Elizabeth decided to adopt. Baby William Cathcart joined their family. Baby Maria Cathcart came to live with them two years later. Elizabeth decided it was time to stay home and raise the children. She gave up teaching at the elementary school. It was hard to leave it behind, but no task was more important than raising their children in a Christian home.

B.J. Cathcart had a secret that no one but Elizabeth knew. His preaching was so powerful that crusades were now being scheduled outside the United States, but he did not share another thing that drove him each day: healing.

He had decided early on that the strange and wonderful power that came upon him from time-to-time would not be used in public. He had no desire to run a TV sideshow where desperate people would come to him to be healed.

However, whenever he could, he would go off to hospitals, nursing homes and wherever the Spirit led him to lay his hands on people who were terribly ill and without hope. He did so with the stern admonition that no one would ever share what had happened to them if they were made whole. He took Christ's warning to "do your good in secret" as Gospel truth. He wanted no recognition for anything that the Master did through him. It was Christ's blessing on others, not his.

As strange as it may appear in a world saturated with cell phones, closed-circuit cameras, laptops, the NSA and TSA, B.J. Cathcart's secret remained hidden from the media and exposure. Even the most dreaded diseases disappeared when the Master led him to minister to someone. He wept with them at their healings, and prayed for them to become strong members of churches that were Christ-centered.

Time passed. B.J. turned 40. The nation grew more apostate as young people turned their backs on organized religion, and older people fell away. There had never been a greater need for the truth to be preached, and the crusades reached millions while millions more walked in darkness.

B.J. often thought of Agnes. Because he missed her he made an effort to return to Greentree each year, as promised, and to reunite with his family. He was filled with love for Elizabeth, his dear children, and the members of his church. He poured himself out daily for the needy, and the Lord refilled him to go on. He loved, and he was loved in return.

His body, mind and spirit belonged to the Lord. He gave everything he had, but there was one thing lacking. The only person he had ever told about it was Elizabeth, and he had wept in her arms when he revealed it to her. It was a pain that could not be relieved, an itch that could not be scratched, and a torment to his spirit.

Elizabeth had held him and comforted him. She prayed silently that one day the Lord would bring him the healing he needed. She loved her husband so much. She did not want to see him suffer so terribly. He gave everything of himself. Her plea was that the terrible wound in his soul would be filled.

### Chapter Six

B.J. parked the car and locked the white Nissan Maxima, a rental from Hertz. His own car was a light beige, four-year-old Ford Escape.

He kept things a long time. His last car had been eleven years old when he traded it in. He had never owned a new car in his life. He didn't plan to buy a new car. There were far more important things.

He looked around the seedy, run-down neighborhood. Two-story buildings were stacked together, side-by-side. Some were boarded up, and others were in various states of disrepair with peeling paint, sagging porches, and the signs of urban decay.

It was not the safest of neighborhoods either. People on the street eyed him suspiciously.

The house before him looked just like the others on either side of it. He mounted the steps and looked for a doorbell. There wasn't one, so he knocked on the door. No one came. He knocked again and stood there for what felt like an eternity, wondering if this was the best idea…or if he was crazy for coming here.

His staff would be out of their minds with worry if they knew where he was at this moment. He was too important to place himself in jeopardy. That's how they saw it. They knew nothing about what he was doing on this day.

The crusade was in Houston's NRG stadium and the first two nights had been jammed to its 71,000 seat capacity. Tonight promised the same. They were there for four nights. Thousands had come forward to accept Christ.

B.J. told his secretary that he was going to see a dentist because he thought he had lost a filling. It was a reasonable explanation for why he was going out for an hour. He had promised to call her when he was returning. As he stood on the dilapidated steps, suddenly the door opened. An old woman in a threadbare housedress looked out at him.

"What do you want?" she demanded.

"I am here to see Mr. Reynolds," B.J. said.

"He isn't here," she said.

B.J. looked the woman in the eyes. She shifted her gaze. He knew she was lying.

"I know he's here. I want to see him now!" he said in the commanding voice that had been heard by millions around the world. There was a power in it that made the old woman step back.

She looked up at the tall man in the doorway.

"I said, he's not here," she said, a little less confidently.

B.J. heard a voice coming from a room to the right of the hallway where the woman stood.

"Who is it? Tell him to go away!" the voice said.

B.J.'s normally kind face in that moment was stern as he said to the woman, "I am not here to be put off from seeing him. Both of you have been watched for a long time. I know he's here and I will speak to him now!"

There was fear on her face then. "Are you with the police?"

"No, but if you don't let me see him now I'll have to take action," B.J. said.

"We didn't do anything wrong!" the woman whined. Her fear was growing stronger. She looked like she believed he might hit her.

"No one said you did. I must see him. It is very important. I won't stay long. You have my word," B.J. said.

The woman knew that she could not stand in his way any longer.

"He's in there. Don't take long. He's not well. He's old and sick. I'm not well either. I want to close the door. I don't want others to see us standing here. This neighborhood isn't safe."

B.J. stepped into the house and moved forward as the woman closed the door.

"You've got company," she said loudly in the direction of a room off the hallway.

The shabby hallway was covered in peeling paint and ancient wallpaper. There were rooms to the right and left, and a doorway at the rear led into the interior of the house. An old staircase ascended upwards from the hall to the second floor where B.J. assumed there were bedrooms. He smelled cooking odors now that he was inside in the house. The woman must have been in the kitchen when he arrived.

B.J. stepped to the doorway on his right. There was a man sitting in an old, torn recliner with his feet raised up in the footrest. He was bald and unshaven. He was unkempt, and his eyes were bloodshot. An oxygen hose hung from his nose. The hose descended to a tank by the right side of his chair. The man's clothes had seen better days, and the shoes on his feet had holes in the soles. The sound of the man's wheezing was loud in the small room. The room was as dirty and disheveled as the man in the chair.

"What do you want with us? We don't have any money. There's nothing of value in this house. Go away and leave us alone!"

B.J. knew the man in the chair was 83 years old. He had him researched carefully long before he had ever decided visit him.

"You are Jason Reynolds, are you not?"

"That's none of your business! Why are you here? Did someone send you? I told you, there's nothing here for anyone. I'm sick. You can see that, can't you? Why would you want to come here? There's nothing we can give you. All my money, all of it, was gone long ago."

It was hard for the man to speak and he began wheezing harder.

"See! See! I don't have the strength to speak to you. I could die right here, right now. Why don't you leave?"

B.J. stepped further into the room, and the man's eyes grew wide.

"Please, please don't hurt me. I don't even know who you are. Why are you bothering me?"

"I've come to ask you a question, Mr. Reynolds. One question, that's all."

"What? What question? What if I get the answer wrong? Are you going to hurt me if I get it wrong? I did a lot of bad things years ago. I spent time in prison. I paid for my crimes. Things were bad then. The business fell apart. I lost my job. I cheated the company, took money. They found out about it. I lost everything. Everything. I've been living with nothing for years and years. Joyce, she takes care of me. She didn't do anything. Please, don't hurt her. Please!" the man said.

The desperation in the old man's voice and the fear in his face were too much for B.J. to bear.

"I didn't come to hurt you. I don't even know you. But I have learned much about you. I had you investigated. I wanted to find you if you were still alive. I have never hurt anyone, and I don't plan to start now.

"However, you hurt me, hurt me in ways that you never knew. You hurt my soul, did terrible damage to me," B.J. said.

The old man said, "Hurt you? How did I hurt you? I don't even know who you are. Now that I see you more clearly you look like that preacher fellow on television that's in the city now, but you can't be him. You would never come to a place like this. Who are you? Why did you say I hurt you?"

B.J. sat for a long moment silently. Then, he said in a quiet voice, "You are my father."

The look on the old man's face was one of disbelief.

"How could I be your father? I don't have a son. I never had a son. I gave away my son long ago. I didn't want him. His mother is dead—"

"Yes, my mother Ann died when I was born. The doctor asked you to take me and care for me. I am your son. My grandmother Agnes Cathcart raised me. I've had a wonderful life because of her. She has been gone many years now. I'm married. I have two children. You have two grandchildren you've never seen. I've been all over the world. I have been privileged to speak to millions in my work. I've met presidents, kings, heads of state, and ordinary people just like me from all walks of life. I have been blessed beyond words, and you had nothing to do with me. I was despised and rejected, just like the One I serve. I did not even know that you existed until my grandmother told me about you on the day she died.

"From what I have learned you were a monster. My mother was beautiful, just like her mother. Both of them were beautiful people in how they cared for others. But you—you didn't care about anyone except yourself. My mother must have seen something good in you. She married you, after all. This is my question: what did Ann Cathcart see in you Jason Reynolds? Why did she love you? What was it about you that allowed her to stand before others and proclaim her marriage vows, vows taken not only before those present, but vows declared before almighty God Himself? Tell me father, what did she see in you? Did you even love her at all? And why do you hate God so much?"

This last question was torn from B.J.'s soul itself. He roared as a lion would roar.

"Why? What do you blame God for doing, or not doing? Why did you treat me as if I was nothing but a piece of human garbage to be thrown away like nothing but trash? How could you hate a baby—your own son? How, in God's precious name, how?"

B.J. was on his feet looming over the old, helpless man in the chair. His face was contorted in pain and tears flooded his face. His fists were clenched. He had never allowed himself to feel rage against another human being in all his life, but he felt it now, and he was nearly out of control.

He wanted the answers to his questions. He wanted to strike this old man. And then reason took hold of him.

He sat down hard on a chair and in a loud voice exclaimed, "Help me understand! Please! In God's name, help me! I am your son, your only son. Tell me, did you love my mother? Did you?"

Jason Reynolds knew then that this was his son, and his face went red with shame. No one had ever asked him such questions in a lifetime of selfishness. He had made a miserable wreck of his life, and now he was confronted with something he had never dreamed he would have to face: his horrible and petty self. He screamed, and the sound was terrible in the room.

"Yes! Yes, I loved her, but I loved my own needs more! I loved your mother. I convinced her to love me because I was good looking and I could be charming then. My parents were Bible-thumping fundamentalists who believed in administering the rod as often as possible when I was growing up. They abused me in their frenzied religion. They made me hate God! No God of love would ever treat me the way they treated me. I knocked my father down when I was 16 and left home for good. I told your mother they were dead. I did not invite them to our wedding. There, I've said it. I loved her, but not enough!

"I did not love you because you would have kept me from my dreams. I wanted money—as much money as I could get! Are you satisfied now? Now you know the truth. Will that set you free? I'm dying! I have lung cancer. I won't live out the month. Does that make you happy? Will that make us even?" Reynolds said.

B.J. sat for a long time staring at the man. He neither spoke nor moved. Then, he stood up and stepped toward his father.

The old man pushed himself back in his chair as far as he could go, a sheer terror contorting his face.

B.J. reached out and placed his hands upon the thin, withered shoulders of his father. There was a fire burning within them.

Jason Reynolds felt the strange heat in his shoulders and did not understand what was happening. He howled in fear. The power grew in B.J.'s hands. It swept through Jason's body. The old man had never felt anything like it in his 83 years. He stopped yelling and became quiet.

When B.J. was finished he stepped back and looked into his father's eyes.

"We will never see each other again, but something has happened to you that will change you forever.  You are no longer the same. My Master is real, and He has touched you in a mighty way," B.J. said.

"What did you do to me?" his father asked in a hoarse voice.

"You have been healed. No one on earth could heal what you were dying from. Yet, you are healed. Your body is whole. As to your mind and spirit, that will take time.

"Your punishment, father, is to live until you are finally called home. That may not be too long at your age, but one thing is certain. One thing is irrevocable and cannot be changed. You have been healed, and the One you denied is the One who has done unto you what could be done by no other. I must forgive you, and I do. I forgive you of everything."

As B.J. spoke, tears began flowing down Jason Reynolds' face.

"You are forgiven, and it is God Himself who has healed you," B.J. repeated. "Now, you will finally believe as I believe. He is everywhere, father. You cannot escape Him. It's obvious that your parents knew nothing about Him. What they did to you was terrible, and what you did to me was terrible, but you must forgive them, as well. They did not know what they were doing anymore than those who nailed my Master to the cross knew what they were doing when they did that!

"I'm leaving now. And you," B.J.'s face was filled with light when he spoke, "you are smitten of God. He has claimed you for his own. Be at peace, father. It's time you were."

When B.J. closed the front door behind him the old man cried in anguish, "My son, why did I forsake you?"

THE TROUBLE

WITH MURPHY

# THE TROUBLE WITH MURPHY

Murphy sat down and stared at the lawnmower. Why wouldn't it run? He had tinkered with it for an hour. He checked off what he had done: cleaned the sparkplug and adjusted the gap, checked the oil, cleaned the air filter, and checked the throttle settings. He checked the choke, washed everything and let it dry, and cleaned the dried grass from the blades and underside of the mower. He'd tried to start it, failed, replaced the sparkplug with a new one, and went through everything again. He tried to start it, failed again, got out the manual, read through the "Problems Starting" section. He did everything that it said and failed again. He got a drink of water, ate a sandwich, scratched his head, and finally gave up.

This was dumb.

He felt dumb. He felt like a failure. Meanwhile, the sun was shining, the grass was growing, the lawn needed cutting, and the Boss was going to be unhappy with him, again.

Maybe he needed a stronger word? Not dumb, but borderline stupid. O.K., maybe borderline wasn't strong enough? How about just plain old garden-variety stupid? What if he added inept, brainless, incompetent? Would that be enough to describe his failures?

Murphy stared at the lawnmower. Maybe he could will it to start up, sort of a mind-over-matter kind of thing? He squeezed his eyelids together and projected, "Start!"

He stood up, set the throttle, and yanked on the cord. Nothing!

The day had started when he got up. Well, actually, he hadn't gotten up. Murphy rarely dozed except when he was standing up. Let's say that he became aware. The trouble with Murphy was that he was usually lost in thought, and he was always thinking about stuff.

The real trouble was he was easily distracted. He would be trying to do one thing and thinking about another. This was not good. Things happened. Accidents befell him. Plumbing broke, electrical fixtures shorted out, appliances breathed their last, on his watch!

Vehicles ground to a halt with broken engines, doors malfunctioned and wouldn't open. Pictures fell off walls and the glass broke into a million pieces. Hangnails that were ignored required major pedicurial attention—was that a word? Everything he touched blew up, fell apart, broke down, or got busted!

Murphy was a mess in search of a place to happen.

Repairs that he made always cost three times what he had expected. Between twisted fingers, skinned knees, an aching back, muscle pain, sunburn, windburn, rotator cuff problems, dust and sneezing, hiccups, headaches, sprains, shoulder separations, and the heartbreak of psoriasis, Murphy endured being the main handyman of the community. He was the Jack-of-all-trades and Master of None, or so it seemed.

He raised his eyes and looked at the lawn. Was it his imagination, or could he actually hear the grass growing while he looked at it? He wanted to shout, "Stop it! Halt! Don't move!"

The yard looked like it was light years in size. As he stared it was expanding before him. It was maddening!

Murphy answered to the Boss, and the Boss answered to no one. He was the Big Guy, Number One, and King of everything. The truth was that the Boss was always really nice to Murphy, but Murphy would pretend that the Boss would be really angry with him since he never got his work done because of some oversight on Murphy's part. It was a way of adding to his personal anxiety level when things went south on him. He spent most of his time puzzling out why this was.

It wasn't that others didn't like him, but it was his job to make sure things worked right. At least, that is was what he thought when the Boss assigned him to the job.

Before he had taken the job, he was oblivious to things mechanical. Like everyone else, he took them for granted. When his own things broke before he had taken the job, he had ignored them. His place was piled up with various things that were busted and in need of repair. He had stopped inviting others to visit. He was ashamed that his personal space looked like a junkyard. He had no idea why the Boss had chosen him for the job.

Murphy sighed heavily. He pulled up a chair, sat down, and resumed staring at the mower. Then, he looked up. The Boss stood, smiling a few feet away from him. The Boss never got mad at Murphy, but that didn't make him feel any better. The Boss had more patience than anybody!

"What's the matter, Murphy?"

"It won't start. I've tried everything, checked everything, changed the plug, cleaned the filters, and done everything I can to get it to run. The yard will be out of control if I can't get it running. Look at it. It's growing while we stand here!"

"It's grass, Murphy. It's supposed to grow."

"Yes, that's true, but I like to keep things neat and in order, because that's my job," Murphy muttered.

"That's O.K. If it grows a little longer what's the big deal? It's not the end of everything. If you don't get it cut today you can cut it tomorrow," the Boss said.

"Yes, Sir, but if I can't get the mower started, I can't cut the yard by hand with scissors. That would take forever!"

The Boss looked at Murphy with another smile.

"When did time become such a big deal to you? You've got all the time you need to get this done. Do I look upset?"

"That's what makes me upset! You never get mad at me. You never take me to task for anything. You just let me go along tinkering with this thing, adjusting that thing, oiling another thing, painting the thing over there ..."Murphy said.

"I understand," the Boss said.

"There you go again. You are always so kind and understanding. You never raise your voice. I try to do everything right for you. I—"

"But, that's *my* job, Murphy," the Boss said. "You have your job, and I have mine. I don't expect you to do everything right. Yes, I know you know that I like things to be perfect, but I never expected that you would be perfect all the time. You have to make allowances for yourself. Cut yourself some slack. If I'm not upset, why should you be?"

"I'm sorry, but I want to do everything right all the time," Murphy said.

"Look, if I had expected perfection I would not have assigned you to this job. I chose you for this job precisely because you're not perfectly perfect. I don't expect you not to have things go wrong. After all, you're a role model for so many."

The Boss laughed. "Don't get mad at me, or yourself," he said.

"Yes, but—"

"No, no buts. If you could remember everything, I wouldn't need you. I like you just the way you are. Now, you said you checked everything, right?"

"Yes Sir, I did," Murphy said.

"What about the fuel? Is there fuel in it?" the Boss asked.

The look on Murphy's face was priceless.

The Boss smiled a great smile and stifled a laugh behind his hand.

Murphy stuttered, "Uh, I didn't even think to look in the tank."

He unscrewed the cap and looked in. It was bone dry. With a sheepish grin, he looked at the Boss.

"No fuel! That's the last thing I would have thought of! It can't run if I don't put fuel in it! Man, am I a dummy!"

The Boss was laughing so hard that Murphy felt embarrassment sweeping through himself. His face turned a bright red.

Finally, the Boss got control, stepped closer to Murphy and put his large hands on his shoulders. He looked Murphy in the eyes.

"You know, I've never told you this, but you are one of the most famous persons I've ever had. I have avoided telling you this, because I didn't want you to get all puffed up with pride. When I say you're a role model, I mean it. Why, practically everyone knows your name! You, Murphy, are a household fixture all over the world. They have even written books about you. I picked up a copy for you."

The Boss started chuckling. When he finally managed to regain control, he pulled out a book.

"After you put fuel in the mower and cut the yard you might want to sit down over there on that bench to read ..."

The Boss started laughing so hard that even Murphy couldn't avoid being caught up in the hysteria.

Finally, the Boss looked at Murphy and managed to say, "I-I, whoeeee, this is so funny! Ha, ha, ha! Aah, ha, ha! I mean, gosh, I—" He laughed some more.

"I can't stand it! Please, Murphy, take the book. I've got to get back to work. Ah, ha, ha, ha! Oh, man, I can't stop laughing! Here, read it. You'll enjoy it!"

Roaring with laughter, the Boss thrust a thick book into Murphy's hands and walked away.

Murphy looked down at the book's cover. The title was in big letters, but there was a misspelling in it.

It read, "*Murphy's Lwa.*"

The

# CURSE

# THE CURSE

Mr. Prescott was antisocial. Everyone at Parson's Retirement Home thought so. He kept to himself, rarely spoke to anyone unless he couldn't avoid it, and when he was in the complex he was in his room with the door closed. His English accent proved to the other residents that he wasn't from the area.

Early in the morning at daybreak he would be found walking along the line of dense evergreens that grew along the eastern edge of the large yard that stretched away from the buildings of the Parsons facility. On the other side of the trees there were Amish farms that went on for several miles. Opposite the property there was a large red brick elementary school surrounded by an equally large lawn. The playground area was located behind the school.

Ephrata Elementary was home to grades K-4, and the middle school on the other side of it housed grades 5 through 8. The high school was a half mile down the road. Prescott walked in every kind of weather, rain or shine. It was as if he was searching for something.

It was early June and the schools were closed for the summer.

Albert had no close friends. That was fine with him. He avoided small talk and found the dialogue of others to be boring. He preferred reading to mingling, and appeared to have no family or outside friends because no one ever came to visit him. He had been at Parsons since the facility opened.

He was of average height, slender, and his hair was worn long. His face was unwrinkled. He could have been anywhere from 50 to 70. No one knew his exact age. His hands were those of a scholar or man of leisure. Age had apparently been kind to him.

Mr. Prescott said he had been married late in life, and that his wife had died of pneumonia years ago. When he had come to Parsons he was asked what he had done before he retired. He said he was an anthropologist, and that he had traveled the world seeking ancient artifacts, digging in ruins, and writing papers and books.

The people who came to Parsons were mostly women whose husbands had died. There were only a handful of men at the facility, but Albert avoided everyone.

He had lived in Egypt for many years. While there, he had grown a beard, traded in his western clothes for that of a Bedouin, and "gone native" in order to blend in.

Prescott spoke passable Arabic, and he had convinced many that he was native to Egypt. When he finally came to America he remained off-the-grid. He had the money to live comfortably, and he had moved to Lancaster County, Pennsylvania. He bought an old, but well-preserved house in the small historic community of Strasburg east of the city of Lancaster.

Albert Prescott maintained his anonymity for years. When he sold his home and moved into Parsons Retirement Home, he did so because he thought that the people of Strasburg had begun to regard him strangely. He did not lack money. In fact, he had so much of it that he could have lived in luxury anywhere in the world, but his desire not to be noticed over-shadowed every possible consideration. He had chosen Pennsylvania because of reasons that he never dared reveal to anyone. His quiet, untroubled life was based on a terrible lie.

There are urban legends everywhere. Stories often take on a life of their own, and the tale of the disappearance of a young Pennsylvania anthropologist was discovered by a graduate student at the University of Pennsylvania doing research for a paper. Helen Brown was looking at old archives in the library.

She came across a newspaper article from the Philadelphia Bulletin detailing the disappearance of a doctoral student in anthropology named Richard Fenner. The young man had gone missing in Egypt, and his assumed death was attributed to foul play. What was intriguing was that his body was never found.

His grieving family had traveled to Egypt to help with the
search. Fenner had been in Cairo seeking to join the Howard
Carter expedition in the Valley of the Kings. He had arrived in the
city on March 20, 1923, and he carried documents attesting to his
skills, along with a letter of recommendation from a distinguished
professor of anthropology.

There were photos in the article of Carter and others at the site
of the discovery of King Tut's tomb and its fabulous treasures.

Apparently, young Fenner never arrived at the site, having
disappeared somewhere between the city and the excavation. The
young man's presumed demise was a minor footnote in the story
of the incredible find made by Carter and his benefactor, Lord
Carnarvon.

The death of Lord Carnarvon, on March 25, 1923, gave rise to
the legend of the curse of King Tut, later portrayed in movies. Lord
Carnarvon was reported to have died from an infected mosquito
bite.

Helen Brown was fascinated with the story. What had happened
to Richard Fenner? Where was his family located? Were his relatives still alive? She wanted to find out.

Helen's boyfriend, Daniel Edmunson, was an FBI agent at the
Philadelphia office. They had met at the home of a mutual friend
in Society Hill at a party. She decided to discuss the story with him
over lunch.

He laughed and said, "You can't be serious? First of all…talk
about a cold case! Wow! You're talking about something that
happened so long ago that there would be no DNA evidence that
we could begin to find, and it happened in Egypt! I'm in the FBI…
not the CIA! Does this Fenner have any relatives? Even if he does,
who would remember anything about this from back then?"

"But aren't you just a little bit fascinated, Dan? An American is
murdered on foreign soil. He is connected with the greatest Egyptian tomb discovery in history! There's the so-called curse of King

Tut's tomb that cost the lives of people involved. I think it's totally intriguing! How would you go about tracking down his relatives? Could you help me with this?"

The look on Dan's face was one of exasperation, but it turned to a smile when he looked at her. He had been thinking about marriage—and he knew she was the one he wanted to spend his life with—so he took a deep breath.

"O.K.," he said, "I can do this much. I'll look into it…on my own time, of course. If I can trace his family members I will let you know who, what and where. Then, you can take it from there. That's all I can promise. I don't expect to find anyone who would remember anything this many years later, but as long as you are intent on playing Nancy Drew, I'll do my best Sherlock Holmes."

A busy month passed for Dan and Helen, and then her phone rang one Thursday night.

"Hi! I've got a break for two days. Are we going to see each other this weekend?" Helen asked.

"I've found something, Helen."

"Found what?"

"I found something about Richard Fenner. I found a relative of his."

"Oh, gee. I've been so busy I forgot about what I asked you to do. Who is the relative?"

"I've been digging around, and it seems he has a niece still alive. He was 23 years old when he disappeared. She's the daughter of his older brother, Harold Fenner. She was five years old when he went missing. She is 99 years old now. Lives in a nursing home in Doylestown, Pennsylvania."

"That's incredible, Dan. At that age she may not even remember her own name, much less anything about her Uncle Richard."

"The ball is in your court, sweetheart. My workload is nuts. Domestic threats are off the charts. I'm afraid you'll have to look into this on your own."

"How did you ever track her down, Dan?"

Doing a bad German accent, Dan said, "Vee have our ways at der Bureau, fraulein!"

Helen laughed. "O.K., you did your part. Now I will do mine."

"Bye, Helen. I'll see you Saturday."

"Bye. Thanks again!"

A month went by. Helen had made some calls, arranged a contact, and drove to the Bellewood Home for the Aged in Doylestown. She arrived and entered the building. From its appearance it had to have been built in the 1930's. Somehow, this seemed appropriate.

Feeling a little guilty for identifying herself as a distant relative of Ms. Alicia Brooks, she confirmed that the woman's madien name had been Fenner, and was taken to a small but comfortable room by one of the people who worked there. She carried a bouquet of flowers.

Alicia Brooks was seated in a wheelchair by the window. She looked up as the two women entered her room. She saw the flowers and smiled.

Helen had used her real name when she made the contact. The old woman said, "Helen…how good it is to meet you. Thank you for coming to see me! Please come in and sit with me!"

Helen was surprised by her response. The old lady's body might be shot, but there was nothing wrong with her mind.

Helen thanked the orderly and asked if there was a vase available for the flowers. The woman said she would locate one and left the room, closing the door behind her.

Helen turned to her host, and the woman indicated a nearby chair. Helen sat down.

The smile had disappeared from Alicia Brooks' face.

"I have no living relatives anywhere. Who are you, and what do you want? If it is money you're after, I have none. I am a ward of the state, missy," she said.

Helen felt herself blushing at the woman's words.

"Mrs. Brooks, I'm not here for money. I'm here for this."

Helen took out a copy of the newspaper story and handed it to Alicia Brooks, who read through it and then looked up. There were tears in her eyes.

"He was my one and only uncle, and I adored him! I didn't understand all the things that happened at that time, but I have had more than enough years to think about it. The family tried to find him. My father even mortgaged our home to pay for the trip to Egypt. His parents went there and stayed for three months. It came to nothing. When the depression came my father lost everything. Life was hard then…harder than you could imagine. What is your interest in this? Why have you come here?"

"I'm so sorry, Mrs. Brooks. I did not come here to bother you. I'm a graduate student at the University of Pennsylvania. My boyfriend is an FBI agent in Philadelphia. He located you. I found the article in some old archives. I wasn't sure if he would find a relative of your uncle, let alone someone who would remember anything at all about the case. That's why I came here. Do you recall anything about what you learned from your family at that time?"

"It's so long ago, and I rarely think about it. I will 100 years old on my next birthday. The curse of being that old is that everyone you ever knew, or held dear is gone from your life. Sitting in this chair, well, I might as well be in prison. Richard's parents—my grandparents—did all they could to find him. They came home exhausted from the experience. My grandmother died a few months later. I believe it was from a broken heart.

"You see, Ms. Brown, Richard's life held such great promise. His parents were ordinary people with little money. My father, Harold, had achieved more than his parents, but Richard was a doctoral candidate! He was so bright! No one in our family had ever graduated from college, or gone on from there. My grandfather was dead a year later. I believe Richard's death killed them both! My maternal grandparents had died years before that. I finished high school, but my education ended then. As I said, life was hard.

"When Richard disappeared, the light went out in the eyes of our family. I have never forgotten him. His warm smile, the way his smile made his eyes turn up, his wit, charm and joy of life! He could make you feel alive and filled with hope just by walking into a room. He loved me. I was his only niece…an only child. I loved him so. And now, you are here, reminding me of that pain from long ago!"

Impulsively, Helen dropped from her chair to her knees and took the old woman's hands in her own.

"Mrs. Brooks, I never intended to bring you this pain again. That is the last thing I want to do. However, there is a mystery here. I'm not sure if it will ever be solved. If it could not be solved back then, I don't know if we can find a thread of evidence now…but I would like to try. I would like your permission to see what I can find out.

"Richard was a graduate student. I am, too. That was our only connection, but now that I have met you, well, such a terrible thing may have taken place long ago, but perhaps God may have planned our meeting. I will not promise you that truth will be found or that justice will be finally served, but you have my word that I will do my best to see if there is anything anyone can discover, even at this late date. Like Richard, I am an anthropologist. We are a tenacious bunch. I am used to digging after facts. I don't give up easily, and besides, now that we've met perhaps you could tolerate me in your life in the future. Yes, I came under false pretenses, but there was no other way I could see to justify your acceptance. I would like to be your friend, if not your distant relative."

At that, Alicia Brooks smiled a great smile.

"Oh, my dear, that would mean so much to me! It is very lonely here. I would love to have a visitor. I'm sure you're very busy at school, but when you have time, please come to me, and bring your boyfriend. What's his name?"

"Daniel. He goes by Dan."

"I've never met anyone in the FBI. That would be interesting, too!"

"Thank you so much, Mrs. Brooks. Please, call me Helen. Before I go, is there anything else you remember about your uncle's disappearance?"

The old woman sat still with her eyes closed for so long that Helen thought she might have fallen asleep.

Finally, she said, "I recall one more thing, but I am not sure how it fits together. It may have nothing to do with my dear Richard."

"What is it, Mrs. Brooks?"

"It's a name."

"What name?"

"Prescott. Yes, Prescott."

"Is that a first or last name?"

"I don't know. I'm not even sure I remember why it strikes me at this moment. It has some connection with Richard, but I cannot recall what it is. I'm sorry, but if I remember more I will let you know immediately. Now, I am quite tired. This whole conversation has excited me and worn me out.

"Please, Helen, stay in touch with me. There is no one left in my life. It would be so good to have contact again, especially with someone your age. I have much to learn about this present time. Perhaps you could teach me about cell phones…and computers. I know nothing about them."

Helen rose to her feet. She leaned down and gave Alicia a kiss on the cheek.

"You have a new friend," she said. "I will come again as soon as I can. My schedule at school is quite busy, but I will visit you again. Thank you for sharing your memories with me. I will see what I can find out, and I will contact you through the office here. If we can discover who Prescott is, I will let you know. I have to get back home now. Please, get some rest."

At that moment the woman orderly opened the door. She had a glass vase in her hands.

"Sorry, I had to attend to other residents, but this should do the trick," she said.

"Thank you. I think the flowers will be perfect in it! Mrs. Brooks and I are distantly related, and I will be returning to see her from time-to-time."

Helen placed the flowers in the vase.

"Is there somewhere I can get some water for them?"

The orderly said, "I'll take care of it for you."

Helen handed the vase and flowers to the woman and she left the room. Helen turned back and smiled at Alicia Brooks.

"Well, cousin Alicia, it's been so good meeting you. Have a pleasant afternoon. I will see you again as soon as I can."

The old woman smiled.

"Thank you, Helen…but please don't wait too long. When one is your age, one has all the time in the world, but when you are my age… each minute that passes is that much closer to eternity."

Helen laughed at the joke.

"I understand. I will say so long for now, but not goodbye. If I figure this out, I will let you know right away. If not, I will still come and visit you. I was raised by my grandparents. I know what love feels like…as well as loss. See you soon!"

With those words Helen turned and went through the door.

*Chapter Two*

As Helen drove back to Philadelphia she thought about her conversation with Alicia Brooks. She wanted to find the truth, but, even more than that, she wanted to visit the old woman and be her friend. Her parents had divorced when she was a child, and she had gone to live with her maternal grandparents at the age of 5.

Their home was a loving one. Her grandmother cared very much about seeing that Helen had a good home, and did all she could to make Helen feel welcome. Her grandfather would have never been accused of being a warm person. However, Helen knew he loved her, as well, even though he was always serious and a man of few words.

After a year of addressing her debts, Helen's mother had moved back home and joined Helen. Helen grew up in that household, attending elementary, middle and high schools in the small town in the Pennsylvania hills, earning a scholarship to Penn State. Following her graduation, she had applied to the University of Pennsylvania to do her graduate work.

Helen told Dan about her visit with Alicia Brooks, and he was sympathetic to the story of the lonely old woman and the death of her beloved uncle. Helen told him about the name, Prescott, and admitted that it was impossible.

"There must be a million people with that name, Dan. I don't know if it's a first or last name. How do I start this? I'm so busy at school I don't have time to think!"

"We'll both have to think about it. If there is a connection to the story, we'll have to find it. It will take time. And yes, I would like to visit Mrs. Brooks with you. That would be fun. Being that old—and that sharp, from what you said—it would be interesting to learn more about what life was like so long ago, especially from someone who was alive back then."

Two weeks slipped by. Helen read everything she could about the expedition that found King Tutankhamen's tomb. Howard Carter's discovery was one of the greatest stories in the world when it had taken place. She read about Egypt and its tombs, the Valley of the Kings, what Carter went through to secure permission to excavate the tomb, about the fabulous treasures, the people involved, and the curse.

She developed a fascination for Carter's benefactor, Lord Carnarvon. George Herbert, the Fifth Earl of Carnarvon, was an extremely wealthy British aristocrat born in 1866. He loved two forms of amusement more than any other: breeding race horses and driving fast cars. Driving had turned him into a near invalid when he was involved in a terrible auto accident in 1901 in Germany.

By the time Carter met him, Lord Carnarvon was weak from his injuries, and he was residing in Egypt, having taken up an amateur's interest in Egyptology and what might be discovered in the ancient tombs. Lord Carnarvon realized he lacked the professionalism to do what he dreamed of doing, so he chose to fund Carter in his efforts.

When King's Tut's tomb was unearthed, the world was fascinated with the monumental discovery, and even more so when Lord Carnarvon became extremely ill and died, having been bitten by a mosquito that apparently had carried a deadly disease. The man became ill after nicking the bite with a razor while shaving. The ensuing infection cost him his life.

His body was returned to England and buried in an ancient hill fort on Beacon Hill. Burghclere, Hampshire, England, not far from his ancestral home of Highclere Castle, the castle used in the popular television show, Downton Abbey. The curse promised that anyone opening or violating the tomb would be doomed. Carnarvon's death seemed to validate the curse, which spawned stories and books, and even movies about the tale around the world.

Today, there is a belief, based on scientific evidence, that Lord Carnarvon died because of a bacteria present on the walls of the tomb that had been carried by the mosquito. With that, the so-called curse had been laid to rest, so to speak.

Richard Fenner's disappearance and presumed murder was not mentioned with the exception of the story that Helen had discovered. The name Prescott did not appear in anything she found. She was ready to give up. It was the end of the trail.

Unknown to her, Dan had not been idle in his quest to find out who Prescott might have been, and what that person's relationship could have been to Richard Fenner.

The Federal Bureau of Investigation came into existence with a handful of agents in January, 1908, more than a decade before Howard Carter's discovery, and the FBI would largely become known for being very good at what it does.

Dan knew of a special program based on an incredible algorithm that had the ability to connect the dots when nothing made sense at all. He sought permission from his chief to run the quest through the program to see what would show up. He had been putting in a huge amount of time on his regular duties, and his chief, when he understood the mystery of Fenner's disappearance, gave him the go-ahead.

It only required an hour to turn up a result once the data had been entered. One name had appeared. The name was Prescott.

The full name was Albert Prescott. Little was known about the man. He came to the U.S. in 1936 from Cairo, Egypt. He was British. He had no family in the states. He had apparently made his fortune in selling artifacts to various museums and wealthy individuals in Europe before he moved to America. Shortly after he arrived he slipped off the grid.

The most notable event in 1936 was the Olympics held in Germany. The great Jessie Owens had shown Adolph Hitler's champions what an American athlete could do in competition, and the mad man had refused to shake his hand. Three years later Hitler's armies swept through Europe and ignited the free world into action.

Howard Carter made his fabulous discovery in 1923, and Prescott was selling artifacts around the same time. The link was a tenuous one, but it was a link, nevertheless. Many of the artifacts handled by the man in his dealings were later identified as lesser pieces from Tutankhamen's tomb. The question was: How did Prescott come into possession of them, and what was his possible relationship with Howard Carter and Lord Carnarvon?

Two weeks slipped by. Dan got a rare Saturday off and he drove Helen to see Mrs. Brooks. The old woman was delighted to meet Dan, an FBI agent, no less. The day was comfortable, so they were given permission to take her to the gardens behind the home.

It was quiet there, and Dan and Helen told Alicia Brooks all about what they had discovered. The old woman was excited.

"Do you think Albert Prescott knew my uncle Richard? Is that possible?"

"The problem, Mrs. Brooks—"

"Please, call me Alicia, Daniel."

"Yes Ma'am, but please call me Dan. The only person who calls me Daniel is my mother, and she does that only when she is angry with me."

The three of them chuckled.

"I could never be angry with you, Dan. My life has gone from nothing but loneliness to one filled with two wonderful young people who have come into my life. Thank you for trying hard to find out what happened to my dear Richard so very long ago. You can't know what this means to me. He was the brightest light in my childhood. Even if you cannot find the truth, the very fact that you are sitting here with me in the sunshine touches my soul. Being old is not easy, especially when you are as old as I am. Your youth and strength touches me. If I could, I would rise up from this chair and dance. That is how happy you've made me."

Helen had tears in her eyes, and Dan swallowed hard. He was not given to displays of emotion easily, but this old woman had struck a chord in him. She reminded him of his paternal grandmother, Margaret, in whose presence he had spent many warm moments as a boy. She had been gone for some time now, but he still missed talking to her.

"What I meant to say is this: Prescott arrives in America,

and not long after that he disappears. We don't know what his connections were. He certainly is no longer alive. We have a lot to do here to find out what might have happened to him at this late date. Helen has done all she can on her end. I can do more, but it will take time. I'm treating this as what you may have heard called a "cold case" on one of those silly TV crime shows. This case is very cold…maybe even frozen solid."

They all laughed at his joke.

"However, I have access to resources that the best police departments lack. I was able to find the connection using something I cannot even talk about with anyone. Yes, the trail is very cold, but I spend my days sifting through seemingly unrelated data to track down bits of information that may lead our people to finding those who are coming to this country with the intention of harming us-"

"Do you mean terrorists, Dan?" Alicia asked.

"Yes, Alicia, and we are very good at what we do. However, this Prescott, as far as I know, was no terrorist. They had them back then, too, but they were called by different names. Albert Prescott is connected to this story somehow. He sold things that should not have been in his possession. How did he get them? Did he know Howard Carter or Lord Carnarvon? I have to establish not only where he went after he came to America, but if anyone in Egypt at that time met the man and made any record of him. It's not going to be easy. I'm FBI. It's the CIA who may be able to help. I plan to have lunch with a friend there next week."

The following week Dan met John Abramson for lunch. They had been boyhood friends. Serving as agents in the two major tradecraft agencies in America kept them very busy. It had been nearly a year since they'd last seen each other.

"So, your love life has gotten interesting, Dan. Helen sounds like she might be the one. When are you going to pop the question?"

Dan laughed. "I believe in long engagements."

"You mean you're engaged already?" John asked.

"No. Maybe by year's end I'll ask her if all goes well. However, that's not why I wanted to see you."

"I thought it was because of our friendship?" John teased.

"Of course. But we're both in the business, and I have a story to tell you about something I'm working on for Helen, and for someone else who is special, too," Dan said.

When Dan finished his tale, John said, "The case, as you describe it, is so old that it is probably quite dead—beyond finding anything out."

"True. But we have technology now that no one dreamed of back then," Dan added.

"O.K. Point taken, but technology, as far as I can see, is useless in this case. What you need is someone in Egypt who remembers something. I suspect that there's no one alive who can help you there, but I will try to find out anything I can. I'm owed a few favors, and I think I can cash one of them in. Now, are you going to invite me to the wedding?"

Dan smiled at his friend. "Only if you agree to be my best man, or should I look for someone less wary?"

"Wow! So this girl really is the one after all?"

"I think so, but, like I said, there's no hurry here. It'll happen when the time is right," Dan said.

"In that case, I would be honored to serve. When can I meet her?"

"We'll try to find a time when you and I aren't running everywhere. You're chasing them over there, and I am looking for them here. Let me know when you'll be stateside again and we'll get together. Now, let's get to that lunch. I'm starving!"

The Egyptian quest proved to be useless. John called in his favor but nothing and no one existed that could bring light to the subject. To make matters worse, there are thousands and thousands of people named Prescott in the United States, including a huge number named Albert Prescott.

If Albert Prescott disappeared in 1936, did he marry? Did he have children? Were there surviving grandchildren or even great-grandchildren alive today? Endless questions needed answering if they were going to get anywhere. How many people would have to be questioned to find out if anyone who knew anything was still alive? If the man had a son, or sons, that would be easier. However, if a child or children were daughters, they had certainly taken their husband's names if they married. The task was not simply daunting. It was probably impossible.

What happened next was unexpected.

Chapter Four

Alicia Brooks had a dream. There were many things mixed together in her dream, but the thread of one thing stayed with her when she awoke on a Wednesday morning. She immediately thought of Helen and Dan.

Both of them had given Alicia their cell phone numbers. They had even gotten Alicia a cell phone of her own, and Helen put her "on her plan"—whatever that meant.

It had taken time to get used to the thing, but Helen had programmed Dan's cell number and her cell number into Alicia's phone. The phone was in the drawer of her nightstand by her bed. There was a typed piece of paper with it outlining how to turn on the phone, how to make a call, what buttons to push if she had an emergency, and what numbers to push if she wanted to call Dan or Helen. Helen suggested that Alicia should call her, not Dan, because of his work, unless it was something she had to discuss immediately with him.

Alicia opened the drawer and took out the phone and the paper. She followed the instructions and pushed the right buttons.

The phone rang. A male voice answered, "Hello."

Dan never answered with his name. Wrong numbers happened. Given his line of work, he maintained secrecy.

"Is-is this Dan?" an old woman's voiced asked.

"Alicia-Mrs. Brooks? It's me, Dan! Are you all right?" The concern in his voice was very real.

"Oh, dear, yes, I'm all right. But I remembered something—"

"What is it?"

"A conversation from long ago. I was in my bedroom after Richard disappeared. I heard my parents speaking in their bedroom. They were talking about my grandparents. Apparently, they had received a sum of money from an unknown source. There was no way to know who had authorized the check. I think it was for thousands of dollars. I don't remember how much it totaled. There was no letter with it to explain why the money was given to them. My father said that the check had his parents' names on it. I think it was from a bank in England. Oh, I'm sorry, but that would be in British pounds, wouldn't it? Anyway, the check had been mailed from Egypt. It was a mystery. I had a dream last night, and this is what I remembered this morning. It's like that when you are old; you can't remember what you had for dinner yesterday, but recall things that are positively ancient."

"Mrs. Brooks—"

"Alicia."

"Yes, Alicia, do you want me to call Helen? Are you sure you are all right?" Dan asked.

"Would you, please? I'm all right, but I'm not very good at using this phone. Please tell her that I am thinking about her. I hope this is of some help."

"Of course. I will call her right away. Thank you. I can't promise it will come to anything, but if it does, I will let you know immediately. I hope to see you soon. Have a good day!"

"Thank you, Dan," Alicia said. "I'll look forward to seeing the two of you, when you have the time."

"Goodbye, Alicia.

"Goodbye."

Dan sat at his desk for a long moment. He would call Helen in a few minutes. He thought about what Alicia Brooks had said. A check from England mailed from Egypt. The year 1923 was so long ago. How could anyone expect to find financial information from that time? He did not have the name of the bank, and how would he ever find out where in England it was located, or if any record of the transaction had been made? How would he find out if the check had been cashed, or what the amount was? It was impossible! The whole thing had taken on a life of its own.

Dan decided to sit down with his chief.

Supervisory Special Agent Marcus Anderson liked Special Agent Daniel Edmunson for his work ethic, intelligence, character, and determination.

"Dan," he said, after hearing the full story, "I see why this is fascinating. There is a mystery here, and we all like mysteries, as long as we can solve them. What do you want me to do?"

"How can we find out where a check written on a bank in England in 1923 to an American couple named Fenner came from? Do you think there is even a way to track down this information?" Dan asked.

"I have no idea, but, to start with, I'll need the first and last names of the couple. I'll take this from there. I have a contact over there. We're in the same line of work, so to speak. If I find out anything I'll let you know immediately."

He paused, smiling. "Have you popped the question yet?" Anderson asked.

"Everybody is asking me—does it show that much?"

"In the movies, they call it love. You have it all over your face whenever you talk to her on the phone. She has to be the one, or this is quite an infatuation you've got going here."

"Sir, you will be the second person to know when I ask her to marry me. I promise."

"Who'll be the first?"

"Helen," Dan said, smiling at his chief.

A week passed and Supervisory Special Agent Anderson called Dan to his office.

"The check was in the amount of 5,000 English pounds, a tidy sum, as they might say, for those times. It was a check from a law firm in London. No reason can be found for issuing the check. The law firm still exists. It has many wealthy Brits among its clientele. The fact that I was able to find this out at all is something of a miracle. I won't go into why. That's all we'll probably discover. Sorry. That's the best I can do."

"Thank you, sir. I really appreciate it. We may have come to the real end of the trail."

"If I know anything about you at all I suspect that's not true. 'I give up' isn't part of your vocabulary. That's why you work for me. Mine either. Let me know if you discover anything else. The case intrigues me, too."

"Yes sir," Dan nodded. "May I ask one more thing? Is it possible to find out who the clients of that law firm happen to be?"

"That could be very difficult, Dan."

"I understand, sir, but perhaps an inquiry could come from your contact in England? If it was worded in such a way that, shall we say, a rich individual was asking whether the firm was adequate for his needs, perhaps dropping a few names would be enough to stimulate new business from another person with a great deal of money?"

Anderson laughed out loud. "You're really something, Dan! I love the way your mind works. Yes, that might be enough to elicit information. I'll run it by my contact. If he's willing to try it, perhaps we'll find out what we need to know."

"Thank you again, sir."

A week went by. Dan's workload was piling up. Terrorism was front page all over the world, and the FBI was gearing up along with every other agency involved in American counter-terrorism.

Helen had her hands full, as well. She was spending hours on her graduate thesis, and when she wasn't in the library or online, she was typing chapters, checking for errors, re-typing and re-reading it all for the umpteenth time.

Both Dan and Helen were making calls to Alicia Brooks on opposite days. One of them phoned her mid-mornings, and the other in mid-afternoons. The idea was to make her feel good about having friends in her life.

She had taken a real interest in them, as well. She felt towards them like a grandmother—admittedly a very old grandmother, would feel. In turn, relieving her loneliness was paramount. They talked about everything with her, and she loved to hear their young voices go on about what they were doing and about all the news they heard in their world. She was more alive in her mind and spirit than she had been in many years.

Dan's chief called him to the office on Monday of the following week.

"My contact decided to try your approach. It worked. He faxed me this list a few minutes ago. I promised that only you would see it, and that I would destroy it immediately. Look it over. See if anything catches your eye. Apparently, this law firm is very well-connected. There are some real heavyweights on their client list. Please, look at it here since I can't copy it, and I'm going to shred it after you read it."

Dan took the list, sat down, and looked through it. It read like a Who's Who of British blue bloods. Halfway down the list a name caught his eye. He felt his pulse quicken and his intuition began sounding alarm bells.

It couldn't be…but it was!

Dan thought he knew where that check had come from long ago. He looked up. Something told him not mention what he had found until he could verify the truth.

"Thanks, sir. There really are some big people and companies on this list. Those guys must be making a ton of money. Guess we chose the wrong line of work."

Anderson laughed. "I couldn't agree more. Did you find anything?"

"No, but I saw some things that were interesting—"

"You're not going to tell me? After I went to bat for you?"

"No sir, I didn't mean it that way. What I meant is that I had no idea that such famous people like that lived in Britain, or that companies that big and well-known need law firms in London. I guess I shouldn't be surprised. People and companies like them probably have law firms all over the place. I guess they really are a big deal. I don't think anyone on this list could be involved in this ancient story. If a company did it, it would have to have been around back in 1923. I would have to find out if the company existed then. The individuals on the list are alive now, too, and none of them go back to 1923.

"The real truth is this makes no sense at all. I'm sorry to have bothered you with it. I'm just trying to find some peace for an old woman I met. I like her a lot. She reminds me of my late grandmother. She's going to be a hundred years old. I promise I'll avoid bringing my private life to work from now on. You have enough on your plate—and so do I."

Anderson said, "Dan, one of the things they taught me in Management 101 is that we are to always be concerned about people's private lives, especially in this line of work. You're a fine special agent with a real future. That's not going to change because you asked my help on this. I am glad to help—and, frankly, I like mysteries. That's why I do what I do. Figuring things out can be tiresome, but when it works, the rewards are fantastic. Now, both of us have stuff to do. If you find anything else that is helpful let me know."

"Yes sir, and thank you again!"

## Chapter Five

The world has grown increasingly dangerous since the events of 911. Surveillance techniques, technology, computerization, the Internet, spyware, hacking, encryption, etc. have combined to create an environment that ought to be incredibly beneficial to mankind, but not when people who live mentally in the 7th century A.D. now use social media to recruit impressionable young people to become brutal murderers of so-called infidels.

Dan Edmundson faced the onslaught at work every day. His preoccupation with the mystery of Richard Fenner's disappearance was something that was not allowed to replace his normal duties. Protecting the Homeland was job one.

However, he could not keep his mind from returning to one name on the list his chief had shown to him. It tied Fenner even more strongly to the players in that incredible discovery back in the early 1920's. What was the connection? In fact, how was a man named Albert Prescott, who had not arrived in America until 1936, long after the tragic events of 1923, related to Richard Fenner? That made the least sense of all!

What was the key that would unlock the secret? The name Dan had seen on the list should have no connection to the Fenner family, but that man had to be the one who sent the check to them—but why?

There was no way to prove anything. No real evidence existed, except a check received and, Dan assumed, cashed and spent long ago.

He decided that it was time to give it up. Dan would tell Helen about the name on the list, but he did not plan to tell Mrs. Brooks. He did not want to upset her. If Helen agreed that it was a strange conclusion, and that there was absolutely no way to prove anything, they would stop the nonsense and get back to work.

They would continue to see Alicia Brooks as often as they could.

Their affection for her grew stronger each time they spoke to her.

He met Helen for lunch and told her about the name.

"Doesn't it strike you as utterly strange, I mean, weird, even, that someone by that name might have sent that check, Dan?

"Helen, I am at the end of this. I have dug for all the information I can. I even got my boss to help me, and he was the one who got the list with the name on it. It was my leap-of-faith that drew the conclusion of a possible connection, but that does not connect at all with anyone named Prescott years later. Mrs. Brooks cannot remember why she remembers the name Prescott. Someone must have said something to her when she was young, perhaps one of her parents? Maybe it is something her mind made up? There is no way to go forward from here.

"Albert Prescott, circa 1936, is long dead, and it would take us a lifetime to track him down and find out why he fell off the face of the earth. Whether his intentions were good or evil, we'll never know. I can't spend too much more time on this. I suggest we drop it, go and tell Alicia about our decision to stop, and simply spend time with her from now on. What do you say?"

"Dan, I never expected that you would get so wrapped up in this, and I love you for it—yes, I said love. You're the sweetest man I've ever met. The way you care for Alicia is heartwarming. Not many guys your age would give a person like her the time of day.

"I like old people. I was raised by them. You know that, but what you don't know is that we can learn so much about life from them! We take everything for granted, but they were there when things began.

"I want to adopt her as another grandmother, with you, if you're willing? I'm not sure how much time she has left, but you've seen her face when we walk in her room! She's fantastic! Maybe all she did was finish high school when the Great Depression hit and the whole world fell apart, but she has volumes of experience we lack. We things from her that aren't in any textbook anywhere."

Dan's eyes were shining. "Helen, you used the word love. If it's O.K., I'd like to show you how I feel about you. I was going to wait until the end of the year, but I don't want to wait any longer. I work in a world that grows scarier and nastier every day, but I know the work I'm doing makes a difference. I can't talk about my work with anyone, but that doesn't mean that I don't need you in my life."

Dan reached into his pocket and took out a small box. He opened the lid.

Helen's eyes grew big and a great smile spread over her face. The ring was absolutely beautiful. She was breathless in that moment.

"Helen, will you spend your life with me? Will you take my hand and walk with me every day? We can share a grandmother, too. We'll just have to adopt her as our very own!"

The people at the other tables in the restaurant around them were rising from their tables and aiming their phone cameras.

"Yes! Oh Dan, my love, yes! I will be your wife!"

Cheers from people around them in the restaurant were loud and long.

The month of August had arrived. It was warm, but, not as warm as it normally could be in Philadelphia. Late summer in Philly can be brutal. Dan and Helen had chosen Christmas to be married. They had talked about waiting a year, but they wanted to be sure that Alicia would be at their wedding, God willing, so Dan suggested Christmas Day. His paternal grandparents had married on that date in 1925. Helen thought it was a wonderful idea.

Alicia Brooks agreed, as well. She would turn 100 years old on October 25th. She promised them that she would be their grandmother, honorary or otherwise, as long as they cared to have her.

Dan and Helen took Alicia on outings to the Philadelphia Art Museum, the Franklin Institute, Independence Hall and other attractions in the Delaware Valley.

They did not talk about her uncle anymore.

One day Helen suggested that they take a trip to Longwood

Gardens. As the threesome made their way about the lovely place, Helen picked up a brochure on Lancaster. Dan, was from Connecticut, and had never been there. Helen had visited several times when she was in high school with her family. She decided they needed to plan a trip there, too.

A week passed, and they drove by Longwood and continued on the road to where the GPS took them to the Lancaster area. They preferred back roads to congested main routes, and they loved getting off the beaten track for lovely scenery.

They made the turn off Route 41 at Gap, Pennsylvania. They drove through the valley, passing Amish buggies and farms as they made their way into the delightful town of Strasburg. They parked, got the wheelchair out, and the three of them went for a stroll. They reached an ice cream parlor on a corner, and agreed getting a cone was a splendid idea.

They found a table and made room for Alicia's wheelchair. They ordered their ice cream and had a great time eating, talking and laughing. When they finished, Dan went to the register to pay while Helen eyed a rack of brochures. One caught her eye. She picked it up and started reading through it. It was titled Strasburg Oddities.

Helen opened the brochure. There were several pages. In an article titled, *What Ever Happened To* there was a list of 10 strange things with descriptive paragraphs. Many of them were funny, whimsical…and then she came to the seventh item on the list and a chill went up her spine. She read through it again. She stuck the brochure in her purse as Dan took Alicia's wheelchair in hand, and the three left the shop.

They returned to their car and spent a lovely day in the Lancaster area, avoiding the shopping malls, but enjoying the back roads, Amish farms, and many pleasant places to stop. They chose carefully because wheelchairs are not always convenient in some environments. Their concern was for Alicia and what kind of day she was having. When they returned her to the home, she was tired but smiling.

"This has been one of the most wonderful days in my life, dear hearts. God bless you both. You'd better get home and get some sleep," Alicia said.

They hugged and kissed her and returned to their car. Before Dan turned the key in the ignition, Helen said, "Let's sit for a moment. I have something to show you."

Helen opened her purse, took out the brochure and handed it to Dan.

"Turn to page 5, and go to item 7," she said. "Please read it."

Dan did as instructed. His eyes grew big. He read through it a second time—and then a third. He turned to look at Helen.

She said, "What do you think?"

"Dear Lord," Dan said. "I think we've found Prescott."

Helen said, "Yes. I think so, too."

*Chapter Six*

Dan had returned to the Bureau and got permission to use the special program again. This time the search took a half-hour. He had asked for all patterns regarding the name Albert Prescott in the Lancaster County, Pennsylvania area from 1936 through the present day.

It appeared that an Albert Prescott had purchased a home in Strasburg, Pennsylvania in 1950, long before Lancaster had become a popular tourist destination. He had moved from Philadelphia. He lived there until 1998 when he had disappeared. No one knew what had happened to him.

Someone with a similar name became a resident of the newly opened Parsons Retirement Home in the town of Ephrata, Pennsylvania in 1999.

*Perhaps this was only a coincidence?* Dan called Parsons to find out. "Does an Albert Prescott live there, or has he moved on?"

"Who wants to know?" Parsons was wary.

"I'm an agent with the Federal Bureau of Investigation," Dan said, which was true, "and we believe a relative of Albert Prescott's has been found dead. I would like to visit him tomorrow if possible."

Dan said this in a very official sounding voice, which the young woman on the other end of the phone found very believable.

"Yes, Mr. Prescott lives here," she said. "Should I tell him you will be calling on him?"

"No, that won't be necessary," Dan said. "I will be there early in the morning."

"You'd best be early," the young woman said. "He takes his morning walk at 6:30."

"Thank you. I'll be there."

Dan called Helen. "Can you go with me tomorrow? We have to leave your place at 5:00 a.m. if we are going to see him. He apparently walks in the mornings. I was told he is outside at 6:30. I want to speak to him away from the building.

"Yes, I want to go. Even if it's the wrong man we need to know," Helen said.

Both of them were yawning when Dan picked her up. They got coffee at a drive-through and hit the highway. They pulled into the driveway in front of Parsons driveway at 6:25 a.m.

Dan parked the car and looked around. The sun was up but it was very early. They got out of the car and walked towards the entrance. Helen saw the figure of a man across the large yard near a line of trees.

"I bet that's him." she said.

They started walking across the grass and their shoes were immediately soaked with heavy dew.

Dan and Helen walked steadily. When they were about thirty yards from the man he became aware of them and turned around.

"Who are you? Keep away? I will yell for help." the man said.

"We mean you no harm, Mr. Prescott. We've come to ask you a few questions," Dan said. "I called here yesterday and told them I was coming. I'm Dan Edmundson and this is my partner, Helen Brown. I'm with the FBI."

The man seemed flustered. "The FBI? What could you possibly want to speak to me about? I haven't done anything. Please…don't come any closer. I'm old. I cannot run from you. That's why I live here."

"Please, sir," Helen said. "We're only here to speak with you briefly. We mean you no harm. Is there a place to sit near here where we can talk for a few moments?"

Prescott looked around wildly. "There are benches right over there by that flower bed. I walk here alone every morning. I like to be alone. I have no friends here. I don't live here by choice. What could you possibly want with me? I've lived here a long time…since it opened. I've done nothing. I've never bothered anyone. I rarely go into the nearby community, and then only when I have to. Please, leave me alone!"

Prescott looked like he might try to run. He would not make it far from the look of him. He looked frail in the morning light. He also possessed an uncanny resemblance to someone Helen had seen before. She could not recall who it was. His British accent sounded very precise. His voice was pleasant, but he sounded like a man who was used to being obeyed.

Helen eased forward while Dan remained behind.

"We assure you that we are not here to harm you at all. We want to show you a newspaper article about something of importance. We are not even sure you are involved. You couldn't possibly be old enough to know about it, but you might have had an older relative who knew something. Could you spare us a few minutes? We won't keep you long, and then you can get back to your morning walk," Helen said, motioning toward the benches. Her manner and voice seemed to have a calming effect on the older man.

"Yes, well, I suppose I could give you a few minutes. The benches over there are probably wet with dew. They probably won't be comfortable. We could talk right here. What is it that you have to show me?"

Helen handed Prescott a copy of the newspaper article about Richard Fenner's disappearance and asked, "Do you need glasses to read this?"

"Glasses? Heavens no. My eyes are fine." He took the article and read through it. He stopped, looked up, and Helen thought she saw the hint of tears in his eyes.

"I don't know anything about this," he said. "Why have you come here?"

Dan said, "We have been researching this story for many, many months. Your name was brought up by a source—"

"What source? I have lived here since 1999 when they opened, but this…this tragedy happened long, long ago. Good Lord. 1923? How would I know anything about that?" Prescott said, with emotion in his voice.

Helen saw that the man's face was filled with apprehension. Instinctively, she reached into her pocket and took out a brochure. She handed it to him.

"Please turn to page 5, item 7 and read," she said.

Prescott looked at the cover of the brochure and his eyes grew big. They both saw fear in his face. "Page 5 … item 7 … you said?" He opened the brochure and looked furtively at the place she mentioned. His eyes looked wild. Again, he looked like he might try to run.

"What does that have to do with me? Is this some bizarre kind of joke? Has someone put you up to this?"

"Is that little blurb about your grandfather? It's the same name as yours. That man disappeared. Is he related to you?" Dan asked.

"No! How could it be? I know nothing about that! If you don't leave me alone, I am going to start screaming as loudly as I can.

Please, leave me! Get away!"

In as calming a voice as she could muster, Helen said, "It's going to be all right, Mr. Prescott. We did not come here to harm you. We'll leave now. We'll leave you alone. You like to be alone, don't you? You're always alone with your thoughts. There is much to think about, isn't there? Come Dan, let's go. Mr. Prescott, we will leave you now. Time will go on like it always does. Oh, by the way, the young man in the story…he had a niece. We have adopted her as our friend. I'm sure you would like her very much if you met her. She wants us to find out the truth. She will be 100 years old in October. Imagine that? Think of the things she has seen! She has lived a long, lonely life wishing she could see Richard again, but that was not to be. Goodbye."

Helen turned on her heel and began walking with Dan a few steps behind her when a voice rang out.

"Wait. Please wait. Please! I can't stand it anymore. I can't go on. Please, come back. I will talk to you, but only this once. And if you tell anyone, I will deny everything."

Dan and Helen turned around and walked back to the man.

Helen said, "Who are you, really?"

"You must believe what I say. Otherwise, there is no point in me saying anything."

"What does that mean?" Dan asked.

"I am George Edward Stanhope Molyneux Herbert, the Fifth Earl of Carnarvon. I was born in 1866," Prescott said.

Dan laughed. "That's impossible. Why, you would be—"

"Yes, I am that old," the man said.

"That's impossible," Helen added. "No one could possibly—"

"Live that long, Ms. Brown? But, you see, the Curse is quite real."

"What curse?" Dan asked.

"The Curse of King Tut's Tomb. However, it is not a curse that brings death. In my case, it is a curse that brought life. I loved the fast life as a young man—fast horses and faster cars. Loved them greedily until my accident in Germany in 1901. It left me as weak as a child. I developed other interests, after that. I went to Egypt and met Howard Carter. What a marvelous find!

"When the mosquito bit me it infected me with this terrible malady. I thought I was going to die. I wish that I had. You can't know what this is like. I am as weak as I ever was, but I don't age. God help me. I live on and on and on. It is like being a living mummy. Decades pass by painfully, people die all around me, and after awhile people begin to look at you with suspicion. "Why isn't he aging like me? Like the rest of us?" they wonder. What is different about him? Is he a devil?"

And so, I have to move on. I cannot abide in any one place for more than 20 years. I stayed in Egypt as long as I could. Then, I loved Strasburg too well, and stayed there too long. I must leave here soon. Life is a living hell for me."

Helen said, "If this could possibly be real …" she paused, the realization of what she was asking slowly dawning on her, "who is buried in your tomb on Beacon Hill?"

"A dear young scholar whom I had hoped to meet by the name of Richard Fenner."

Dan's face clouded with anger. He said with great force, "Did you kill him? If you did I will see to it that whatever life you have left is even more miserable!"

Prescott did not flinch. He showed no fear. In a voice that showed he was used to giving orders rather than receiving them, he said with clear distain, "Mind your manners, Mr. Edmunson. No one speaks to me in that tone. I have never killed anyone. Poor Richard Fenner was rushing to our site when his drunken idiot of a driver drove off the road, killing the both of them, not far from our excavation. He died in the accident.

"I also died, or so everyone thought. But I revived. I hid myself. Locals took the bodies of Fenner and his driver, stripped them, dumped them in a pit, and covered them with sand. Then, those same people stole the vehicle.

"Poor Howard Carter rushed to the scene, but found nothing. Confused, he went back to his work. I learned later, that he thought Richard Fenner had changed his mind about joining the dig. When Richard's parents showed up later searching for him, he was overwhelmed with remorse, having discovered that Fenner really had disappeared.

"I dressed in a disguise. Having lots of money is sometimes a good thing. I paid handsomely for information and had Fenner's body recovered. I knew that something incredibly strange had happened to me.

"I decided to stage my own death. It's amazing what money can do. Given the impact of the elements and the clothing, no one looked too closely to see if Fenner's body was mine.

"I lived in anonymity in Egypt for years. Then, I came here. I lived in Philadelphia. I discovered that people were eyeing me strangely as the years slipped by. So, I moved to Strasburg. I stayed there far too long. The same thing happened. Finally, I came here."

"Have you no remorse for Richard Fenner?" Helen asked. "His parents never found out what happened to him. Our dear friend, his niece says they both died of broken hearts. She has grieved for him all her long life."

For the second time, she thought she saw the gleam of tears in the man's eyes.

"I-I sent them money once. Five thousand pounds."

That was the clincher. Dan and Helen were convinced that this was actually Lord Carnarvon. They stood in silence for a long moment.

Finally, Dan said, "Well, what are we to do with you? You didn't murder the poor man, but you have been living a lie for so long that it is unbelievable. You've hurt people deeply."

"Yes, I agree. I am sorry for the selfish things I've done, as all men will be. But, if you turn me in, at first they won't believe anything about this. How could I be who you say I am?

"Even if they do believe you, what would they do with me? I would become an object of research, poked and prodded in their desire to extend life. Perhaps, using me, they could discover eternal life, but the human body cannot last indefinitely.

"The announcement of my existence would also create a dreadful problem for my heirs and the present Earl.

"I believe that I am one-of-a-kind, a cruel anomaly that will never be repeated. Now that you have found me, you must decide what you will do.

"There is one thing that I can do, immediately. I will see to it that Richard Fenner's niece does not have to worry about money anymore. The decision is yours to make. I am so tired of living this way, but I am also afraid to die. Do as you will."

*Epilogue*

Alicia's 100th birthday was celebrated at a restaurant in Philadelphia. The entire event was paid for by an unknown benefactor. It was a wonderful party.

The wedding of Dan Edmunson and Helen Brown was spectacular. Their adopted grandmother, Alicia Brooks, was wonderfully comfortable in a seat of honor. Those who attended the wedding said it was incredible.

The couple went on a month long honeymoon to England, Scotland, Wales and Ireland.

"The rich really do know how to live well," Dan remarked during an exquisite private tour of Highclere Castle, conducted by the present Earl.

As to Mr. Prescott, Dan and Helen had agreed: The worst punishment he could suffer was to go on living in anonymity.

# NO LAUGHING MATTER

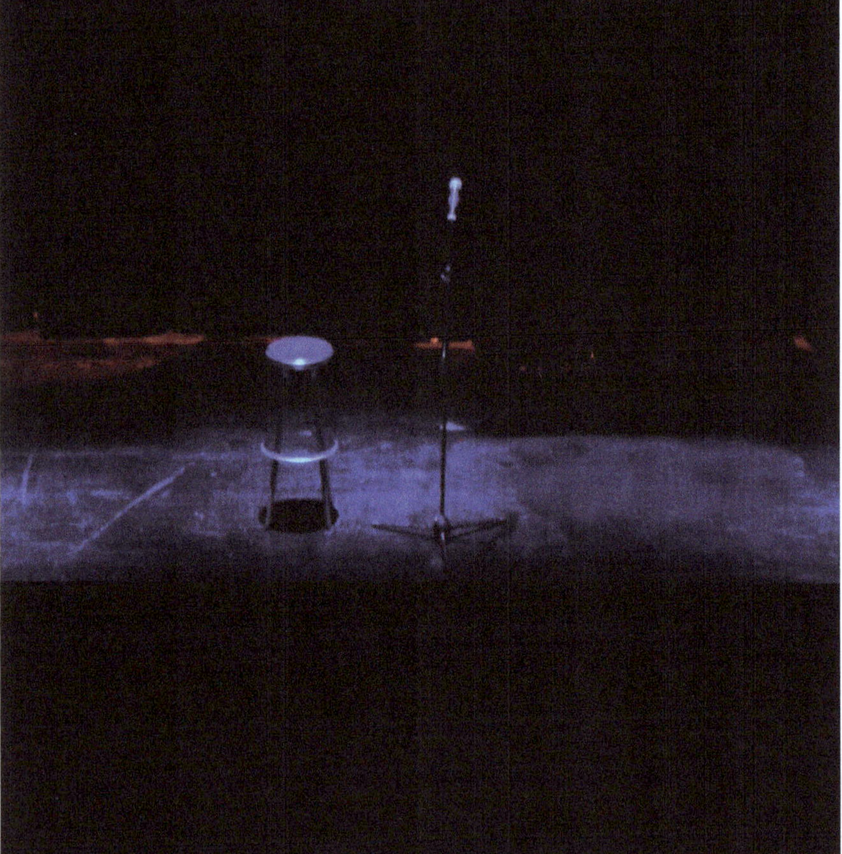

# No Laughing Matter

Kenny Kendrick was a funny guy. He tried working in construction, as a delivery man, waiting tables, bartending, and even playing the trumpet. He was a failure at everything, but he liked to make people laugh. He told jokes. Kenny had a great mind for jokes. He was irresponsible, lazy, devious, and offensive, but when he drank too much he became a real standup comic, at least in his own mind.

His great desire was to be on the circuit. After all, why work for a living when you could stand on stage and get paid to tell jokes? The trouble was that his material was really awful. Twenty minutes of filthy jokes was O.K. in a bar on the tough side of town, but that wasn't what people wanted to hear on the other side of the tracks. Humor is subjective, of course, and working for sandwiches and drinks was fun for Kenny…until he had to pay the rent.

He went to the best clubs and watched the comics work. The best of the best made it to television, earning big money. His dream was to get a great gig in Vegas.

Kenny was very good at something else, as well: envy. He envied the ones who grabbed the brass ring and went to the top. He envied the comics who had great material, perfect timing, and who could reduce audiences to laughing so hard that they were crying. He wanted what they had. There was just one problem. He was so lazy that he wouldn't even stand in front of a mirror and practice his technique, such as it was.

His idea of funny was gutter humor. He never noticed that some people in the audiences, even in the seediest dives, were cringing at his constant stream of profanity, blatant maligning of women, and his never-ending emphasis on sex in everything that came out of his mouth. Only men laughed at his jokes, and they were the kind of men who frequented places that were not visited by polite society.

Kenny was oblivious to his own shortcomings. However, his envy level went off the scale when he thought about the success of the best comics in the business.

In his opinion, Larry Lane was King of the Comics. Whenever Lane appeared on a TV show, Kenny was watching. When Lane put out a CD with new material, Kenny stole it. He never paid for what he could take from a store. If Lane came to Philadelphia, Kenny would finagle a ticket by any means necessary to be in the audience on opening night.

When Lane was cast in a sitcom on NBC, Kenny was salivating with desire every time he watched an episode.

Kenny grew up in Pittsburgh, Pennsylvania and left home right after high school. He had no desire to go to college or do anything special in life. To him, life was bars, girls, working when he could not avoid it, and running scams and cons when he could get away with them.

He spent every waking moment seeking the shortest distance between effort made and money received. He was the kind of guy who would walk a mile to avoid picking up a brick.

He had never gone home again. His parents had high hopes for him, but he didn't like them because of their expectations. He wanted nothing to do with them after he fled the area. They had to be content with his younger brother and sister, who were far better people than he ever wanted to be.

Kenny schemed, lost one part-time job after another, drank away his money, and continued to appear on stage at the only bar that would allow him to do standup on Saturday nights. The Blue Heron Bar was a real dive. The owner let him go on and do his set at midnight when patrons were totally fried and unable to pay attention.

Kenny was lazy. He never changed his material, only altering the order of the jokes from one week to the next. He was paid in sandwiches and beer.

He lived in a run-down hotel near the bar, and he was in arrears on his rent. He was facing homelessness when his luck changed.

Larry Lane was coming to the area for two nights to be on stage in Atlantic City. Kenny was in Philly, but he would manage to be there, no matter what. He would take a bus and see the show the first night.

One of Kenny's other problems was gambling. Whenever he went to a casino —which wasn't very often because he was broke most of the time—he hit the slots. He never had enough money, or confidence, to play craps, blackjack or roulette. He preferred the anonymity of the one-armed bandits because he didn't have to talk to anyone. He would be lucky after Lane's show if he could get out of the casino with enough money to catch a bus back to Philadelphia.

Sitting in the front row at Lane's first show, having scammed an old woman out of enough money to buy the best seat in the house, he laughed along with everyone else. Larry Lane was really on this night. His timing was impeccable, his jokes and routines were all new, and he was in high spirits.

Mid-way through the show Lane chose Kenny to come up on stage. He did a bit that made Kenny look like a real idiot, but Kenny didn't care. The audience roared. When Lane shook his hand, he was directed backstage instead of back to his seat. It was very dark immediately off stage, but he moved ahead towards a lighted hallway.

Someone should have been there to re-direct him back to the theater, but that stagehand had been called away momentarily, so Kenny moved through the hallway not knowing where he was. He saw a door with a star on it, and he decided to open it. He slowly opened the door. There was no one in the room. It was a dressing room. It was, in fact, Larry Lane's dressing room. He closed the door behind him. He looked around. On a table surrounded by lights he saw a thick notebook.

He quickly picked it up and was astounded to discover that it was filled with jokes and bits that were absolutely A-list material. He scanned the pages quickly. This was a goldmine! In that moment Kenny Kendrick decided to cross the line all the way.

He tucked the book under his arm and left the room. He entered the hallway and continued moving in the direction he had been walking when he found the dressing room. It led to an exit door that opened onto another hall, which took him to an exit at the side of the building.

Kenny stepped outside and found himself on a street next to the casino building. The Atlantic City boardwalk was to his right. He turned left and followed the streets back to the bus station. There would be no gambling this night.

When Kenny got back to Philly he went to his quarters and sat up reading through the material in the notebook.

~ ~ ~

When Larry Lane discovered the theft, he was furious. The notebook contained brand new material that had been written by some of the best joke writers in Hollywood. He had only tapped the surface of what lay between its covers, and he vowed that he would never come to Atlantic City again. Las Vegas was Lane's home base, and if he ever came east another time it would only be to New York. The notebook represented many thousands of dollars out of his pocket!

Suspicion led to questioning of everyone in the stage crew, but no one had seen anyone near his dressing room, and the mystery of who took the notebook wasn't likely to be solved.

Then, Lane remembered the guy he'd called up on stage during his act. The guy's name was Len, or Ken, or something like that. He had gone backstage after the bit. Maybe it was him, but there was no way to find out who the guy was. It was hopeless.

~ ~ ~

The notebook was a life-changing tool for Kenny. He read through it carefully, and then read through it again. He realized for the first time in his life why someone like Larry Lane was light years ahead of guys like him. The pages were filled with sheer comedic genius.

He wasn't a dummy. He had liked English in high school, and he even did pretty well in his school work, but all he wanted was to party and have a good time. He had screwed up a B+ average because he didn't care, and Ms. Richards had given him a C for his final grade.

However, this stuff was dynamite. The jokes were superb, but the genius lay in the set-up of each joke. The descriptions of the bits were perfect, and Larry Lane was the master at carrying it off. The writers had even included built-in pauses for perfect timing. They had described the necessary facial expressions, what words to emphasize, the body language – all of it!

The trouble was that Kenny could not use a word of the material as it was written. If he did, he'd be in jail. Larry Lane was a multi-millionaire. Kenny Kendrick was a low-class slob living in a fleabag hotel in Philadelphia without a job or a steady income.

How could he turn this to his advantage? He didn't have a clue.

In the middle of the night there was a knock on Kenny's door. He awoke and stumbled to the door and looked through the spy hole and saw that someone was outside his door.

He was afraid to open it. It could be a cop. Maybe they traced him to Philly? He stood there shivering in the darkness, holding his breath, trying not to make noise.

A voice spoke from the hallway.

"Mr. Kendrick, I advise you to open the door. I have something to discuss with you. It's important. There is no need to be afraid."

Kenny was still afraid. He screwed up his courage and slowly opened the door.

A man stood in the hallway. He was dressed in old fashioned clothing and wore a cape over his shoulders. He was smooth-shaven and his skin was pale. He wore very big, dark sunglasses.

Kenny thought absently that that made no sense. Why wear sunglasses inside a building?

"Yes, what is it? What do you want?" Kenny asked.

"Aren't you going to invite me in?" the man asked. His voice was deep with a strange accent as if English was not his first language.

Kenny said, "This place is a real dump, and I'm not dressed."

The man laughed, and the sound sent shivers up Kenny's spine.

"I've seen far worse, Mr. Kendrick. I can't give you this information if you don't invite me in. It will not take but a few moments."

His statements were oddly formal and sounded old-fashioned.

"What's the deal?" Kenny asked.

"The deal, Mr. Kendrick, is that I know what you did, and I can turn it to your advantage."

Kenny feigned innocence. "What I did? I didn't do anything—"

"Ah, but that is not the truth, is it? You shall speak the truth, and the truth shall set you free. Isn't that right, Mr. Kendrick?"

This last statement was said in a tone of mocking condescension.

Kenny felt his face grow red.

"I was asleep. I've been here all night!" Kenny declared.

"Then why do you have something that doesn't belong to you? You see, Mr. Kendrick, I know all about what you did. Mr. Lane is furious—"

"Good God, did he send you?"

The man smiled, and his smile was frightening. It reminded Kenny of something he'd seen in a horror movie on TV

"God, Mr. Kendrick? You offend me. No, Mr. Lane did not send me. He knows nothing about you. However, it is hard to keep things hidden from me. I make it my business to go where I am—needed. You need my help, Mr. Kendrick, but I cannot provide that help unless you invite me in. Say the word and your life, such as it is, will become far better than you could ever imagine. Deny me and I will seek someone else who needs, my help. What's your decision?"

Kenny stood for a long moment staring at the man.

"All right, come in. You're going to wake up the whole place if I don't get you out of the hall." He opened the door wider.

The man in the hall sighed deeply, and his frightening smile grew broader.

"Thank you, Mr. Kendrick. You will regret it deeply, but think of the fun I will have." He stepped into the room.

Kenny Kendrick was not able to recall much of what happened after that. He ended up signing some sort of contract agreeing to abide by the rules that were in it. In exchange, he would be able to use the material in the notebook, but in such a way that no one, including Larry Lane, would ever be able to accuse him of theft. When the man left Kenny stumbled back to his bed and slept fitfully until noon.

Chapter Two

When Kenny woke up he felt like he had been drinking and his hangover was world-class. He rolled on his right side and felt like he was going to throw up. The fact was that he had not been drinking the previous night because of his trip to Atlantic City. Still, it sure felt like he had had been belting down the booze.

As he lay there he saw what looked like a business envelope on the floor next to the bed. The only amenity in the room, other than the bed, was a folding luggage stand where his suitcase rested. His clothes were piled on top of it. There was no nightstand or dresser. The only window faced onto a brick wall. It was covered by a stained shade that was torn in two places and hung limply three-quarters of the way down to the sill.

Kenny slowly sat up and reached down for the envelope. It was a 9 X 12 white envelope with a self-seal. He opened it and found a copy of a contract, a business card with the name, address, and phone number of a talent agency in New York, and a smaller envelope that contained $1,000.00. There was also a sheet of paper covered in old fashioned, cursive writing.

*Dear Mr. Kendrick,*

*Herein, please find your copy of our contract. The New York agency will start you on your path to success. Purchase a decent interview suit, shoes, shirt and tie for your trip to the Big Apple with the enclosed cash. Burn your old clothing. It's abominable.*

*See you sooner than you might imagine,*
*L.S.*

Kenny's first thought was to go on a binge, spend the money, have a great time, get smashed, and to hell with the whole deal. Who was L.S.? He didn't have a clue. He remembered little of the man in the hallway.

He sat there for a half hour wondering what to do. He looked at the business card. The name on the card was: Talent Ltd. The address was somewhere in Manhattan. Strangely, there was no email or web information.

Every company in America has an email or a website, don't they? he assumed.

A decision had to be made. Kenny stood up, then immediately sat down hard on the bed. He was dizzy and nauseous. Then, as if by magic, he felt better. In fact, he felt like a million bucks! He hadn't felt this good since he was a kid!

He stood up. Yes, he would do what the note said! He was going to New York. He was going to the agency to see what they could do for him. He was going to be a star!

Kenny went to a clothing store in the neighborhood and bought a modestly-priced, dark grey suit off the rack. He also purchased a white shirt and a tie with the help of the sales clerk, a young lady who happened to be the daughter of the owner. Shoes were next. By the time he was done he had spent $436.00 of the money.

He put his old clothing in a dumpster, bought a small suitcase and placed his underwear, toiletries, odds and ends, and the notebook in it. He took a cab to the bus station. He had never taken a cab before.

It was fun to pretend that he was actually somebody who could afford to take a cab anytime he wanted.

As the bus made its way up the New Jersey Turnpike he watched the scenery with interest. Kenny's mind was churning with possibilities.

When he got off the bus, he went to a cab stand and took a cab to the address on the card. He was surprised to discover that the building was not far from Times Square. It was a real high rent district! Kenny was impressed.

He took the elevator to the 30th floor. When he stepped out he looked to his left and right along a hallway extending in both directions. There were doors to offices on both sides, all of which were closed. Before him an ornately paneled door contained the name Talent Ltd.

He went to the door, opened it, and saw a blond receptionist seated behind a desk typing on a computer keyboard. There was an area to his left with a coffee table and several comfortable-looking armchairs in rich mahogany-colored leather. To his right there was a coffee and tea station, and next to that was an entrance to a kitchen area.

The woman behind the desk was spectacular. She looked up and smiled at him with a dazzling smile.

"Mr. Kendrick? We've been expecting you. Mr. B will see you in just a moment. Please, help yourself to some coffee or tea and have a seat."

Kenny thanked her and he went to the seating area and sat down.

His stomach was too nervous, and he felt like he needed a drink.

An hour dragged by, then two. There were no magazines to look at, no TV screen, and nothing to relieve the tension. Mid-way through the third hour Kenny stood up and approached the receptionist.

"Pardon me, but did something happen to Mr. B? You said he

would see me in just a few minutes when I came in, and it has been—"

The look on the woman's face did not match her voice. She looked positively enraged, but her voice was soft and persuasive.

"Mr. Kendrick, it has only been five minutes since you arrived. Have you looked at the clock?"

Kenny had been watching the clock. The hours had dragged by slowly. Now, when he looked again, he saw she was right! Only five minutes had passed. He felt his face redden. He was embarrassed. He must have fallen asleep and dreamed that over two hours had passed.

"Sorry," he mumbled. "I'll just sit down again."

Kenny returned to his seat. Another hour slowly dragged by, and then another …

He was beginning to wonder if this was some kind of a cruel joke when a short, squat man in an expensive suit entered the room from a door on Kenny's left. The man's head had an odd shape to it. His jet black hair was slicked back, and his eyebrows, the shape of his face, his nose, cheeks and eyes reminded Kenny of something.

What the devil was it? Then, Kenny realized that the man resembled a giant rodent. A rat. His teeth were pointed when he smiled at Kenny, completing the image.

"Mr. Kendrick, I'm Mr. B. Thank you for waiting. I hope I didn't take too long?"

Kenny stood up. He was at least a foot taller than his host.

Mr. B. extended his hand, and Kenny shook it. He withdrew his hand immediately. The man's hand felt like touching something slimy, wet and distasteful. He tried to hide his revulsion.

"I-I'm sorry. It did seem like a long wait, although now, when I look at the clock, I see that it has only been 15 minutes."

"Yes, a minute can sometimes seem like an eternity," Mr. B. said. "Please, come to my office. We'll talk there. Thank you, Miss A. Please tell our next appointment that I will be with them shortly."

The rodent-man led the way with Kenny following.

*Mr. B. and Miss A? Didn't these people have names?*

They entered the cavernous. Enormous windows provided a spectacular view of the city. An incredibly expensive desk built of some exotic wood filled the left wall of the room. Plush chairs and a sofa were arranged in a seating area to the right.

Kenny was directed to a chair in front of the desk by Mr. B., who sat down in an enormous black leather chair behind the desk. In contrast, Kenny's chair was hard and wooden.

It felt like he was back in middle school again. The chair was uncomfortable, and he shifted in it to find a better position. Mr. B's chair was higher, and he looked down at Kenny, his black eyes reminding him even more of a rat.

"Welcome to Talent Limited, Mr. Kendrick. That's what the Ltd. stands for in our firm's name, and there is humor there, indeed."

Rodent-man chuckled, and the sound was evil to Kenny's ears. He shuddered.

"Your first gig will be at Carolines on Broadway this Saturday night. Next week, it's the Comedy Cellar, and after that—"

Kenny's eyes were practically bugging out of his head.

"But, my God, they're the best clubs in the city! I'm not ready—"

"Please, don't mention God, Mr. Kendrick! He has nothing to do with this. His name makes me, uncomfortable. You are ready, Mr. Kendrick. By Saturday your dreams will come true. Remember, we have you under contract. You would not be here if you weren't ready. We make sure you are. It's in the agreement. May I call you Kenny?"

"Of course, Mister, uh, B. Why do you use an initial as your name?" Kenny asked.

Rodent-man smiled and said, "My name is too hard to pronounce. B is easy on the tongue, so to speak. Once again, may I call you Kenny?"

"Yes, sure, fine. But I can't possibly—"

"Here's the deal, Kenny," Mr. B took the tone of an adult speaking to a small child. "We guarantee that you will be ready. When you leave here you'll go to the 40th floor of this building. A suite has been assigned to you there. There is a complete wardrobe waiting for you in your sizes. You will be given a bank account with \$20,000.00 in it.

"Your appearances at Carolines and the Comedy Cellar have been booked for months. Kenny Kendrick, you're a star in your own right! It will be standing room only. When you take the stage all eyes will be on you! Our contract automatically supplies you with all you need. That's only the beginning. You've also been booked on every network TV show that really matters in this city.

"A month from now you leave for Hollywood. You'll be making a pilot for a new TV show that will begin this fall. You're the star! You're also booked at Second City, iO West, and ComedySportz in Los Angeles. You have a major role in a movie that begins filming in October in the Valley. The biggest names in comedy will co-star in the film with you.

"When the New Year begins you'll be headlining for a month at The Mirage Aces of Comedy in Vegas, and then your tour will start. You'll travel the world appearing at the best comedy clubs on earth, Kenny. Now, go to your suite, open the notebook and start reading. You have a week to prepare. You'll be ready by week's end. Trust me."

At that, Kenny felt like he wanted to bolt from his chair, take the elevator, race back to his hovel in Philadelphia and hide under his bed. He took a deep breath.

"How can I do this? I don't have that kind of talent—"

"You're precisely right, Kenny. That's where we come in. We make dreams come true, hence, our name. You may have limited talent, but you also have us behind you. You can't screw this up. We won't allow it. When you take the stage on Saturday you will be ready."

Kenny looked at what he'd come to think of as Rodent-Man. The beady eyes stared back at him, the sharp teeth visible in an evil smile.

"O.K., I'll do it. I go to the 40th floor and get off, right?"

"Yes, that's what I said. Your suite will be on the right when you get off the elevator. Your name is on the door. We won't see each other again for awhile. Your dream is coming true, Kenny. It doesn't get any better than that, but it can get worse. Now, I'll say goodbye. I have another appointment waiting."

Mr. B. stood up and led Kenny to the door. When Kenny passed through the reception area there was a woman sitting in a chair waiting for her appointment. She appeared to be nervous. He smiled at her.

She smiled tentatively in return.

Impulsively, he walked up to her and said, "Hi, I'm Kenny Kendrick."

He did not expect what happened next. She jumped up from her seat, her eyes wide, with a big smile on her face.

"Oh!" she said, "Kenny Kendrick! You're the most famous comedian in the whole world!"

She extended her hand, and he took it. She was positively gushing.

"I'm, I'm Sandy Stewart. I'm going to be a singer. If I get big enough, maybe I can do a show with you one day. This is so great!"

Kenny looked at her closely. She was not unattractive, but she wasn't spectacularly beautiful either. She was going to need help in the appearance department.

"What kind of singing do you do?" Kenny asked.

"All kinds, but I'm not all that good. Pretty ordinary, actually—"

"However, you signed a contract …" Kenny began.

It was like a dark cloud passed over her face. She said, "Yes,I did. I don't remember much about it, but I'm here."

Kenny released her hand.

"Well, Sandy Stewart, good luck." He smiled. "Perhaps we'll see each other around."

As he left the offices, he heard Ms. A, the receptionist, say, "Mr. B. will be with you in just a few minutes, Ms. Stewart."

Kenny thought, *But don't hold your breath, or you'll be dead.*

He took the elevator to the 40th floor. When it stopped, he stepped off and went to his right. Sure enough, there was a door with his name on it. He opened it and found a suite that was beyond his wildest dreams.

Kenny toured the rooms and discovered everything that was promised. A huge walk-in closet contained more clothes than he had ever seen outside of a men's store. There was an ornate desk in his bedroom. A checkbook with his name on it was lying on the desk. There was a bank statement next to it from the bank that had its name on the checks. The statement said he had $20,000 in the bank.

He made his way to the kitchen. The refrigerator was stocked with his favorite foods. He opened a beer and stood by the windows, looking down at the city. If this was a dream, he hoped that it would not end.

He wanted to turn on the TV and veg out, but he went to the bedroom and got the notebook instead. He sat down and began reading. Hours passed. Night had come to Manhattan. Kenny read through the night.

When the sun started to rise above the city, he made his way to the bedroom and fell asleep in his clothes. He slept like a drunken man for 12 hours. When he awoke, he took a shower and dressed in new clothes.

He could get used to this.

He heard a knock on the door. He went and opened it. A waiter stood in the hall with a cart.

"Dinner, Mr. Kendrick."

Kenny stepped aside and the young man pushed the cart into the suite. He uncovered the plates and turned, smiling.

"Will there be anything else, Mr. Kendrick?"

"No, thank you."

Kenny stood there for a moment, and then he felt foolish.

"Just a moment, please."

He went into his bedroom and took a $50.00 bill out of his wallet. He had a lot of money. His bank statement said so. He went back into the living area and handed the bill to the waiter. The kid's eyes grew big.

"Wow, thanks Mr. Kendrick. I didn't expect—"

"No problem. Keep the change."

The waiter left the suite pushing the cart, and Kenny looked at the food. It looked delicious.

While he ate, he continued reading through the notebook. He was finished eating and went into the bedroom. There was a full-length mirror on the door of the walk-in closet.

Kenny Kendrick, the greatest comedian in the world—at least in the minds of those he had met since he arrived in this place—began practicing in front of the mirror.

Rodent-man had promised that he would succeed. Well, he would see about that. Saturday night was coming. He was afraid. He had never been so afraid in his life. He remembered something his father used to say to him when he was at home. The old man said, "Kenny, be careful what you wish for, because you just might get it!" He never understood what that meant. He was sure his father was wrong. He had gotten everything he wanted, hadn't he? What's not to like?

Saturday came, and Kenny Kendrick found a limo waiting for him on the street in front of the building. As promised, a standing-room-only crowd awaited him when he stepped on stage at Carolines on Broadway. The fear was raging within. It was now, or never. He forced a smile and told his first joke. The fear evaporated. The audience roared with approval. Kenny Kendrick owned the stage and could do no wrong!

*Chapter Three*

Ten years slipped by. Kenny Kendrick was delirious with success. He was the biggest comedy star in the world. Anything he put his hand to could not fail. Movies, TV, tours, comedy albums, talk shows, New York, Hollywood, London, Paris—he owned the world.

He had everything that money could buy, but all of it did nothing to change him inside. He was still the grasping, needy, selfish person he had always been when he stepped off-stage.

People thought of him as wonderful. If they knew what he was really like they would have shunned him and never paid another nickel to see him again. It was a sham, an act, and he pretended to care so that he would be adored.

For a man so loved in public, his life was empty in private. He had had three wives in a decade, and he was alone again. He had a semi-permanent place in Vegas. He left the town to do movies, TV and tours, but he always returned. He had been signed to a five-year deal at the Bellagio, and they were willing to work with his schedule so that he could go off and do other things regularly.

Kenny heard that his dad had died. He didn't bother to send a card. His brother Frank tried to call him two years after that to tell him that their mother was very ill, but he refused to take the call. He didn't care.

His manager wanted him to support a children's charity because he thought it would be great PR. He declined, saying that his schedule wouldn't allow involvement. He hated children and had no time for them.

In his fifth year of success his former hero, Larry Lane, had come to see his show. After it was over, Lane came backstage to shake his hand. Lane looked at Kenny and said, "You know, you remind me of me when I was younger. I'm not sure why, but congratulations! That was a fantastic show!"

Kenny bit his lip and said, "Yeah, I always wanted to be you, and now I am."

Lane thought that was a strange reply, but he didn't say anything.

When Lane died of a heart attack at his Hollywood home two years later, Kenny went to the funeral. He had sent flowers, as well, along with a card that read, "Thanks for all you gave to me."

The Kendrick estate outside Vegas was set on two acres. It was gated, protected, and lovely. There was a housekeeper and gardener at the estate. Being in a gated community afforded him double protection, too. Kenny liked it that way.

He drank heavily, but he hid his drinking so that no one would know. His employees knew about it, but they also knew that they would be unemployed in a heartbeat if they said anything to anyone.

By every measure, Kenny was a success beyond whatever he had dreamed of years before. He was also disillusioned, cynical, paranoid, and envious of every new young comedian that dared to make "good press," as he thought of it, in the tabloids. His word carried weight, and he had vindictively destroyed several up-and-coming careers by things he did and said behind the scenes. He made enemies.

His home was his palace, and he spared no expense in decorating it. He never gave parties, preferring instead to attend public functions and shows in Vegas in order to maintain his lifestyle.

The three wives had signed pre-nuptial agreements, and all three of them had little to show for their marriages. They had been stage-struck when they married him, and, shortly thereafter, they felt like they had been run over by a stagecoach. While he never hit one of them, his verbal abuse could peel the skin off a buffalo. His caustic mouth was filled with judgmental statements that were like pouring acid on a wound. Kenny Kendrick was just plain mean and nasty!

In the grand living room of his mansion there was a glass case, hidden in a large wall safe. When he was home for an extended period, he would take the case out of the safe and place it on a marble pedestal in his foyer. He kept it locked away whenever he was on tour, doing a movie, or traveling. The case contained Larry Lane's notebook.

When the case was in the foyer, he would stand and gaze at it several times a day. It had been the key to everything, and he gloated over it.

His housekeeper and gardener had seen it, but they knew better than to ask about it. They were paid not only for their work, but also to keep silent. Kenny's connections were such that he would willingly pay to have anyone killed who dared to cross him. You did not mess with the Great Kendrick!

He had been touring in Australia and New Zealand for six weeks when he returned to his home. He opened his safe to get the case and it was not there! Someone had taken it. He had a hundred thousand dollars in the safe, three Rolex watches he had received as gifts but did not wear, and $50 thousand dollars in gold coins. The only thing missing was the notebook.

In a fit of rage he fired the housekeeper and gardener and then opened a new bottle of whiskey. He could not call the police. He could tell no one about the missing notebook. After all, he had stolen it himself. How would he ever explain that to anyone? He got very, very drunk.

When he awoke at 3:00 a.m. he rang for the housekeeper and lay there in a stupor. He then remembered that he had fired her and the gardener. He sat up in bed. Had he heard strange noises in the house? It was a very big house. He had an alarm system, but had he remembered to re-set the alarm after he sent his employees packing?

What if someone had gotten in? What would he do? He had a pistol in the bottom drawer of his nightstand, but it wasn't loaded. He opened the drawer and took out the Beretta 9-millimeter. The shells were in a box in the drawer.

Kenny was frightened. He fumbled in the dark trying to load the pistol. He was afraid to turn on the light. He realized he couldn't load the gun if he couldn't see what he was doing. He turned on the light by his bed.

Like everything else in his life, he avoided doing anything that he didn't want to do, or he had someone else do it for him. The man at the store had shown him how to load the gun, but now he stared at it helplessly. He had good intentions of going to a range to practice firing it, but he had never gotten around to it. Now he was in a state of panic.

Kenny's bedroom was huge. There was a fireplace in it that he rarely used. When the weather got cold he simply turned up the heat. He avoided anything that required physical effort of any kind. He was a star Others were supposed to wait on him hand and foot!

It was a gas-fired fireplace. All he had to do was use the automatic control to turn it on, but he had the housekeeper do that for him.

She was gone. There was no one to help him. On the fireplace hearth there was a totally useless but decorative set of wrought-iron fireplace tools in a stand.

Kenny picked up the poker in his right hand and went to his bedroom door. He stood there for five minutes listening with all his concentration. The room was cool but he felt sweat on his brow. He was ready to totally freak out!

He heard nothing but silence. Maybe the person on the other side of the door was holding his breath? He was so afraid that he was shaking.

Slowly, carefully, and as silently as he could, he turned the doorknob and gently eased the door open. The hallway was empty. There were nightlights burning throughout the huge house, but he was afraid to step out of his room.     Finally, he screwed up what little courage he had and stepped into the hall. Nothing moved. He began a systematic search of the house. Thirty minutes later he had determined that he was alone, and that all the doors to the house were secured and locked. The alarm was set. Everything was in order. He felt relieved until he approached the front door. Something was lying on the floor. The light was dim. What was it?

He bent down and saw that it was an ordinary plain white business-sized envelope. Nothing was written on it. He picked it up and saw it was unsealed. Perhaps the housekeeper had left it for him. She was in tears when he drove her out of the house.

Kenny made his way to the huge kitchen, turning on lights as he walked there. He turned on all the lights in the kitchen, and those that had dimmers he cranked to full power. He would drive the darkness away.

He sat on a stool by the huge granite-topped island and opened the flap of the envelope. There was a single sheet of folded paper in it. Kenny unfolded it and read.

*Dear Mr. Kendrick,*

*We have the notebook. All good things must come to an end. Your contract is ended. In due time, we will collect what we are owed. We look forward to seeing you again, soon.*

*Very truly yours,*
*L.S.*

Kenny Kendrick was terrified. He ran to the powder room off the kitchen and threw up all over the floor. His housekeeper was gone. There was no one to clean up the mess.

He then ran from room to room, turning on every light in the house. When all the lights were shining he made his way to the bar and poured himself a water glass full of whiskey and drank a third of it in one gulp. It burned his throat and he choked on it.

He now remembered the man who had come to his hotel room years ago, the one who had worn sunglasses in the night. He had come with the contract. Now, he had taken the notebook. What was going to happen? He was so afraid he could not think straight. He drank more whiskey. He would start drinking and stop thinking.

He couldn't begin to know what he owed to the man. He had burned the contract long ago. He did not remember what it had said, and he had not cared. He was, after all, Kenny Kendrick, the funniest man in the world.

### Chapter Four

The phone rang the next morning. It was Artie Miller, his manager.

"Kenny, hey, I hope I didn't wake you up. It's almost noon. I know you like to sleep in."

Kenny was groggy from booze.

"You could have waited till afternoon. I don't feel that good right now."

"Well, I would have waited but I wanted to let you know, I got some bad news here. Hate to tell you, but the movie deal fell through—"

"What? What happened? Who—" Now Artie had Kenny's attention.

"The studio head called me a couple minutes ago. Seems the money people aren't on board. He said they decided not to go ahead with it"

"Artie, it was a three-picture deal worth millions! You could retire with what that would bring in. What am I going to do?"

"Kenny, I know it's bad, and there's more. Geez, I'm sorry, but the Bellagio called, as well. They're exercising a clause in their contract. We're out and some new kid is in—"

Kenny screamed in rage. "*What new kid? What the—*"

Artie had clamped his hand over the phone so he wouldn't hear the expletive.

He counted to 10, and then said, "Look, Kenny, you're the star. You're known all over the world. Man, this is no big thing. When the rest of the people in this town hear you're available you'll have to beat them off with a stick! Relax! Cool down. Take a deep breath. Don't get your blood pressure up. Look, I'm on this. Bad things happen—"

"*Not to me, they don't!*" Kenny raged.

"I'll make some calls. Please, Kenny, do something to vent the anger. I care about you. This will pass. I'll call you later. Get some more sleep. You sound like you need it. I promise I will get back to you this afternoon."

Artie tried to sound encouraging. "Remember, the British tour is booked. You have a weekend in Atlantic City coming up. You've got

Reno next month. I can set up more dates to make up for these—glitches. Don't worry. I'll get back to you by 5:00," he said and hung up.

Kenny sat holding the phone and staring at it like it was a poisonous snake. His whole world was falling apart!

*A new kid?* There wasn't a new comedian on the planet that could touch Kenny Kendrick when it came to talent!

Kenny took a long shower and put on his robe. He wasn't hungry, but he forced himself to eat a bowl of cereal in the kitchen. He was going to have to find a new housekeeper and gardener. Maybe if he called them and begged them to come back?

He went into the huge great room and put a DVD of one of his movies in the player. An hour into it, he fell asleep.

The ringing phone woke him up. He reached for it and knocked it off the table. Swearing loudly, he reached to retrieve it. He looked at his watch. 3:20 p.m.

It was Artie. He sounded nervous.

"Kenny, uh, man, I—"

"What? What's the matter?"

"I don't know what's happening. Maybe the stars are out of alignment or something, but the British tour is off. Atlantic City canceled. I called everybody in town. Nobody's interested. I can't believe it. This is really bad karma, Kenny. I tried everyone. Everybody is making excuses. Nobody gives me a straight answer. The only thing left is Reno ..."

Kenny was numb. He sat staring at the TV, his mind raging. He watched as on screen he made a fool of himself in the movie. When that scene played in theaters, people were laughing so hard they were out of control. Now, his life was disintegrating, and nobody cared. What was he going to do?

"Kenny, speak to me!" Artie said.

"I don't feel so good, Artie. I'm going to hang up now—"

"Wait! Don't do anything rash. You want me to come over?"

"No, no. I just want to be alone. Let me alone. Don't call me unless something good happens. I don't want to know anymore bad things today—"

"Kenny!"

Kenny hung up the phone. He needed booze! Booze would make it go away.

A month slipped by. Then, two months. Kenny did not leave the house. Most days he did not even shower, shave or get dressed.

To his credit, Artie called every day, several times a day. He was Kenny's only friend. Kenny had been his meal ticket for a decade, and the guy was a pain in the backside, but Artie lived very well thanks to Kenny. He had tried having other clients in the beginning, but Kenny was so demanding that he had to give up his other talent to serve Kenny Kendrick exclusively.

He stopped by the house, but Kenny would not let him in. The yard was overgrown, and the town's enforcement official had pounded on his door demanding that he take care of it.

Artie had enough money to retire. He hired a lawn service to keep after things at Kenny's house. Kenny did not care. Booze was his friend, and he was either zonked or sleeping most of the time. The days of the great Kenny Kendrick were gone.

Artie felt sad. As nasty as Kenny could be, his talent had been enormous. Artie wished he had an answer, but no one wanted the great Kenny Kendrick anymore.

*Chapter Five*

The phone rang and Kenny picked it up thinking that it was Artie calling. A voice he did not recognize said, "Mr. Kendrick?"

It was morning, so he had not opened the new bottle of whiskey yet, and he was relatively coherent.

"Yes, who is calling?"

"My name is Damien, Mr. Kendrick. I understand that you might be available for a live performance. Is this true?"

Kenny sat up in his chair.

"What? You have a gig for me? Yes, well, I could possibly work you into my schedule. When and where are you talking about, and have you spoken to my manager?"

The caller laughed softly.

"I haven't spoken to Mr. Miller. Is that a problem?"

"No, it's not a problem. I can deal with that. So, where is the show, and when do you want me?" Kenny asked.

"The show will be at a private estate this Saturday night. It will be quite late, actually, at midnight. Very important, uh, people, will be there. Is the time a problem for you?"

Kenny thought the time was late, but beggars could not be choosers.

"Where's this estate? Who owns it? And what's the pay?"

"The estate is outside of town, in the desert. The owner is a very powerful individual who maintains a very low profile. He doesn't use his name because he prefers to remain anonymous. As to the pay, it pays well."

"Mr. Damien, what you describe is unusual. You won't tell me who wants me to appear, and how much the compensation is for my show. I'm Kenny Kendrick! I don't work for peanuts. What are we talking about?

The caller laughed softly again.

"What is the greatest amount you have ever been paid for a standup routine, Mr. Kendrick?"

"I get millions for movies, Mr. Damien. My TV shows have earned me more millions. The Bellagio pays me $25,000 per performance, and I—"

"Yes, Mr. Kendrick, I hear you, but the Bellagio no longer employs you. They've hired a new, young comic. As to the movies and , well, I understand that your prospects have not been good lately."

"Who told you such things?" Kenny blustered. "They should get their facts straight. I've been taking some time off. I needed a break.

I've been rehearsing a whole new routine. I'm ready to go!"

"Perhaps, but you still did not answer my question. What is the most you have ever made for a stand-up performance?"

Kenny thought for a moment.

"I was paid a hundred-thousand for a command performance in London last year. That's the most for a single appearance. Why do you ask?"

Damien said, "This will pay more than that."

"How much more?" Kenny asked.

"The pay is over $600 thousand for the show. Do you find that to be enough to take to the stage again?"

Kenny could not believe what he had just heard.

"You're serious? Is this for real or some kind of joke?"

"No, it's quite real, Mr. Kendrick. If you agree, a limo will pick you up Saturday night at 11:00 p.m. in front of the gate. You'll be driven to the estate and the show will begin at midnight. This could be a very big break for you at this point in time. I would keep the information about this quiet. That way, you can keep all the money. You won't have to share it with your manager. You'll be paid in cash when the show is over," Damien said.

Kenny swallowed hard. This wasn't movie scale, but it was *a lot of money*!

"You said the gate. Did you mean outside the complex? Why not come to my door?"

"No, it's best we do this our way. Be outside the gate just before 11:00 p.m. In fact, I know that the gates are automated after 10:00 p.m. for residents with the pass key. There is no guard on duty at that time. Bring your pass key with you, and when the show is over the limo driver can take you to your front door. It's simpler this way. Be sure to wear your tux."

"What about a contract? Can I get this in writing?" Kenny asked.

"Mr. Kendrick, this is strictly a cash and carry affair. My employer insists that it be done this way. Just as you don't have to make a record of this transaction, neither does he. Do a great show and get paid a great deal of money. It's simple, yes?"

"Yes, yes, you're right. O.K., I will be waiting in front of the gate. I'm looking forward to it."

"Not as much as we are, Mr. Kendrick. I'll look forward to meeting you Saturday night," the caller said and hung up.

Kenny stood up from the chair he had fallen into when the man said he'd be paid $600 thousand dollars! It was time to sober up. It was time to start living again. He had a second chance. The old Kenny Kendrick was dead. This was the new and improved Kenny Kendrick!

Kenny decided to start his day by doing laps in the pool. His former gardener had also worked as his pool man, so the pool needed a lot of attention. Kenny had done two laps when he noticed the dead animals and insects floating in the water. The pool had not been cleaned or chlorinated in a long, long time. When he saw the dead rat, he quickly got out of the pool and ran to the shower.

The days slipped by.

~ ~ ~

Kenny was standing in his tux in front of the gate when a long black limo pulled up. He was used to limo drivers getting out and opening the door for him, but no one got out of the driver's seat. He stood there for a minute, feeling both angry and foolish, and then he reached out, opened the rear door, and got into the vehicle.

He was the only one in the passenger compartment. There was a fully stocked bar. The window between him and the driver was closed. It was also black. He could see nothing through the glass. He wanted a drink, badly. He had stopped drinking three days earlier to get ready for this night. His hands were shaking.

He finally gave in to his desire and poured himself a glass of the best whiskey in the small bar. However, when he tasted it he made a face and set the glass down. It tasted strange. The thought that came to him was that it tasted ancient! It was as if it had been made a thousand years ago and had been sitting that long before he attempted to drink it. What a weird thought!

The limo traveled smoothly over the main highway leading out of town into the desert. Several miles out of town it turned off the main road onto a dirt road. This new road was not smooth. The car bumped along and Kenny swore.

He was nervous, and the car's air conditioning was not working. He was hot and sweating. The windows were tinted so dark that he could not see where they were going.

He tried the button that would lower the window next to him, but it didn't work. He saw a button that would activate the window between him and the driver, but that didn't work either. He leaned forward and rapped on the glass partition, but there was no response. He was starting to feel panicky. He wanted to get out of the car and breathe fresh air.

Suddenly, the car came to a stop and his door opened. Kenny bolted from the limo, ready to give the driver a piece of his mind, but there was no one there. He looked around and saw that he stood alone in the desert. In that moment the car door closed, and the limo started to back up.

"Hey, wait! Stop!" Kenny yelled. "Don't leave me here! Come back!"

The car continued backing up, turned around, and took off.

Kenny chased after it until he could not catch his breath. He stopped. He was sweating, his shirt was soaked, his tux was rumpled, and he was enraged.

He screamed a string of obscenities into the night, but there was no one there to hear him. He looked up at the sky and saw millions of stars in the blackness.

Kenny Kendrick was a creature of cities, hotel rooms and casino stages. He knew nothing of the wilderness, and he did not want to find out anything about it. Now, he was alone. He was vulnerable and afraid. Thoughts of snakes and scorpions and coyotes formed in his mind. He was going to freak out, again.

"Mr. Kendrick, I've been waiting for you."

Kenny whipped around so fast, he felt his back crack. He winced in pain. He had been drunk and indolent for two months, and his inactivity had taken its toll.

There was a very tall, black figure standing next to him in the darkness. He jumped back in terror, ready to run.

"Please, Mr. Kendrick, I'm Damien. I spoke to you on the phone. I've come to lead you to the estate. It's not far from here. Please, follow me."

It was difficult to see what Damien looked like in the darkness. Kenny thought he had caught a glimpse of his eyes, but they looked red instead of white. *Maybe the guy had a hangover?* He hoped so.

"O.K., I'll follow. You know where we are. I haven't got a clue."

The tall figure turned and started walking, while Kenny followed. They had walked about a hundred yards when Damien stopped.

"We are here," he said.

Kenny looked ahead into the darkness. He saw a vast shape rising up from the desert. There were no lights, but he thought he saw flickering torches.

"What is this place?"

"It is the estate. This is where you'll do your show."

"Why aren't there any lights?" Kenny asked.

Damien laughed and said, "Because, we are environmentally friendly. There's no electricity out here in the desert."

The way Damien said the word "friendly" sounded to Kenny like an obscene joke. He felt a chill race up his back.

"This is it? You've got to be kidding! I've done shows in some pretty poor clubs, but this is a new low. In the dark it looks like some kind of castle or something."

"Be that as it may, this is the place where the show goes on. Follow me," Damien said.

As they drew closer to the great shape looming over the desert in the night, Kenny began to make out more details, and what he saw was frightening. It did look like a castle, a black and foreboding place which might be filled with all manner of things.

They came to a drawbridge that crossed a moat. As they walked over the bridge Kenny thought he saw shapes moving in murky water. He would not want to fall into that water.

They passed under an archway and moved forward, Damien leading and Kenny following. Flickering torches gave a surreal appearance to the place. It looked a thousand years old. Kenny was becoming more nervous with each step.

They stepped into a vast foyer. The ceiling was so high that Kenny, looking up, could not see it in the darkness. He thought he saw things moving in the air above him. They looked like bats.

In a shaking voice, Kenny asked, "Where's the stage. I'd like to get this over with."

Damien did not reply. He simply kept going forward. Finally, after walking down a long hallway lined with torches, they came to a great doorway. Damien said, "We're here."

They stepped into a vast chamber. There were tables and chairs everywhere, and a low stage to their right. All of this was lit with more torches. Kenny wanted to turn and run for his life.

"That limo was hot! The air conditioning didn't work. Where's the dressing room? I've got to freshen up? It's warm in here, too. How do you cool this place?"

Without answering, Damien pointed to the rear of the stage, then turned and walked away.

Kenny said, "Well, that was rude! Who do you think you are?"

The tall figure continued down the hallway in the direction they had come and disappeared.

Kenny watched him, ready to yell more obscenities, but the atmosphere of the room was so oppressive that he kept silent. He turned, stepped up, and walked to the rear of the stage. There was a doorway there that he had not noticed. It looked positively ancient. There was no modern door handle. In fact, there was no handle at all.

He pushed against the door, but it did not move. He pushed harder. It still did not move. Then, he pushed with both hands as hard as he could. The door moved an inch, then two, and finally swung inward on screeching hinges.

Kenny entered a small room lit by a single, flickering candle on a stand. It looked like something out of a medieval movie. However, this was no stage prop. There was a mirror-like piece of what must have been some kind of metal on the wall. It showed a poor, distorted reflection of Kenny and the room.

In disgust, he did his best to smooth his tux and his hair. Was it his imagination or was it getting even hotter? He felt the sweat running down his back and his shirt was sticking to him. There wasn't any-thing he could do about improving his appearance in the heat and the dim reflection in the so-called mirror.

Kenny gave up and returned to the door. He pushed on it. It would not move. He swore and pushed even harder. It was solid and immovable. He felt trapped. He began pounding on the door and yelling for help. His hands were becoming bruised and his voice was hoarse from the exertion and yelling.

Finally, after what felt like an hour, the door moved slightly. Kenny got his hands in the crack and pushed with all his might. The door opened just wide enough for him to slip through the opening, and leading with his left shoulder, he forced himself through it.

He was filled with desperation that was rapidly becoming panic. The rough surface of the wooden door scraped the right side of his face. He finally freed himself and stood on the stage.

He looked out, and to his wonder, every table was occupied and every seat filled in the vast room. Everyone was dressed up like they might have been at one of his shows at the Bellagio, except for one thing. Their clothing looked very old, like something from the 1920's, and here and there he thought he saw tears and rips in their garments.

No one was saying a word. They were dead silent!

Kenny took a deep breath and moved to the center of the stage. The lighting had not improved. He could not see the back of the room, but he sensed it was huge, perhaps bigger than any room he had ever played.

At front and center there was a small table that was only big enough for one, and the chair behind the table was empty.

Kenny noticed that there were familiar figures at the table to the right of this small table. Two people sat at it. Then, he remembered. It was Mr. B. and Miss A. from the agency. The blond was as stunning as ever, but her costume was no longer modern. Mr. B. grinned wickedly.

Kenny suppressed the urge to bolt for the door.

Suddenly, everyone in the room rose to their feet.

Kenny saw someone walking through the crowd from the rear of the vast room. The man was dressed in old fashioned clothing and wore a cape over his shoulders. He had on huge sunglasses, and the light was so dim in the room that Kenny wondered how he could see. He did not appear to be looking to the left or right, but straight at Kenny. This must be the host, the guy with the money who was running the show. He made his way to the small table and sat down. Everyone else sat down.

Kenny looked out as far as he could see. The room had grown far hotter, and the sweat was pouring from him. He was drenched. He had never sweated so much. It was awful.

Kenny noticed something strange. There was no food or drink on any of the tables. People at casino shows were eating, drinking, laughing, talking and enjoying themselves. When Kenny Kendrick did a show, they became silent out of respect for his performance, but waitresses and waiters still brought them their drinks.

The silence in the room was deafening. Kenny thought he was going to melt with sweat.

The man at the small table turned his head to his right. Mr. B.

stood up as though he had been given an order, though no words had been spoken.

"We are happy, in fact, we are delirious to have the great Kenny Kendrick as our entertainment this evening," Mr. B. said. "Tonight's show is one hour, sixty seconds in each minute, and sixty minutes in the hour, exactly. At the shows end, Mr. Kendrick will be paid the agreed upon amount."

Kenny thought this was a very strange thing to say, but he remained silent, afraid to say anything.

"You were told that the pay would be over $600 thousand dollars, and this is true," Mr. B. continued. "The exact amount is $666,666.66, a tidy sum, indeed. Let the show begin."

Kenny took a deep breath and told his first joke. There was no microphone, but his voice carried through the vast room. The crowd remained silent. No one laughed. It was unnerving.

He told his next joke. He was using his "A" material. He knew that everything, everything depended on making this crowd laugh, but the dead silence continued. His sweat flowed like a river, making his clothing soggy. He was a flop, and sensed that if there was ever a crowd that needed to laugh, it was this one!

Kenny told jokes for what felt like an hour. He glanced at his Rolex and was astounding to see that no time had passed. It was midnight, the witching hour.

He told more and more jokes, but no response came. He was growing desperate. He had never played a crowd like this.

Then, he began to notice something terrifying. The people at the edges of his vision no longer looked like people. Their appearance was changing. Now, they looked like monsters with gaping jaws filled with horrific looking teeth.

Kenny felt like an hour had passed. He had gone through all his best material. Now, he was reduced to jokes so old that they were stupid. He was telling the obscene jokes that he used in bars long ago, before he had ever stolen Larry Lane's notebook.

Kenny glanced at his watch again. It wasn't even a second after midnight! *What the hell was wrong?*

A voice spoke from the crowd. It was Mr. B.

"Mr. Kendrick, there is just one problem here. At my office, you commented on the problem of time, assuming that time works the same way, everywhere. Unfortunately, here, in our kingdom, a second really is an eternity. I am afraid that this hour will never end."

Suddenly, Mr. B. was down on all fours, and his teeth had grown very long, indeed. Kenny quinted into the room. Everyone looked like monsters to him. His terror was escalating at mach speed.

In that moment, he looked to the right of Mr. B. and saw two things. The notebook—his beloved notebook—was lying on the table, and the one sitting at the table had removed his sunglasses.

Kenny looked straight into the eyes of the one who sat there. In that moment he understood what the initials L.S. stood for. He was looking into the eyes of the most malevolent spirit in the universe!

Kenny screamed in terror, and the vast room filled with laughter for the first time, but it was no laughing matter.

# CHAIRMAN
## OF THE
# BORED

# THE CHAIRMAN OF THE BORED

Francis Franklin Fredericks III, or Frank to his closest associates, was born to privilege and wealth. The family estate near Hyde Park, New York fell into the category of "old money." There was nothing nouveau riche or pedestrian about Frank Fredericks. The 25-room manor house, 12-room guest cottage, 8-room servants' cottage, six-car garage, barn and horse stables, dock on the Hudson and its boathouse, tennis court, and the 3-hole golf course plus putting green, all set on a pristine 50 acres, practically screamed patrician!

The garage housed a Rolls, Bentley, Ferrari, Cadillac Escalade, Lexus and a tram used to take guests on a tour of the grounds. Lawn and garden tools used by the maintenance staff were housed in a building hidden by a grove of trees at the edge of the 10-acre landscaped gardens and yards.

There were three swimming pools, as well, and one of them was housed in its own building. This structure also contained a complete gymnasium, weight and equipment room, and two handball courts.

The Fredericks family lacked nothing. They also had homes on Martha's Vineyard and in Venice, Florida. Their fortune, built on railroads, steamships, and Manhattan properties, had passed from one generation to another. They employed people to manage their estates and homes. They did not work. Work was most definitely beneath them.

At 51, Frank Fredericks still had his hair and physique, thanks to genetics, two personal trainers and his gym. His wife, Adrienne, also kept her figure through vigorous workouts. Their two children, Sarah and Lance, lived in New York and Denver, respectively. Lance was a new attorney in a prestigious Denver firm, and Sarah did not work. She was married to a noted surgeon and spent her days dabbling in New York art circles and patrician causes near and dear to her heart.

Frank and Adrienne wintered in Venice, summered on Martha's Vineyard, and spent the rest of their time at the estate. Life was a series of parties, celebrations, New York plays, garden parties, yachting, society weddings and events. They donated to self-congratulatory charities, supplying hospital suites and the like, for which they were honored at dinners for their magnanimous giving and toasted accordingly.

Life was very good. In fact, it was absolutely splendid! Someone who lived an ordinary life would probably kill for such an existence. A poor soul who spent her days under a bridge, or scavenging garbage cans and pushing a shopping cart containing all her worldly possessions would have thought she had died and gone to heaven if she was suddenly thrust into the Fredericks' lifestyle.

There was just one problem. Frank Fredericks was bored out of his mind. He did absolutely nothing to contribute to society. He realized this on the morning of his 51st birthday.

He had awakened in his fabulous bedroom on the third floor of his estate, and he lay there, staring at the ceiling. His first thought was, *What is the meaning of my life?* His second thought was, *What will I be remembered for?*

Adrienne lay next to him, sound asleep. She did not have an appointment until noon, and that was at their tennis court with family friends. She continued sleeping. She had no idea that the man next to her was experiencing a mid-life crisis of major proportions!

He wanted to sit up and yell, *What the hell does it all mean?* It would have frightened his wife, and being a man of generally mild temperament, it would have been totally out-of-character! He took a deep breath. Perhaps if he went to the gym and beat the punching bag, he could get rid of the unfounded anxiety in his normally placid mind! It was maddening!

Frank got out of bed and went to the enormous 750 square-foot bathroom. Every luxury that could be found in a bathroom was in this one. It was opulent, with gold-plated fixtures, crystal chandeliers, marble, two sunken tubs, a massive shower, a sauna, and a soaking tub.

He stared into the huge mirror. His medium brown hair was in disarray from sleeping, there was stubble on his face, and his blue eyes were slightly red. He needed to go to the gym, but first he would go to the pool and swim laps. Frank left the bathroom, went down the hall to the elevator, and on to the sub-basement where there was an underground tunnel to the pool house. He went to his locker and put on his bathing suit.

Frank entered the pool area and walked to the diving board. The 50 foot by 40 foot pool was 12 feet at the deep end. He usually did 50 laps three mornings a week, but today his mood was somber. He dove into the pool and began his laps.

He was on his twentieth lap when he was startled by what he first thought might be a hallucination. He stopped, treading water. Someone was sitting on the diving board. The morning light coming through the windows was dim because the day was cloudy.

"Who's there?" he asked. There was no response.

He was suddenly afraid. "I asked you who you are. Answer me!"

The silence was frightening. Frank swam to the side of the pool and pushed himself up onto the edge. The figure on the diving board had not moved.

"How did you get in here? If you don't answer me, I will call the police."

There was still no response. Frank stood up, debating what he should do. Whoever was sitting on the diving board might be dangerous or harmless; there was no way to tell. His world of luxury and parties had not prepared him for anything like this.

The phone was in the locker room, and his cell phone was in his bedroom on his nightstand. He convinced himself that discretion was the better part of valor, and he was about to walk towards the exit when a voice said, "You called. I answered."

"What did you say?"

"You called. I'm here."

"I didn't call anyone. I don't know you. You should not be on my property or in this building," Frank said, screwing up his courage.

"When you awoke today, you asked what the meaning of life is. I have come to answer your question."

Whoever the person was on the diving board, his voice was deep. He stood up and appeared to be very tall.

Frank stepped backwards, ready to run.

"How do you know what I was thinking when I woke up this morning? Are you spying on my home, and who the hell are you, anyway?"

"It is my business to know. I am here. You called. I have come. Ask me."

"Ask you? Ask you what?" Frank stammered.

"Your question."

"Is this some sort of joke? Did someone put you up to this?"

"Ask the question, Frank."

"You need to leave here, now. I've had enough of this. It's time for you to leave. If you leave now I won't call the police," Frank said, feeling both fear and anger at the same time.

In a commanding voice, the tall man standing in the dim light said, "You have one chance to ask the question!  Ask it now!"

Frank said, "O.K., if you'll leave now I'll ask the damn question, if that will satisfy you! What is the meaning of life?"

"I thought you'd never ask," the man said, and he laughed a frightening laugh.

Frank was ready to run as fast as he could go, but the room was growing dark. There was a mist in the air. It was getting hard to see. He could not make out the man in the dimness. It grew darker and darker. What was happening? He needed to see. He had to get away from the pool house. In the darkness he put his hands out. What he felt frightened him so badly that he drew back, tripped and fell down.

His heart was hammering in his chest. His breath was rapid and shallow. He was on the verge of a panic attack, ready to yell in terror.

Then, the darkness began to lighten. He had been wet and wearing a bathing suit, but now his body was covered with clothing, and it was itchy and uncomfortable. He noticed an odor, actually a stench. Where was it coming from?

As the light grew stronger, he saw a dirty brick wall before him in the dim, early morning light. Against the wall under what appeared to be a mound of dirty blankets, sweaters and other soiled clothing he saw human hair. This was what he had touched.

Frank shrank back in horror. *Where, in God's name, was he? How had he come to be in this place?*

He looked down and saw that his body was covered with filthy, grimy clothing, and he almost screamed. *What was happening to him? Had he lost his mind?*

In that moment, he heard the voice of a woman, but it was an ancient voice—a voice that sounded as if ages had passed since it last spoke aloud.

"It's too damn early to go to the park! Why are you awake so early? Didn't you drink enough of that crap you love so much last night? Answer me!"

Frank pushed himself back harder, and he felt a wall behind him. His heart was pounding in his chest. Nothing in his life had prepared him to find himself in such a place.

Finally, he managed to gain control of his raging emotions. He said, "Who are you, and where am I?"

The woman sat up and stared at him for a moment. Her hair was gray in the light, stringy and matted. Her face was covered with grime. She opened her mouth and he saw she was missing teeth. He could not distinguish the color of her eyes, they were so bloodshot.

"Ah, your mind has finally turned to mud, hasn't it, Frankie, dear? You know damn well who I am and where we are. I'm your loving friend, Angel—your one and only friend. We're in New York, the greatest city in the world, and this is the penthouse suite. You, on the other hand, are an idiot.

"Why did you wake me so early? You know I don't like to be

touched before 11:00. The breakfast crowd hasn't even been to the park, yet. The pickings will be slim. I'm hungry today. I'm so hungry I could take a bite out of you, but I can wait."

She turned to look at him more closely. "What's the matter with you? What's the rush?"

He said, "You, you called me Frankie. How do you know my name?"

The woman's eyes grew big. "You really have lost it! We've been living in this alley for two years! We met outside the Port Authority three months before that. I've been on the street for five years, and you have been on it longer than I have! You, the big money man with the plan! You, the man who figures the angles and cuts through the haze to win the prize! The great man, himself, who said you threw it all away because you could never drink enough of that crap you call the Nectar of the Gods!

"I'm the one who agreed to watch your back. I'm the one who showed you the park. I'm the one who brought you to this alley, the safest alley in the city! No one but us knows about this alley, because it's protected, and they don't know it's here!

"You owe me! I've listened to your stories about your money and houses and wonderful life every day. I'm sick of them, and I'm sick of you. You make me want to puke! So, you've finally lost your mind! Don't expect me to take care of you. I have enough trouble. I don't need any of yours!"

Frank's mind was raging again. "I don't believe you! A few minutes ago I was standing by the pool at my estate. This must be a dream— a nightmare!"

"You're out of your mind, Frankie, completely nuts! You've been layin' here all night, just like me. There's no pool and no estate. You've had delusions since I met ya'. You belong in Bellevue in a padded room. I'd tell you to act like a man, but you never have acted right. I've had enough! Get outta here and don't come back! If you do, I'll open you up like a can of tuna!"

The old woman had thrown off her filthy blankets, and she was holding a butcher knife in her right hand.

Frank scrambled to his feet.

"Get out!" she screamed, poking the knife in the air before her. "Get out, or I swear to God—"

Frank turned and ran towards what appeared to be an opening between walls. It was. He made a right turn and saw another wall opening. He took this as fast as he could move. He came into an alleyway between two tall buildings and ran down it, towards an opening to the street. When he burst onto the sidewalk, he almost bowled over a well-dressed man.

The man swore at him, "Don't touch me you crazy—"

Frank didn't wait to hear the expletive.

He ran as fast as his filthy clothes allowed. He was filled with terror. He ran until he could not run anymore, and when he stopped he was five city blocks from where his nightmare had begun. He stopped, panting, trying to catch his breath. His sides ached from the exertion. He felt sick and faint. This wasn't normal. He had been in good shape before he awoke in this dream.

It was still early in the morning. He looked around. The shadows of Manhattan's buildings blocked the light from where he stood, and the dim light obscured his vision. As the light became stronger he saw his reflection in a store window and stood staring, aghast at his appearance.

His clothes were mismatched. He wore a filthy denim coat, and under this a soiled sweater. His hair was long and wild in its disarray, and there were streaks of dirt and grime on his face. His eyes were bloodshot.

Ancient, khaki pants covered his legs. The knees were ripped and there were stains all over them. Dirty sneakers with the tops worn through were on his feet, and he could see yellowed socks through the holes. He looked like he was a thousand years old, like so many of the street people he had seen and ignored in New York.

This had to be a nightmare. He reached up with his right hand and slapped himself across the face. The blow hurt, and he was sorry he had hit himself. As he stood there, someone placed a quarter in his right hand. He turned, but the man was already 10 feet away from him. He looked at the money.

Frank had never thought about money before. He had so much of it that it meant almost nothing to him. He took everything in his life for granted. The quarter lay there in his palm. He wondered if there was more money on his person. He searched the pockets of his coat and pants, but found nothing. He reached under the sweater beneath his coat and into the breast pocket of his shirt. He found something and pulled it out.

It was a small, cloth bag with a pull string. Frank opened it and found three crumpled dollar bills, two dimes and three pennies. He dropped the quarter in the bag, hid it in the shirt pocket, and pulled down the sweater.

His fortune amounted to $3.48!

Suddenly, he became aware that a New York cop was standing a few feet away from him.

"It's time to move on, Frankie," the cop said. "You know I don't want you on the street when the good folk are out and about. No one wants to look at you and Angel! Speaking of Angel, where is she? Is she layin' dead in some alley? Come to think of it, it is a little early for her. She's gotta get her beauty sleep!"

The cop laughed at his own joke. "So, why are you on the street? Lookin' for booze? Man, you gotta a problem, Frankie. You should check into a rehab, but they'd have to hose you down before you got through the door! I can smell you from here. Go on, get outta here!"

Frank said, "If you knew who I am, you wouldn't speak to me in that tone."

"Beg your pardon, your Highness! I forgot about your crazy claims about who you are. Well, I don't care if you're the King of Brooklyn, if you don't get the hell outta here in the next 10 seconds, I'm gonna have you picked up and taken to the tank. When you get the jitters, I hope you shake yourself to death. Move your backside, Frankie. Now!"

Frank turned and rushed off down the street, wanting to put as much distance as he could between himself and the cop. He had been going to tell the cop all about who he was, but this dream didn't allow for it. He had to find someone who would listen to him.

He had gone a block when he reached the entrance to Central Park. A clock in the distance read 6:50. Lots of people were beginning to fill the streets on their way to whatever they did during the day.

As he was standing at the curb staring at the park's entrance, someone placed a dollar in his right hand. Again, when he turned, the person, a woman this time, was already fifteen feet away and heading in the other direction.

Frank looked around. No one was near him. He shoved the dollar in a pocket in his coat, making a mental note to move it to his stash when he got somewhere private.

He crossed the street and entered the park.

Frank was not familiar with Central Park. In fact, he had never gone into it. He saw an information kiosk that was closed. There was a map encased in clear plastic affixed to the front of the small booth. He walked over and looked at it. The legend showed him where he was, and he carefully noted the layout of the park. He was at the entrance at the southwest corner.

He picked up a discarded map from the ground. With $4.48 to his name, only due to the unsolicited kindness of strangers, Frank would not be visiting any attractions, taking a horse and carriage ride, or enjoying any of the amenities inside Central Park's 843 acres. Looking as he did, he would be hard-pressed to avoid people. He had no wish to end up in the tank, whatever that was.

He needed money to get clean. He needed a long, hot shower, a haircut, shave and new clothes. No one would believe anything he said if he didn't change his appearance, but how could he get money?

Beg? *Just how did one beg for money?* He had seen vagrants on the streets of New York and elsewhere over the years, but he had never given any of them a penny. He was afraid of catching something, so he avoided them.

Now that he looked like one of them, he tried to remember how they had asked for money. He had seen street musicians playing, but they were different. They usually had instrument cases opened for donations, or perhaps a nearby bucket, and, of course, they were trying to entertain passers-by.

What could he do? If he could just get money, maybe he could take a bus to Hyde Park?

He was thinking about this when he looked up and saw two cops approaching him.

"It's time to get off the street. Gonna be a nice day, lotsa people in the park. They don't want to see the looks of you! Spoils their appetites," the big, beefy one said. He looked Irish.

The other cop, who was smaller and looked Italian said, "Yeah, you gotta find someplace to be real quick, paisano. Nice people don't need to see you. It's time to leave the park. We have other things to do 'stead of botherin' with you!"

"But, where can I go?" Frank asked, pleading with them.

"We don't care, just so it ain't here," the Irish cop said. "Now, vamoose! I don't want to see you again today. In fact, I don't want to see you on any day! Kapish?"

Frank knew that there was no sense in trying to argue with them. He walked back to the entrance and left the park. He had to find a place where he could get away with asking people for money. He had no idea how much money he would need. He had never purchased clothing for himself. He had a wife and servants to do that for him who kept him well dressed at all times.

He crossed the street and made a right at the corner. There was no place that looked like he could sit down. He had nothing to write with and no way to make a sign of some kind, no cup or container of any kind for money. This was not a neighborhood where he could beg in public.

A man came walking down the street and approached him. He had a friendly face. He said, "Nice day today, isn't it?"

Frank looked at him suspiciously. "Well, I, uh, suppose so, depending on your needs."

The man smiled at him. "Looks like you might need this." He handed Frank a $5.00 bill.

When Frank started to thank him, the man waved him off, smiling, and continued on down the street.

Frank's fortune had grown to $9.48.

Maybe this was the key? Maybe he could just walk along and people would come up and give him money? Yes, and maybe elephants would fly, too!

Frank saw another cop eyeing him up. He turned and started walking back the way he had come.

He resolved that he had to get away from this neighborhood. There were tourists everywhere, and while they might be more inclined to give him money, unlike their jaded New York counterparts, there were far too many cops out and about.

Frank worked his way by side streets and alleyways deeper into Manhattan, and he finally discovered a small park with just a few people to be seen. He sat down on a bench, and he grew sleepy. Soon, he was sound asleep. He had not slept very long, when someone touched him. He sat up in terror.

There was a street person looking down at him.

"What the hell you doin' on my bench? This is my bench! Get up!"

The man was big and dressed much like Frank.

Frank jumped to his feet and started to say, "I'm sorry. I didn't know—"

"This is my bench and my park. Ain't no room for anyone else. You come here again, and I'll make you wish you hadn't! Get outta here! Go on!"

Frank rushed out of the park onto the sidewalk. He started walking again. *Would this nightmare ever end?*

He saw a clock. It was 2:30 in the afternoon. When he'd entered his pool house in what seemed like eons ago, it had been late September. Now, even though it was a warm day in New York, night would bring colder temperatures. He kept moving.

By the end of the day, two more people had approached him and given him small amounts of money. One man had worn a priest's collar, and he had handed $2.00 to Frank and blessed him. An old woman had given him a small handful of change. Altogether, he had $11.73.

Frank looked around as the sun began setting. He had no idea where he was, and fear was settling into his mind like a pall of smoke. *Where would he spend the night?*

He had taken a bottle of water from a street vendor's cart while the man was talking with another vendor, and rushed into an alleyway to drink it. As he came out of the alley, his stomach rumbled. He was hungry, and he had never been hungry in his well-bred life! It was a new sensation, and not one that he had ever desired to have.

It was then that his eyes saw a sign across the street. It read Mason Street Mission. Wasn't a mission a place where they helped people? He thought it might be. He crossed the street and went to the door. There was sign by the door that said, "Open."

Frank opened the door and stepped into a hallway. He saw an inner door with a buzzer and speaker by it. He pressed the button.

A voice came from the speaker. "Yes, who is it?"

"I'm looking for a place to spend the night," Frank said.

"Do you have any money?" the voice asked.

Frank answered quickly, "A little, very little. Not much, at all."

The door opened, and a man of Frank's height was standing there. "We subsist on donations," he said. "How much can you donate?"

The man's face was kind, but there was a hard look in his eyes that belied Frank's initial impression.

"I have a little money, but I need something to eat and a place to sleep. A shower and shave would be great, too. I don't usually—"

"You don't usually look this way? I've heard it before. We can give you some food and a cot. That's all. How much do you have?"

"I can give you $5.00," Frank said, looking down at his torn sneakers, his face warm with embarrassment.

"Well, that's not much, but we've helped some for less. I'll take your $5.00. We can offer you tonight. That's all. As the season gets colder, we get people here who pay more. You'll have to move on tomorrow morning."

"No showers?" Frank said, hopefully.

"No, sorry. Do you have other clothes with you?"

"No, these are all—"

"Never mind. Follow me." The man turned and went down a hallway. Frank followed behind him. They entered what had to be a kitchen, where there was a pot of food on a stove.

"You can sit over there. I'll need the money, first."

Frank gave the man five crumpled dollars. He was served a bowl of stew, a piece of buttered bread, and a small glass of milk.

He ate quickly. Never had any meal he had ever had in his wealthy life tasted as good as this. After he had eaten, he was required to wash his bowl and spoon himself.

"We all must work for our supper," his host said. He didn't know that Frank had never worked a day in his life.

When his task was over, he was led to a large room off the kitchen. The room was filled with cots, and all but one of them was already occupied. One cot mid-way down the right side of the room was empty.

The sound of snoring was loud in the room. Frank approached the cot warily. He would never be able to fall asleep in such a place. He sat down for a moment. Then, he lay down on the cot. In the darkness, the sound of the snoring in the room was too much. How could he sleep with such a din? Moments later, Frank was fast asleep.

*Chapter Two*

Frank opened his eyes. It was very bright where he lay. This did not seem right to him. He had fallen asleep in a large room with many other people, all of them on cots. He also felt very warm. He rolled onto his left side and looked at what was near him.

He saw someone lying on a cot a few feet away. The person looked like a boy. That didn't seem right, either. The room had been filled with adults the night before. The boy was dark-skinned. He looked to be perhaps 8 or 10 years old.

Then, Frank looked at his arm and hand. His skin was also dark. He sat up quickly. He was no longer in the room where he had fallen asleep. This room was smaller, but there were cots crowded together throughout it. Other boys lay sleeping around him. All were dark-skinned. *What was happening to him now? Where was he?*

He stood up. There was a piece of mirror on a wall near his cot. He walked to it and looked at himself. The face of a black male, perhaps 15 years of age, looked back at him. Startled, he yelled, "What in God's name— ?"

"Be quiet, Francis! You'll wake the others. It's not time to work, yet!" said a boy who looked about the same age.

Frank's eyes grew wide. "Call me Frank, not Francis. Who are you? Where are we?"

"Did you have a dream? You know very well who I am: Cidreck, your best friend! We are in the orphanage. Where else would we be?"

"I've never seen you before in my life!" Frank said.

"Are you trying to frighten me?" Cidreck asked, "If so, you're doing a good job of it. You must have had a bad dream—"

"This is a bad dream!" Frank declared.

"Don't yell! Please don't wake them. They need their sleep."

"I'm-I'm white. My name is Frank, and I live in Hyde Park, New York."

The boy who called himself Cidreck began laughing.

"Why are you laughing at me?" Frank demanded.

"If you are white, then I must be green or blue. Your name is Francis. We have known each other since birth. I have never heard of this Hide Perk—"

"Hyde Park, not Hide Perk! This can't be happening to me. I live on an estate that has been part of my family for generations! I am 51 years old and—"

"And you are crazy! The only estate we have is the plantation, and we will be in the fields soon enough. Now, stop it. Don't wake them. They need their sleep! It's too hot today, and we need to rest, not yell at each other. You had a bad dream! That is the only explanation. Go lie down. We'll be in the fields within the hour, and then you'll wish you had been quiet!"

Frank stared at the other boy. This was impossible! He was Frank Fredericks—THE Frank Fredericks—the one and only Frank Fredericks. He was not a black boy living in an orphanage in wherever the hell this place was!

He returned to his cot and forced himself to lie down. He was trying to slow his breathing when a voice called, "Come, my young men. Come, my handsome ones. Awake, arise, the day has come. It's time to do our duty to our country."

Frank sat up. There was handsome black man in the doorway of the room. He was dressed in khaki clothing with leather boots on his feet. His pants ballooned in the military fashion over his boot tops. He wore a hat that looked like a safari hat, for that was exactly what it was. He held a riding crop in his right hand, and he was tapping the palm of his left hand with it.

"Up, up! Get out of bed, sleepy ones. Your work awaits you. It's time to get up. I will be waiting for you. Don't tarry," the man said. "You know the rules."

All of the boys were scrambling from their beds. They looked like they had slept in their clothes. There were 17 boys, altogether, and

Frank saw that Cidreck, two other boys and he appeared to be the oldest in the group. They were grumbling about having to get up.

Everyone started through the doorway, but Frank hung back.

Cidreck turned and looked at him. "Come, you'll miss breakfast. You know the Master gets angry when we are late!"

Frank followed him through the door and into the sunlight. The boys were walking in a group towards a low building next door. When he came in last behind them, he saw that it was a large lavatory with sinks, urinals, toilets, and there were showers visible through a second inner doorway.

He desperately wanted a shower, but then he realized that this was because he had been so filthy in the previous dream, or whatever it was. It was not to be. In less than 10 minutes the boys left the bathroom and walked to a third low building. Frank saw rough-made picnic tables and a doorway into a kitchen.

Two women were standing in the doorway, looking at them. Plates, utensils, cups of water and food awaited them. There was little talking. The boys took their places at the tables. Frank would have stood there by himself, not knowing where to sit, but Cidreck grabbed his arm and led him to his seat.

The food was unfamiliar to him, and Frank stared at it. One of the women asked, "How do we begin the day?"

The boys answered in union, "With prayer!"

The second woman asked, "What do we pray for?"

"Strength and protection!" the boys proclaimed.

The first woman continued, "And to whom do we pray?"

All of the boys said together, "The Lord God."

The second woman said, "Francis, you will lead us today."

Frank sat silently thinking that there must be someone else in the room named Francis, who would speak. The silence went on for a moment.

Cidreck poked him in the side and whispered, "Pray, Francis, or you'll be punished!"

Frank did not attend church, although he had donated money to charities. He had not spent much time in his life thinking about anything other than his own needs and enjoying himself. God played no role in his daily existence, but now he was afraid of the women who stood in the room, staring at him. He frantically searched his mind for how to respond.

The boys were growing restless. A younger boy two tables away muttered, "What is wrong with him?"

Frank opened his mouth, "Lord God, we pray for strength and protection. Please—"

He didn't finish his sentence. All of the boys shouted, "Amen!" and fell to eating as quickly as possible.

Frank joined them, keeping his head down and avoiding eye contact with anyone.

The food was bland. He was thirsty, so he drank the water in his cup.

Five minutes later, the boys stood up and began filing out the door.

Outside, they boarded an old, rickety bus that awaited them. The driver of the bus was a very old black man, and he did not acknowledge them when they took their seats.

The day was becoming hot, and Frank felt sweat under his shirt and on his face. The overseer, or whatever he was called, sat in the front seat by the door next to the driver. The windows of the bus were open, but even the breeze was hot. There was no relief as the bus pulled away from the orphanage.

Frank read the sign on the building.

*Malawi Means Progress*
*Do Your Best!*

He had no idea what it meant. Cidreck was sitting next to him on the aisle, and Frank was next to the window. They were about mid-way in the bus. He whispered to Cidreck, "What is Malawi?"

Cidreck had started to laugh, but when he turned and looked

at Frank, and he stopped laughing. He whispered, "Is it the dream again, Francis? What is the matter with you? It is our nation. We live here. I came to the orphanage a month after your mother died. Don't you remember? How can you not remember? My father had died and my mother was in the hospital dying. We are all that's left. Malawi is our home.

"Now our life is toil at the plantation. They give the money we earn to pay for our room and board at the orphanage. This way, no one else must pay. No one in Malawi has much money. You know this. We are the poorest of the poor. That's why we work!

"I think that maybe you need to see a doctor! What kind of crazy dream makes you think such things? You're not an old white man! You're 15 years old and black, same as me. We'll be working on the plantation when we die! Just like all the others!"

Frank did not know how to respond to this. He had never heard of Malawi. He had never cared for anything but his easy life and the endless parties, celebrations, events, chamber music, golf, tennis, horseback riding, swimming and the sights in the beautiful and protected places where he spent all of his time.

The Republic of Malawi is a landlocked country in central Africa bordered by Mozambique to the east, south and west, Zambia to the northwest, and Tanzania to the northeast. It is sometimes described as the poorest nation on earth with an annual average income of $226.00 a year. Roughly 9% of the 16 million people are infected with HIV/AIDS, and 50,000 people die of the disease yearly. The low life expectancy of 50.3 years and high infant mortality rate complete the picture of a terribly impoverished nation.

About the size of the state of Pennsylvania, Lake Malawi covers about a third of the land area. One of the least developed countries on Earth, Malawi is rural and depends on agriculture to survive. The main crop is tobacco, representing 70% of Malawi's revenue. Tea and coffee make up another 20% of the exports, with sugarcane, cotton, corn, potatoes, sorghum, cattle and oats producing 10%.

Elephants, hippos, big cats, monkeys, lemurs and a great variety of birds are seen in Malawi. Africa's Great Rift Valley runs from north to South.

Frank knew nothing about this, and his eyes would have glazed over if had ever had to read about it. His world was as wide as his riches and a sixteenth of an inch deep. No one had ever taught him about the world's inequities, and he had never had a desire to learn about them.

The bus lurched along on its over-aged springs, banging hard and causing its occupants to feel every pothole and rut. The day had grown hot and sweat was running down Frank's face. He stared at the countryside through the open window.

They came to the gates of the plantation. Plantation was over-stating what it was. It was merely a farm comprising about 30 acres of tobacco fields. The so-called Master stood in front of a small, low building that served as an office. Barns for the harvested tobacco were adjacent to the office.

The man was in his 40's. He had dirty blond hair, blue eyes, and fair features, but there was nothing kind in his face. He was wearing sweat-stained khakis, scuffed brown boots, and a wide-brimmed hat.

When the bus rolled to a stop, the black overseer stepped down from the bus, and the boys came after him, forming two rows for inspection. Frank kept his eyes down and followed Cidreck. They were in the second row, with Frank on one end of it, while Cidreck stood next to him.

"We have a lot of work today," the Master said in a low voice. His British accent sounded somehow too formal for the scene.

"The younger boys will be in the field, but I need six to fertilize today. Pick the six, Maurice, and let's get started. The day is wasting as we stand here in this damn heat!"

The black man with the riding crop turned and chose the six biggest boys. Cidreck and Frank were among them.

Cidreck muttered, "Oh, God, he will kill us!"

Maurice heard this and stepped forward quickly. He grabbed Cidreck by the front of his shirt with his right hand and smacked the boy across the face with his riding crop.

Cidreck yelled in pain. The blow left a welt on the boy's face.

The overseer stepped back and said, angrily, "Do any of you have anything else to say?"

The other boys remained silent. Frank was terrified. He had never witnessed violence so close in his life. He stared at the ground. He did not raise his eyes to the man.

A long moment passed, and then the overseer said, "Good. Go get your equipment. You'll be told where to go. Move. Don't tarry. There's much to do."

The nation of Malawi does not pay attention to child labor laws. There was no Division of Youth and Family Services or other agency that was going to come to the rescue.

Two large corporations controlled 90% of the tobacco production in Malawi, and the system was set up to keep the farmers of the nation poor an unable to reap the full benefits from their labors and crops. Manual labor was the preferred method of getting things done, because the wages paid were miniscule, and the process of fertilizing crops did not involve the health and well-being of those who did the work.

Fertilizers, pesticides and other chemicals were not properly handled or stored. Exposure to all sorts of deadly elements is routine for Malawi farm workers.

78,000 Malawi children work on tobacco farms from January through May each year, and they cannot attend school. While their pay is supposed to be a minimum wage of $1.12 daily, the quality of the tobacco leaves usually makes that amount even smaller.

Children also suffer from green tobacco sickness, a form of

nicotine poisoning. When wet leaves are handled, nicotine from the leaves gets absorbed in the skin and causes nausea, vomiting and dizziness. This can permanently change brain structure and function.

Frank and the other boys began the process of fertilizing a field. Because he had never done a day's work in his life, Frank stood helplessly at the edge of the field before him, not knowing what he should do. It was at that moment that he felt the lash of the riding crop on his back and fell to his knees, screaming out loud. A second blow knocked him facedown to the ground.

Rough hands reached down and pulled him to his feet. He was turned about, and Maurice, the overseer, held him with crushing hands to his upper arms, his face inches away from Frank's.

"You stand here, boy, like a statue! You are here to work! Have you become stupid? Do your job! Get to work. Otherwise, I will beat you, until you do!"

Cidreck, who stood a few feet away, said, "Your pardon, overseer, but Francis awoke this morning with a stomachache. He is not himself—"

"Do I care about such things?" Maurice asked, sneering. "He will work, or I will see that he wishes that he was never born into this world!"

"I will see that he works. Come, Francis, follow me. Let us get to work. We have much to do," Cidreck said.

Frank staggered towards Cidreck and the other boy grabbed his hand and whispered, "Do as I do, Francis. Watch me. Please. He will beat you bloody, if you don't."

Cidreck showed Frank how to spread the fertilizer they both carried. The overseer stood watching them for what seemed an eternity. Frank went through the motions until he understood what he was to do.

Cidreck whispered, "Step away from me. We will use what we have and then replenish our supply. I will show you how. The dream has made you forget who you are. Follow me. Keep me in sight. We will be here a long, long time today."

Frank moved away from Cidreck. They were moving through the tobacco plants. Both boys were covered with fertilizer. Frank was coughing. Finally, the overseer turned and walked away.

It was still early in the morning, but the heat was fearsome. Sweat streamed down Frank's face and body. The fertilizer was choking him, and the leaves of the plants scraped against his legs below his shorts.

What began then was like a day in hell. At noon, they were given a short break for food and water, and then returned to their task. Frank's young body ached, and his mind raged. *Why was this happening to him? What had he done to bring him to such a place?*

The afternoon lasted forever. When twilight came, the boys staggered from the field, exhausted beyond words. They got onto the bus and rode back to the orphanage.

Because they had worked with the fertilizer that day, Cidreck, Frank and the other four boys were allowed to use the showers first. The water was tepid, neither hot nor cold, but Frank stood in it as long as he could before the others yelled that it was their turn.

The boys went to supper. The women demanded that another boy pray, and they ate in silence.

As they left the mess hall, no one spoke. They went to their room and fell onto their cots. Frank lay in the darkness for a moment. *I am in hell itself,* he thought. *I cannot live through another day.*

He fell asleep.

### *Chapter Three*

Frank awoke to an overpowering stench in his nostrils. He looked up at the ceiling above him. It looked strange. He saw that it was made of cardboard, pieces of fabric, old building materials, bits of wood and other things he could not identify.

He sat up, only to discover that he was no longer a boy, but a man again. He looked at his hands. They were no longer the hands of a black teenager. His clothing had also changed. He was no longer dressed in shorts and a t-shirt. This clothing was stained and ragged. He wore a pair of khaki pants and a long-sleeved polo shirt. Ragged sneakers were on his feet.

In that moment, a woman dressed in poor clothing came through a doorway. The door was made of pieces of wood, aluminum foil, wire and string that held it together.

She looked to be young, perhaps in her middle 20's. She was pretty, but there was a grim look on her face. She looked at him and said in Spanish, "Francisco, we need to hurry. The trucks are coming. If there is to be anything for the children, we must try and get there before the others."

Surprisingly, Frank understood her perfectly. He answered her, and he was speaking Spanish, too.

"Who are you and what is this place?"

"What is the matter with you? I am Maria, your wife! We are in La Chureca. It is where we live."

Her eyes grew fearful. "Did you eat something bad? Francisco, is there something wrong with your mind? We must hurry! We must go now! The others will have picked over everything! There will be nothing left! Come with me now! Get your bags and let us go. There is no time to wait!"

With these words, she went to a corner of the small space and picked up a bunch of old bags that were made of various materials, including plastic and fabric. She passed him and went through the door.

Frank saw more bags in the corner. He gathered them up and went through the door after her. The sight that greeted him was overwhelming.

La Chureca, the "City of Trash," is the largest dump on the outskirts of Manaqua, Nicaraqua. Four square miles in area, over 400 families live there in homes constructed of trash. The carcasses of dead animals, bio-waste, toxic chemicals, heavy metals and toxic fumes make moving through the vast land of waste a never-ending health hazard for those who live there.

Called Churequeros, the inhabitants spend their days digging through trash for food and other necessities, as well as for things that may be worth money or useful in some way. Outsiders who come there are not welcomed, and it is not a friendly place to live.

Frank knew nothing of this. He saw Maria ahead of him, and he followed her. True to her word, she led him to a place where the trash trucks were arriving. At least a hundred people of all ages were already there, waiting in anticipation of what might be hidden in the mounds of refuse, garbage, and worse that spilled from the trucks.

They ran for the trash the moment a truck was emptied of its contents. Maria had picked up two hoes to bring along, and she handed one to Frank when he stepped beside her.

A man, woman and two young boys were next to them. Maria led them a few feet away and began digging in the pile. The odor that came up from it was unlike anything Frank had ever smelled before, and it set off his gag reflex. He could not believe that she was digging in such filth.

She turned to him and cursed at him. "Dig, Francisco! Dig! We need food! Jara and José will come home from school, and they will have nothing to eat! Don't stand there, help me!"

Frank overcame his revulsion as best he could and sunk his hoe into the mass before him. He watched Maria to see how she used the hoe, and he copied her method.

She had uncovered a white plastic bag that was tightly knotted. She grabbed it and tore it open. The bag contained food that was mashed together, but he saw what appeared to be pieces of chicken in it. Maria carefully separated the food into an aluminum dish she had in her pocket. It had a plastic top to cover it. She used a spoon from another pocket, and when she had enough of what she thought was edible, she closed the container and pushed the trash bag away. She looked up and found her watching him.

"Dig, Francisco. That is not enough for today! Dig!"

Frank could not believe what he was doing, but he dug into the pile. He did not find a bag with food, but he did uncover a paper bag. When he opened it with the edge of his hoe he saw an old shirt and what looked like a man's belt.

Maria said, "Save them. We can use them!"

Frank put the items into one of the bags he had with him.

As the morning slipped by slowly, Frank continued his search. He finally dug up a bag with food in it. He would have never touched anything he found, not for all the money he once had, but Maria stepped in and chose more food from the garbage to put into a container.

Shortly after mid-day, he uncovered an old, worn leather satchel, and when he opened it he saw zippered pockets within it. He was about to open one of them when he felt Maria's hand on his wrist.

"Don't open it here," she hissed in his ear, "we'll take it home and look in it there. It might be something important. Put it in your bag!"

Frank did as she said.

The sun moved across the sky. It felt like many hours had slipped by. Frank's back, shoulders and legs were aching.

Maria looked up. "School will be closing soon. Let's go. The children will be coming home. We must be there when they arrive." She picked up her hoe and bags and started to walk home.

Frank followed her.

When they approached their home, such as it was, Frank saw that it had been built into an indentation of a hill of debris. Apparently, the mound of refuse offered some sort of support and protection for the structure.

They entered their house and placed their bags on the floor. The floor was of dirt, but it had been covered over with cardboard and old blankets.

Maria took out the two food containers that she had managed to fill that day, and Frank removed the leather satchel from his bag. He handed it to Maria.

They sat down and she opened the bag and pulled back the zipper on a pocket. It was empty. The second pocket proved to be much better. There was a wad of money wrapped by rubber bands.

Maria yelled in excitement. "Look, Francisco! I was right. If the others had seen this, we would be dead! We must protect it! We can't tell anyone, not even the children. We must hide it!"

Frank had no idea what the money was worth. It was Nicaraguan money. He said, "How much is there?"

Maria counted it. She was excited about her count. "There is over 20,000 cordobas, Francisco!"

"How much is that in dollars?" he asked.

She looked at him strangely. "I don't know. What does that matter? There are no dollars here. Why do you ask such a thing?"

In that moment two children came through the door.

Jara, the girl, was the older of the two. She looked like her mother. She was 10 years old and dressed in mismatched clothing and a worn pair of sneakers. Jose was seven, and he wore dirty jeans, a torn t-shirt with a New York Yankees logo on it, and sneakers. He resembled Frank, but Frank did not know it because he had not seen his reflection in a mirror since he was in the Malawi orphanage.

The children were excitedly talking about something that had happened at school. La Chureca has a six-room school located in the dump, and Maria insisted that both children go to school for as long as they could. Many children spent their days sifting through the trash and garbage with their parents, but she wanted something far better for her children. The odds were against them, but she dreamed that one day they would leave this place.

The money might help that become possible. She had thrust the cash back into the leather satchel when the door burst open.

Apparently, there had been a fight at school. Two older boys had been fighting over a remark that one had made to the other. A teacher had broken up the fight, but not before being hit by both the boys. In the end, the boys had been barred from returning to the school for a month. They would be trash-picking until their punishment was over.

The afternoon ended, and Maria prepared the evening meal. When she presented it to the family, Frank had no desire to eat, knowing where the food had come from, but his hunger was such that he overcame his revulsion and ate with them.

As night fell, they lit an oil lamp and talked for an hour in the flickering light. Then, it was time to sleep.

Jara lay down next to her mother, and Maria pulled an old blanket over them on one side of the small room.

Frank lay down with José and did the same. The boy cradled his head on Frank's shoulder, talking about a book he had seen at school that day. It had a picture of a big house and a beautiful scene on its cover. He wondered aloud what it might be like to go to such a place, and Frank felt tears in his eyes. He knew about such places all too well.

The boy fell asleep. The hut was filled with the soft breathing of those who slept.

Frank could not sleep. He lay in the darkness, thoughts swirling in his mind. He wondered if his nightmare would ever end. He was afraid to go to sleep. To what horror would he awake the next morning?

*Chapter Four*

Frank awoke in sheer terror. He sat up and found that he was in his own bed. The disorientation of sleep gave way to reassurance that it had been a dream, after all. With a sigh of relief, he turned and looked at his wife. She was sleeping peacefully by his side.

It was the morning of his 51st birthday. His wife had arranged a grand party at the CIA— Culinary Institute of America— in Hyde Park that night to celebrate his milestone. All their best friends would be there. His son had flown in from Denver, and his daughter and her husband were coming up from New York.

He was looking forward to it.

What a terrible dream it had been. Never in his life had he had such a dream. It had been so real that it was frightening to even think about it.

Frank got out of bed. The dream had been unsettling. He never thought about such horrors. In fact, he knew nothing about such things because he had never read about anything like what he had experienced in the dream.

To be homeless in New York, a black child in an African orphanage, and a father living with his family in a place where there was nothing but garbage were circumstances that had no reality in his blissful existence.

Still, there was that nagging question that was lurking in the back of his mind.

Frank went to his bathroom, and he decided that a bit of time in the gym would be good for him, but some laps in the pool before-hand would be a great way to begin the day.

He took the elevator to the sub-basement and the tunnel to the pool house. He went to his locker to put on his swimming suit.

He opened the locker and saw something that should not be there. There was a paper bag in his locker.

He stood for a long moment, afraid to touch it. *Was another nightmare about to begin?*

Finally, he found his courage, took the bag out of the locker, and opened it. He reached in. His hand found several items. He took them out, one-by-one and placed them on the bench, next to him.

There was a small cloth bag with a drawstring, a large leaf from some sort of plant, a crumpled piece of paper that looked like money, and a folded note of white paper.

With shaking hands, Frank pulled the string and opened the cloth bag. He dumped the contents on the bench. There was $6.73. He had given $5.00 to the man at the mission to stay the night. This would have been the amount leftover. He picked up the leaf and looked carefully at it. It was a tobacco leaf. His hands began to shake violently. It took all his self-control to pick up the single piece of paper money. It was a Nicaraguan note.

Frank put down the money and picked up the folded piece of paper. He opened it. In flowing script was written:

*"Do you understand the answer to your question,*
*or is more instruction necessary?"*

The party was a great success. Everyone said so. When it was over, Frank, Adrienne, and their children returned to their mansion and went upstairs to bed.

Adrienne Fredericks awoke and looked at the clock. It was almost 2:00 a.m. She rolled over, but Frank was not there.

Concerned, she got up, put on her robe, and went to the bathroom. He wasn't there. She took the elevator to the first floor and went to the living room. He wasn't in the living room.

Adrienne went to the den. She found Frank sitting in front of his computer.

"Are you all right? Is your stomach upset?" she asked. "Is there anything wrong?"

Instead of answering her questions, Frank said, "Adrienne, would you sit with me for a moment?"

"Yes, of course, darling, but I want to know what you are doing up at this hour. You should be in bed. It was a long day."

"Adrienne, have you ever wondered about the meaning of life?" Frank asked softly.

"What kind of question is that? Our life is wonderful. What possible meaning could it have? It's 2:00 a.m. I'm tired. I have a luncheon today, and I'll have to be up by 10:00. You know I need my sleep!"

Frank's face looked serious. He did not have his usual mild look.

"I asked you a question, Adrienne. This is terribly important. I've been sitting here for hours educating myself. It's amazing what you can find out on the Internet. Will you answer me, please?"

"Answer you? Yes, of course. What was the question again?"

"I asked you if you had ever thought about the meaning of life."

"I think it's having fun with family and friends, enjoying each day, playing tennis, swimming, going on vacation, going to the theater, and doing all those fantastic things we do. Is that a good answer, Frank?"

"Once I would have agreed with you, but my ideas have changed," Frank said.

"What do you mean?" Adrienne asked.

"I'm going to explain the real meaning of life, Adrienne. This will take awhile."

"Well, I hope it won't take all night."

"Oh, it will take much longer than that, Adrienne."

"Mercy! How long will it take?"

For the first time, Frank smiled. "Adrienne, my love, that is a wonderful word—"

"What? What word do you mean, Frank?"

"Mercy. It's at the heart of everything. Now, as to how long—"

"Yes, Frank?"

"It's going to take the rest of our lives. First, I have a story to tell. I think you'll find it interesting."

"I hope so, Frank."

"That's another great word, Adrienne."

"What word, Frank?"

"Hope. Let me begin …"

THE
FOREVER
MAN

# The Forever Man

The residents of Madison Acres Retirement Home numbered 83: 79 women and 4 men. The full capacity of the home was 90, and Director Ezra Johnson intended to regain the maximum count by month's end.

February had brought a rash of deaths. Influenza had killed three women and a man. Two more had died of natural causes in March, and the last one had died on April 15th, Income Tax Day. In the modern world, that was enough to frighten anyone to death. It was a poor attempt at gallows humor, and Johnson's laughter was as dry as his personality.

Johnson was 47 years old, wore steel-rimmed glasses, was slight-of-build with a pronounced paunch, and slightly stoop-shouldered. He looked like a stereotype of a man who would occupy such a job. His medium-brown hair was closed-cropped, his eyes were a watery blue, his hands were endlessly restless, and his voice was non-threatening.

He had taken his undergraduate degree in accounting, tested for and passed his CPA exam, and gone to work for the Bettinger Corporation, owners and operators of retirement and nursing homes in seven northeastern states. Madison Acres was about four miles from Lancaster, Pennsylvania, and Johnson was in his seventh year as director.

Johnson had chosen not to marry. His one-story brick ranch home was about two miles from the facility. He spent his free time browsing the antique shops, flea markets, and Amish and Mennonite businesses and operations throughout the Lancaster area.

He was respected and feared by the staff for his meticulous approach to management of the home, and it was his policy to never fraternize with the help. Johnson felt that such relationships could compromise his ability to hire and fire, when necessary. He had no intention of ever allowing himself to like anyone to the point of undermining his ability to do his job.

He had watched his father die an early death when he was laid off from the corporation he had willingly served for 33 years, and he would absolutely not place himself in jeopardy if he could avoid it. Johnson was a "numbers man" in everything he did. If the numbers added up in his favor, he stuck to them. Emotion played no role in the life of Ezra Johnson.

His mother still lived in their two-story clapboard home in Philipsburg, Pennsylvania, and two of his three older sisters also lived in that town. He returned home for holidays, and dutifully sent his seven nieces and nephews cards and sensible money gifts for birthdays and graduations.

Johnson believed in structure, carefully written regulations, annual employee reviews, following strict guidelines, loyalty, truthfulness, honesty and he did not allow anyone under 2 his jurisdiction to stray from the prescribed methods of advancing the corporate agenda and keeping it profitable for his superiors.

The Madison Acres facility was a business first and a retirement home second. It produced money for the parent company, and Johnson saw to it that this was first priority. The marketing approach used by Bettinger was good. The brochures and graphics were informative without being ostentatious. The furnishings were one step above utilitarian. Decorations were kept to a minimum. The food was of sufficient quantity, but bland.

In the world of retirement homes, Madison Acres would be described as second-level. Johnson kept it this way with a tight rein on all expenditures. It was more affordable than the more opulent homes, but the margins were much better. His bosses thought of him as a cold fish, but they respected his rate of return. It was one of the top five most profitable homes in their stable of 27 homes throughout Pennsylvania, New Jersey, Connecticut, New York, New Hampshire, Vermont and Massachusetts.

Three families had been interviewed, and it looked like they would be bringing their relatives to Madison Acres to begin residency by the month's end. All three were women. It is axiomatic that the vast majority of retirement home residents are female. Men simply do not live long enough, on average, to make it to the last lap of life. This thought brought another internal dry chuckle to Johnson's mind. Three more family interviews had been booked, and if they qualified the total count would be 89, just one short of maximum.

The weekend slipped by, and the first interview had been set for Monday afternoon. Interviews two and three were held on Tuesday and Thursday, respectively. As far as fortune was concerned, all three potential residents had qualified with still a week to go to try to add one more to fill every bedroom.

Unless families demanded otherwise, women were housed two to a bedroom. The four men in residence each had their own small room in the east wing. Madison Acres was designed in the shape of a cross, with the longer span housing the offices, nurses' office, dining room, TV room and game room. The laundry facility was housed in a separate building.

Ezra Johnson attended a Methodist Church about a mile from his home. It carried the name of the founder of Methodism, John Wesley. Johnson thought this was appropriate. He went to church so that he could say that he attended church. He did not believe in the faith, but appearances were important. No one suspected that his soul was as empty as his dry smile. His church attendance was also good for business.

The problem on his desk was to find one more person to fill the home. He wanted it operating at full capacity. He was a no-nonsense man who expected others to get with the program, or get out of the way.

He did not expect what was coming. The term "rude awakening" was about to take on a whole new reality for Ezra Johnson. The fun was about to begin.

*Chapter Two*

It was close to 5:00 p.m. on Friday afternoon when Director Johnson became aware that the room had grown darker. It had been a bright, sunny day, and the change seemed to reflect his mood. Tomorrow, the new month would begin without him meeting his goal. He did not like to miss the mark when it came to achieving the benchmarks he set for himself. He felt frustration building inside of him.

He was sitting at his computer reading his email and mentally composing a note to his boss that would tell him the good news that 89 residents were confirmed, and the bad news that they were one resident short. But not to worry, he would fill the slot next week.

His thoughts were interrupted when the sun in his west-facing windows dimmed.

He looked up in irritation, only to see the biggest human being he had ever encountered standing in front of his desk. He was so startled that he almost yelled in fright. He jumped to his feet and exclaimed, "How did you get in here?"

The voice that answered was deep and powerful. "I came in the front door. I assume that is probably how most people come in," the man said.

Johnson looked at the giant. Dark-skinned, with long black hair, dark eyes, and a handsome face, the man was at least seven feet tall and powerfully built. His dark eyes were penetrating.  He wore his hair to his shoulders, and his face was unlined. He was dressed in a dark suit with a white shirt and a red and blue striped tie. His black shoes shone with a brightly polished effect, and his smile was broad. Two suitcases sat on the floor beside him. They looked ancient, and Johnson saw travel stickers all over them.

"What can I do for you, Mister … ?"

"Call me Simon," the man said.

"Is Simon your first or last name? Johnson asked.

"Just Simon will do. I understand you have a room. I need a place to stay."

"Well, Simon, I need a first and last name. Is your family in the area?"

"I don't have a family. I am alone. You do have a room, don't you?" the big man asked.

In his characteristic way, Director Johnson put on what he thought of as his friendly face and said, "Yes, but there are a number of things we need. There are forms to fill out, a background check, financial determinations, and a great deal more. This is not a hotel. People don't just walk in here off the street and expect to be accommodated."

The big man smiled in return. "Perhaps this will help." He reached into his inside suit jacket pocket and pulled out a roll of bills. There must have been thousands of dollars in the roll. He placed the roll on Johnson's desk. "That should cover the initial costs."

Ezra Johnson's eyes grew big. He had never seen so much paper money at one time. The roll was very large, and the bill on the outside was a hundred dollar bill. Nevertheless, he had seen huge checks pass over his desk. Retirement homes were not cheap. The average stay costs a resident $75,000 per year for a semi-private room. A single room costs even more.

"Well, Mister, uh, Simon, our residents don't pay with cash. Besides, you look quite healthy. You don't appear to be the age of the people here. And where did you get all the cash? I hope you didn't rob a bank," Johnson said, laughing softly.

The big man's face grew serious. "I am much older than I appear, Mr. Johnson. As to my finances, I always pay in cash for everything. Banks don't interest me. I do not use credit cards. My cash goes where I go. I am not a bank robber, and I find the idea offensive. I was told you have an opening. I'm here to fill it. From what I read, the average stay in such a facility is about two years. I will pay you in cash for two years right now. Is that acceptable?"

For the first time in his life, Ezra Johnson was at a loss for words.

He stared at the man. Finally, he said, "A private room at Madison Acres costs $82,000 annually. Do you intend to ..."

He did not finish his sentence. The big man reached down, opened one of the suitcases, and Johnson saw that it was stuffed full of hundred dollar bills, bundled in paper wraps. He counted out sixteen bundles, and then peeled off $4,000 from the roll that he had placed on Johnson's desk. "There, that should cover it."

There was $10,000 in each bundle, $164,000.00 in all. Johnson was stunned. He stammered, "But, Mr. Simon, this is highly unusual. We can't accept just anyone. I mean, good heavens, how can I take this to a bank? They would want to know where I got such a huge amount of money. They keep track of large transactions. The government has rules. In fact, where did you get such a huge amount of money, and why don't you use a bank?"

The huge man smiled, "I have lived a long time, Mr. Johnson, and I have been very frugal. I saved my money. I live simply. I have few needs other than to enjoy the company of others. I am at a place and time in my life where Madison Acres would be perfect for me. I'm sure you can overcome the small problem of the money. There are various ways you could deal with it, all of them legal and acceptable. Besides, you had one room to fill, you set your goal, and I am here to help you meet it."

Johnson's face showed his astonishment. "But, how do you know—"

"About your goals? I know many things, Mr. Johnson. I know when the sun will rise and set. I know when the rain and snow will fall. I know the seasons and their rhythms. I know the smell of earth in spring, and the beauty of the world He created. I know a great deal about people of all kinds, shapes and sizes. I have lived all over the world. I travel endlessly. I speak many languages, and I have walked paths both safe and dangerous.

"I have seen love and hate, justice and inequality, compassion and brutality, suffering and death, and the hope that transcends all things.

I was drawn here. I go where there are needs that are not stated, where there are wants that must be met, and where loneliness must not prevail. You are uncertain because you live a life that is orderly and you are always in control. I respect that. The money is there. I fulfill your need. Your rooms will be fully occupied and your superiors will be happy and satisfied. Does this meet with your approval?"

Ezra Johnson stood mesmerized by the man's words. He had never heard such things said, not even in church by trained speakers, and he had a strange thought. The man reminded him of something he had read somewhere long ago, but he could not clearly recall what it was. He should tell the man to take his money and leave, but the truth was that his goal would be met, the rooms would be full, and this was the last day of the month! If he could tell his superiors of his accomplishment, it would be another feather in his cap, and his holiday bonus would be that much larger.

"Do you have more possessions, Mr. Simon?" he asked the huge man.

"The man smiled again. "No, this is all I need, one bag for my money and one for my clothing. And please, just call me, Simon."

"What about your car?"

"I don't have one."

"But how did you—?"

"Get here? I walked," Simon said.

"You walked from where?" Johnson asked.

"From the city named for brotherly love."

"Good heavens, all the way from Philadelphia? Why didn't you take a bus, or a car? You could have hitchhiked."

"Look at me, Mr. Johnson. Who in their right mind in this world would pick up someone my size, carrying two suitcases? I like to walk. It provides me time to think."

"This is highly unusual. However, we do have transportation here. The county provides buses that take our residents to various points. We do not allow cooking or small refrigerators in our suites, and all of our food is provided in our cafeteria. There are vending machines in our community room. Meals are at set times. The rules and regulations are in our handbook.

"The room we have available is a single room. It should be adequate for your needs. If you will allow me, I should put the money in the safe. I can put it into the system in smaller amounts and see that your monthly obligation is met. However, how am I to explain someone who has one name only? There are forms to fill out, addresses required, a Social Security number must be given, and do you have health insurance?"

"Mr. Johnson, I am sure the room is fine. If you must use a last name, use a name that you choose. If you have a name that you like, use it. I don't have a Social Security number. I just arrived here a few days ago from the other side of the world. I am not an American. I was born elsewhere. I don't need insurance. I have money to pay for whatever is needed," Simon said.

"But how do I explain all this? Do you have a passport? Where did you come from?"

"Africa. Before that, I was in Israel. I have lived in Asia, Europe, Indonesia, Australia, South America, and many other places. I travel the world constantly. I have an Israeli passport."

Then, you must have a last name."

"No, I do not."

"How is that possible? You must have an address in Israel, given the fact that you are an Israeli."

The huge man reached into his suit jacket and brought forth a passport and handed it to the Director. He opened it and saw that there was only one name: Simon. There was no address. He looked more closely at it. He had never seen so many international stamps in his life. The man had been everywhere.

"How do you get away with having one name?"

"Simply put, I just do. From time-to-time I must explain this to inspectors, but they seem to accept what I have to say. You can fill out the paperwork so that it satisfies your superiors. Now, could I see the room? I'd like to freshen up in time for dinner."

Johnson handed the passport back to the man. "I'll call my assistant, Helen Buchanan. She'll give you the tour and show you to your room."

"Thank you, Mr. Johnson. I appreciate your kindness. It's good to be here. I have traveled a long way to get here."

Johnson reached across the desk and extended his hand. When Simon took Ezra's average-sized hand in his, the man's huge right hand virtually swallowed it. Ezra felt a strange tingling warmth.  It was a bit unnerving, and he released his grip quickly.

Johnson picked up his phone and hit a button. Helen Buchanan appeared in the doorway a few moments later. She was dressed in a modest gray business suit with a white blouse, and her light brown hair was tied in a bun. A century before she would have been called a spinster.

Helen looked up at the big man, amazed at his size. She wondered how he had gotten into Mr. Johnson's office without her having seen him. He would have had to walk past her desk in order to get into the room.

"Ms. Buchanan, this is, uh, Mr. Simon. He's going to take our remaining room. Would you take him to his room, and then give him a tour? Please make it brief ,because he wants to change for dinner. Thank you."

Simon smiled at Ms. Buchanan.

She said, "Do you need help with your bags?"

"No, it's no problem for me. I've carried a heavy burden many times. In fact, I once carried the heaviest burden ever borne. It was an incredible honor to do so."

Both Johnson and Buchanan thought this was a strange thing to say. Ezra Johnson asked, "What do you mean Mr. Simon?"

"You'll understand when the time is right, Mr. Johnson," Simon said, and smiled. He picked up and his bags, and Ms. Buchanan led him into the hallway. They walked down the corridor and made a turn at the end.

Ezra Johnson watched them until they disappeared from sight. He had covered the money with file folders before his assistant had entered the office. Now, he sat there looking at it. He had never seen so much cash at one time. It was impressive. For just a moment he was tempted, but then he reminded himself how badly things could turn out if someone made the wrong decision. He was not a religious man, and he never expected to be so, but he liked his job and he wanted to keep it.

He turned and dialed the combination to the safe, gathered up the money, placed it on one of the shelves, and locked the safe.

He turned again to his computer. He composed an email to his superior. "All rooms are filled once again. Sincerely, Ezra Johnson. It was time to go home. Fortune had smiled upon him once again. He looked forward to having a long conversation with Simon. The man must have a last name. He wanted to find out what it was.

*Chapter Three*

In the month that followed Simon's arrival, six more women moved into Madison Acres to begin their retirement, but no one created the stir that the giant man did. He was not only massive in size, but also a fascination to everyone who spoke to him. He could talk on any subject, was extremely friendly, sought conversation with all of the residents and staff who were willing to engage with  him, and his stories and tales about the places he'd been and the things he'd seen were better than the boring television shows that droned on and on in the community room.

The sound of his deep voice and booming laughter brightened the dullest days, and when he spoke to someone he made them feel very special. If someone was having a bad day, and there are many gloomy days in such places, he would single out the person who was feeling lonely, or in pain, and do his best to lift his or her spirits. The women who lived at Madison Acres were thrilled when he paid attention to them, and the men, although small in number, saw him as an ally in a world where they were sorely outnumbered.

One man, Charley Higgins, had been a cop in Philadelphia, and he took to Simon immediately. When the two of them spoke together anyone nearby would have thought that they had known each other forever. They laughed and joked, walked the grounds together, and even rode together to the Tanger shopping mall on the county bus.

Simon also did things in secret that only Ezra Johnson knew about. If someone needed something, such as medical equipment,  or something else that might not be covered by insurance or Medicare, he would see that it was purchased and presented to the one in need without taking credit for it. He had made an arrangement with Director Johnson to do this, making sure that no one would ever know who had done the act of kindness.

It was almost impossible to say no to the big man. He would smile his engaging smile, laugh kindly, and people would end up doing exactly what he wanted them to do.

The food at Madison Acres had been adequate, but the choices and cooking were utilitarian, at best, until Simon showed up. During his second week at the home, he walked into the kitchen two hours before lunch and literally took over. The ingredients were the same, but the tastes were fabulous. He used spices in such a way that he could make almost anything taste wonderful, to the delight of the residents. The days of bland meals were ended.

The cooks were enthralled with his skills, and Simon spent hours showing them how to make soups, sauces, salads and entrees in whole new ways, writing down the recipes and ideas so that they could follow them.

Simon had a powerful voice, and he also played the piano. He led everyone in the community room in songs and fun, urging them all to sing along as loudly as they could. He also had fun leading them in charades and other games. The mood of a nursing, assisted living or retirement home can be somber and unhappy, but Simon would not allow anyone to be downcast for very long.

Ezra Johnson observed the changes in the staff. There were far more smiles and cheerful greetings in the morning among his employees. Some actually said that they enjoyed working at the home, and no one had ever said such a thing before Simon's arrival.

The residents were another story. Many had possessed little energy, and those in wheelchairs would spend most days listlessly staring out the windows, or at mindless TV shows that contributed little to their daily life. Now, even those who could not walk were smiling, laughing, greeting each other, and engaging in animated conversations. They were obviously far happier than they had been previously. All of it was due to the presence of the huge man with the big voice and wonderful smile.

The months slipped by and Christmas came. Simon had secretly arranged to give gifts to every resident and staff member, and on Christmas morning everyone gathered near the tree in the community room and opened gifts from an anonymous donor. Cries of joy and laughter went on for an hour as each gift was opened. Each recipient claimed to the rest that the gift was exactly what he or she needed! It was as though Simon somehow knew what was hidden in a human soul, and he gave each one what their heart desired.

The New Year brought a heavy snowfall, and the people awoke to look out the windows and discover the big man wielding a shovel and clearing the walks before employees could get to the task. Under normal circumstances insurance coverage would have prevented any resident of the home from engaging in such activity, but Simon was not an ordinary resident, and Director Johnson was the only one who understood the difference.

## Chapter Four

Each year several residents passed on during the winter, but this year, as the winter slipped by, no one died. Spring arrived, and everyone who lived or worked at Madison Acres looked with anticipation to warmer temperatures, flowers, and the rebirth of the world.

Ezra Johnson had done his best to find out more about Simon, but it was to no avail. The big man would smile whenever they spoke, and when the Director asked him a question about his past, his last name, or anything related to his fortune that seemed to have no end, he would say, "In due time, Mr. Johnson. In due time." And then he would change the subject.

Simon had become the de facto leader of the guests. Under his guidance and urging, the residents of the home did all sorts of things they had not done before. They took buses on day trips to a Phillies baseball game, a tour of the Gettysburg battlefield and the President Dwight Eisenhower farm. They ventured out to Longwood Gardens, Hershey Park and other destinations. No one was excluded. Madison Acres employees went along to enjoy the sights and tend to residents in wheelchairs who also came along. The big man paid for all of it.

The fun and joy of simply being alive was evident in all of them. Eyes sparkled, and smiles abounded, even among the oldest of the people. It was as if life had returned in all its power, and the shackles of aging had fallen away. It was like being reborn.

Director Johnson marveled at the change in the residents and the demeanor of his staff. He saw employees singing, laughing and whistling as they went about their work, and he found himself envying them. He wished that he could drop his guard, lay aside his cynicism for a moment, and laugh along with them. However, he was the Director. He could not stop being aloof, distancing himself from others. He had to maintain control, even if he was the only one who did so.

Then came the day when Simon approached him with a question.

"What church do you go to, Mr. Johnson?"

Ezra was startled by the question. "Why do you ask?"

"I thought that I might impose on you this coming Sunday," Simon said.

"I attend the John Wesley Methodist church a few miles from here. In what way do you wish to impose?" Ezra responded stiffly.

"I wanted to ask if you would take me to church with you. I would like to attend services, and since I don't have a car, I was thinking that you could take me to and from the church this coming Sunday."

The Director said, "Well, I know you attend the chapel services here when outside clergy come each week. Why would you want to go to my church?"

"Each church is a house of God, is it not?" Simon asked softly.

"Yes, but—"

"God is everywhere. I simply want to visit a church. Will you take me?"

There was no way Ezra Johnson could refuse such a request, not after what Simon had spent so freely on the people and staff of Madison Acres.

"I can pick you up at 10:30 this Sunday at the front door," Ezra said. "It's a traditional service. We have a small but loyal congregation. Men wear suits and ties, and women dress—"

"It sounds perfect. I will dress accordingly. Thank you very much. I look forward to it," Simon said. He smiled and turned to go to the dining room.

Ezra's next thought was, *How will he fit in the car?* The Director used a Chevrolet Suburban that belonged to the home whenever he had to take a resident somewhere, which was infrequently, because other staff members normally transported residents when bus transportation was not available. It was one of the biggest SUV's, yet he hoped Simon could fit into it.

The Director pulled up at the front door of Madison Acres promptly at 10:00 a.m. Sunday morning, and Simon was waiting for him. He looked splendid in what had to be an expensive charcoal gray double-breasted suit with a crisp white shirt, yellow tie, and black shoes with such a shine that they actually were mirror-like in the morning sun.

Ezra had put the passenger seat all the way back, but Simon still had to scrunch down to get into the car. The top of his head touched the lining of the car's roof, and his knees were pressed against the dashboard.

The Director said, "I see why you prefer to walk. It must be difficult for someone your size to find a car big enough to accommodate you."

Simon smiled. "I'm not often in cars, but this is a big model. What kind is it?"

Johnson gave him an incredulous look. "It's a Suburban, one of the biggest SUV's made in America. How could you not know about it?"

"You forget that I am not from America. What is an SUV?"

"The letters stand for "sport utility vehicle." A Suburban is one of the earliest SUV models. This one holds up to nine passengers, although I had to put your seat back as far as it will go. That doesn't leave much leg room for the person who might sit behind you. I'm surprised you don't know more about cars. Don't you have such vehicles in Israel?"

"I told you that I am from Israel, but I came here from Africa. I spend much of my time in very poor areas of the world where transportation is limited. I walk a great deal, or travel on buses and trucks that might be available. The back of a truck is often the best place for me to ride."

The Director had had very few extended conversations with the big man or much of an opportunity to question him at length. "Where were you in Africa?"

"I go from one place to another, all over, actually. The people there have been virtually forgotten by the developed world. There is great suffering in many places. I help them as much as I can," Simon said.

"That is very noble of you," Johnson said.

"There is nothing noble about helping someone. It is my task to find suffering and to do what I can to alleviate it."

"Why do you do it? Help those people?" the Director asked.

"Why do you help the people at Madison Acres?" Simon asked, softly.

This question had never been asked of Ezra Johnson, and he stammered, "Well, I, it's not me helping, actually, it's the company I serve. It's my job to run the operation and see that everything is in good order."

"That doesn't answer my question," Simon said. "Why do you help the people who live at Madison Acres? You must have gotten into this work for some reason other than just doing a job. What is it?"

Ezra Johnson had never felt as threatened as he did at this moment. Long ago he had hidden a great secret away from the world, and he had not felt this vulnerable in 20 years. It was a long moment before he answered. He stared into the eyes of the big man next to him.

"When I ask you where you are from, what your last name is, and why you are at Madison Acres—because you obviously could go anywhere and do anything you want, you always change the subject," Ezra said.

"All of us have secrets, Simon. I can't give you an answer. Neither of us has been totally honest with the other. I have broken rules to allow you to stay at Madison Acres. I have written down false information for you on forms. I have kept the truth about you from my superiors, because I don't even know what your truth is! Don't ask me to reveal myself when you are not willing to tell me who you are and why you are here."

There was anger in Ezra Johnson's voice when he said this, and his face contorted in rage.

Simon said softly, "When it is appropriate, you will know what you need to know. I am here because my task is to help others. I asked if you would bring me to your church because there is a task to do there, as well. I go where I am called to go. I do not mean to sound mysterious, but there are things in the universe that few men fully understand.

"I have no wish to pry into your private life, but I am concerned about you. I know that you harbor pain in your soul. I see it. I would like to be your friend, if you would allow me to be."

In his lifetime no one had ever told Ezra that he wanted to be a friend, and he clenched his jaw. "You want to be my friend? I have no friends! Friendship has no place in my life. I will not discuss this further.  I have no wish to continue this discussion. We are here!"

The Director turned off the road and into the parking lot of the church. It was built of gray stone with a bell tower and a cross that gleamed in the pale, spring sunlight. Lovely stained glass windows reflected the light. The window on the street side showed an image of Jesus kneeling by the rock in the Garden of Gethsemane.

People were getting out of their cars and walking towards the double front doors.

Simon was silent. He watched the people through the windshield.

It took a few moments for Ezra Johnson to regain his composure. When he finally did, he exited the car without saying another word to the big man.

Simon ducked his head, squeezed his massive frame out of the front seat and stood up. He looked at the church and its grounds.

Built in 1925, John Wesley United Methodist Church sat on five acres. The sanctuary had been remodeled twice, and its pews could hold 200 people. A parish hall and Sunday school rooms were attached to the main building. A well-maintained cemetery sprawled on the parish hall side of the structure. Hundreds of tombstones were scattered throughout clusters of large, well established trees, including oaks, maples, pines and other varieties. The scene was pleasant.

Simon saw gravel walkways, stone benches, hedges and other nicely arranged bushes and foliage that looked healthy and well-kept.

He turned his eyes to Ezra Johnson and stood, silently waiting.

Johnson had mastered himself, and remembered his manners, along with the fact that Simon had been very good to the people and staff of Madison Acres.

"I must apologize to you," he said. "I do not wish to offend you. You have shown great kindness and compassion for so many. I—"

Simon did not allow him to finish his sentence. "Mr. Johnson, there is no apology necessary. You were kind enough to bring me to your church this morning. Let us enjoy the service and the rest of the day."

The two men turned and walked towards the entrance to the church. They were given bulletins by a smiling man at the door who said hello to Johnson, who, in turn, introduced Simon to him, identifying the greeter as Thomas Bigelow.

When they had walked through the foyer they passed into the sanctuary. The wooden pews, the lighting, and the light streaming through the stained glass windows above the altar created a serene atmosphere.

Simon sighed and said quietly, "I see why you come here. It's quite beautiful, and peaceful, too."

"The attendance has fallen off in the last few years," Johnson said, "but the new pastor just joined three months ago. We hope he can help rebuild up our membership. Many of the people have been here for generations. Our service is traditional. We like it that way, but some people wish we had a more contemporary service."

People were talking, then quieted when the music began. A group of about 12 people, dressed in choir robes were seated to the left of the altar. A white-haired organist with her back to the congregation began playing the hymn, "How Great Thou Art" while people stood, opening their hymnals to the appropriate page and joining with the choir.

They sang three stanzas of the song, and then a boyish-looking young pastor in a black robe left his chair to the right of the altar. He stood at the pulpit. His name was Samuel Blankenship, according to the bulletin, and he opened with prayer. The service continued with more songs from the hymnal, the Apostles' Creed, the Lord's Prayer, another hymn and the sermon. His title was "Live for Today," and he used several passages of scripture to illustrate how life should be lived in the 21st century.

When the service ended several people approached and were introduced by Johnson to Simon as "one of our residents at Madison Acres."

Simon towered over everyone in the church, even the tallest people in the congregation, and the huge man was welcomed warmly. This was the first time Johnson had ever brought a guest to church, and a couple people said that they were glad that he had finally done so. One woman urged him to bring other residents in the future.

When Simon met the young pastor at the door, the two men appeared to bond immediately. Simon asked him if they needed more choir members, and he eagerly said, "Yes, the more the merrier! We need all the help we can get!"

"When does your choir practice?" Simon asked him.

"They practice at 6:30, Thursday evenings. You're more than welcome to come and participate. Bring others, too. If people enjoy singing hymns they can come here and join the choir," Pastor Blankenship said, smiling.

When they got to the car, Ezra Johnson said, "Looks like you made a friend or two today. If you want to come to choir practice I can arrange transportation for you. If you ask others to come with you, maybe we can add some new members to the roll."

"That's a good idea. I'll find out how many want to come with me," Simon said, smiling as usual.

The two men rode in silence back to the retirement home, and when Johnson pulled up in front of the door to let Simon out the big man turned to him and said, "Thank you again for this morning. It has been a long time since I was inside a church and it means a great deal to me. It's good to be in His house again. I'll see you tomorrow, Mr. Johnson."

They said their goodbyes.

As Ezra Johnson drove home where he would have his solitary

Sunday meal, he thought about the big man. He wished that he could be that outgoing, so much so that people were drawn to him. He also wished he could wash away the stain on his soul, and be free of the thing that tormented him. He wished he had a friend who would listen to him and not judge him.

It would be so good to be free to laugh and at ease with others. If only there was some way to tell his story. If only he could find the courage to be as he once was. If only …

*Chapter Five*

On Monday morning, Ezra Johnson was sitting at his desk when Simon knocked on his door.

"Come in, Simon. What can I do for you?"

"I'd like to arrange for transportation to choir practice at the church for this Thursday evening," Simon said.

"That's good news. How many will be going with you?" Johnson asked.

"Well, that's just it. I'm not sure what you have available."

Johnson said, "The Suburban holds nine people, including the driver. That should be good enough for your needs, I imagine—"

"Not exactly …" the big man said.

"How many people want to go with you?" Johnson asked.

"Twenty-three, and there may be a few more. I asked everyone I saw, and …" Simon hesitated.

Johnson stood up from his chair, knocking his half-full coffee cup over and spilling its contents onto the desk.

Simon quickly stepped forward, grabbing a box of tissues from a nearby table.

"TWENTY-THREE PEOPLE?" Ezra Johnson exclaimed. "How did you manage to … ?"

"As I said, I just asked everyone I saw. There are apparently more singers here than I imagined. How can we get them to practice?"

"We have a bus that we use when other transportation isn't

available for large groups. How in heaven's name did you get that many to go along?" Johnson asked him with a look of incredulity on his face.

"You just said it, Mr. Johnson," the big man said.

"I said what?" Johnson asked.

"Heaven's name, that's the name I used. It works every time! So, we have a bus, but do we have a driver?"

"Arnie Henshaw can drive the bus," the Director said.

"You mean Arnie who works in the kitchen?" Simon asked.

"Yes, he has the proper license, and I'm sure if you ask him he'll be able to help out. You amaze me, Simon. This will triple the size of the choir. Most Sundays these days we're lucky if we break a hundred people in the congregation, including the choir!  I never thought to even ask anyone here if they would be interested in going to my church. I don't know what to say."

"You don't have to say anything, Mr. Johnson," Simon said.

"Please, call me Ezra. If one name is good enough for you, it's good enough for me, too. Our congregation will be thrilled with this many new people coming to church. The pastor is going to love it, too!" the Director said.

Simon smiled. "When we're alone, I'll call you Ezra. When others are about, it will be Mr. Johnson. You are the boss here—"

"Some days I wonder about that,"Ezra said, and smiled. "I'll arrange for the bus. Talk to Arnie and tell him about his new duty. Tell him I'll pay him for it."

"No, that's all right, Ezra," Simon said. "I'll take care of Arnie. Keep it off the books. That way you don't have to explain it to anyone. He and his wife Maria have a new baby girl. He can use some extra money to help out."

"I didn't even know he was married," Johnson said.

"That's all right," Simon said. "I have time to ask questions. You have a lot to do. Everyone understands the pressures you're under. You'd be surprised how much you're respected here, Ezra. People know how hard you work. You can't keep track of everything."

"Simon, I need to do more, but there are things I can't do. I can't change the company's policies on spending. I've never met anyone like you. You could move a mountain if you wanted to do it. I don't have your resources, and I don't have your joy. I realize that you're older than I am, but you act younger than I do. You make people laugh. You make them happy. I make them frown and run the other way. The truth is that I don't know how to do what you do. Would you tell me how you do it?"

This was the most honest Ezra Johnson had ever been with anyone in his life, and he surprised himself with what he had said to the big man.

Simon stood silently for a long moment. "I will tell you the most important truth about why I treat others the way I do soon enough, but you can do what I do as easily as I can," he said.

"How is that possible? I don't even know how to be happy. I haven't been happy since …" Ezra stopped speaking.

"Yes? What were you going to say, Ezra?"

"I, I can't say now. Perhaps one day…"

"When you're ready to tell me your story, I will be there to listen," the big man said. "For now, I will speak to Arnie and make sure the bus is ready for Thursday. You might want to give Pastor Blankenship a call and tell him what to expect. I will also give you a full count Thursday morning of who will be going to choir practice."

Simon turned to leave. "I promised Mrs. Stern that I would read to her this morning. She's almost blind. She likes me to read to her in Hebrew. I will speak to you later."

Simon left the office, and Ezra Johnson sat for a long time staring at a photograph on his desk. Memories came flooding into his mind. If only he had a chance to go back in time what he would do differently!

He did not feel the tears on his face. If he could change the past his soul would be at peace. Ezra reached out and picked up the photograph. Once he had been happy. Once he had been at peace. Anger had destroyed everything in his life. How could he tell Simon the truth? How could he go on living with such pain?

He was the most tormented of men, and he pretended that everything in his life was perfect. Everyone around him thought he was always in control. He wore the mask of the self-sufficient. He wanted to stand up and scream at the unfairness of the world, but he did not want anyone to know what had happened. The shame would destroy him.

————

Thirty-four people were on the bus that Thursday evening. The choir director and the pastor were waiting for them when they entered the church.

After all the introductions, Simon took control and began asking each person what their key was. He arranged the first and second sopranos, first and second altos, first and second tenors and first and second basses together. Extra chairs had been set up. Simon turned to the choir director and said, "I have a suggestion for Sunday. There is a wonderful song on page 237 of the hymnal that I've always enjoyed. Would you like to try it?"

The choir director, Agnes Sampson, opened the hymnal to that page.

The hymn was *Lord of the Dance* by Sydney Carter. She looked over the first stanza.

> *I danced in the morning when the world was begun,*
> *And I danced in the moon and the stars and the sun,*
> *And I came down from heaven and I danced on the earth:*
> *At Bethlehem I had my birth.*

The verses that followed were done to a lively tune that could get people on their feet, clapping their hands and singing along.

Mrs. Sampson said, "Well, this is a bit too—"

She never got to finish her sentence. Simon said, "Mrs. Sampson, if you will allow me," and he smiled his great smile at her, "I will direct this piece. We have to get the parts right. This is a wonderful hymn. I'm sure the congregation will enjoy it. Would you be kind enough to use the piano instead of the organ? It plays very well on the piano, and it will be easier for everyone to find his or her note."

The big man had become the director of the choir, and Mrs. Sampson had become the instrumentalist in that moment. One might have thought that she would object, but she was overwhelmed with gratitude by his request. The truth was that she was tired of playing the same hymns, sung by the same voices, Sunday after Sunday. She was excited to see what would happen when all these new people raised their voices, and she sensed that this huge man knew exactly what he was doing.

While Mrs. Sampson moved from the organ to the piano, Simon brought her director's hymnal over and placed it so she could read it easily. He turned to the choir.

"Now, let's begin. I will sing the song all the way through so you can be comfortable with the phrasing, the lyrics, the changes in tempo, the cadence and the unique vision of this song. This is an absolutely wonderful piece, and it celebrates what the Master did for all of us. Please listen carefully. Mrs. Sampson, would you play for me? Let's go through it together."

Mrs. Sampson and Simon began playing and singing, and more than 40 people listened in awe as the voice of the huge man filled the church. Had the Lord Himself had come down from heaven, they could not have been more amazed. Simon's vocal range was incredible and apparently without limitations. The song came to life thorugh his powerful voice. Some of the women were crying when he finished singing. A hushed silence filled the sanctuary when he stopped.

Pastor Blankenship stood in the center aisle with his mouth open, a huge grin on his face. *This man should be singing at Carnegie Hall!* he thought. He clapped his hands and yelled, "Bravo! Bravo!"

The spell was broken, and the newly reformed choir joined the clapping, whistling, and shouting along with the pastor.

It took a couple of minutes for the people to quiet down.

Simon appeared not to notice all the approval. "Now, that is the way we want to do it on Sunday. I'm going to lead you through the parts. I have two rules when I direct a choir. Rule Number One: Smile! Rule Number Two: Don't break Rule Number One!"

Everyone laughed.

For the next two hours they practiced, and Simon led them gently, but firmly to the right notes and phrasing. He said, "For those uncertain singers among us, don't be afraid! Listen to the others who are more certain, but, above all, make a joyful noise unto the Lord!"

Even Arnie Henshaw, who had driven the bus, had become part of the choir. "Yes!" he exclaimed, "Sing with all your heart!"

When they finally stopped practicing, everyone was talking about the song and its joy, the wonderful enthusiasm in its vision, and the powerful message it contained. No one wanted to leave.

Many people came up to Pastor Blankenship to ask about possibly joining the church, and he gladly shook hands, talked to each person, and promised that all were welcome. By the time they were on the bus everyone was excited.

They sang the song, even without the help of Mrs. Sampson's piano all the way home.

Sunday morning dawned and three buses waited in front of Madison Acres retirement home. Everyone was going to see the performance, including Mrs. Stern and four other women who were all Jewish. No one wanted to miss hearing their friends sing.

Pastor Sam Blankenship would refer to that Sunday morning as "The day the miracle occurred at John Wesley church."

The truth was that the congregation did not contain many young people. The majority of the pews were occupied by seniors, the choir members were seniors, and the people from the retirement home were seniors, as well.

But looking around that Sunday, the pews were filled with young families, young singles, children, teens, African Americans, Hispanics, Asians—the whole family of mankind seemed to be present. The church was packed, and extra chairs had to be set up in the aisles to make a place for each person.

A hush settled over the congregation as Mrs. Sampson took her place at the piano and Simon stood up to direct.

When the song was ended the people were on their feet clapping their hands, shouting their praise, and making a joyful noise that went on for five minutes.

Where the younger people had come from, no one knew. How the word of what would happen had been spread in the community would never be determined. All Pastor Sam, as the younger folks would call him from that day forward, could do was join in the celebration as he moved towards the pulpit.

He had a carefully written sermon prepared, but he turned it upside down and stood looking at the happy, cheerful throng in front of him.

He grinned at them, and a lovely young woman with red hair and blue eyes near the front row caught his eye. They made eye contact, and Pastor Sam's life would change again following the service.

As the crowd grew quiet he said, "King David danced in joy before the Lord. How can we do less? Our joy should be taken to the streets and be seen by everyone! He is the Lord of the Dance, and His is the dance of life itself! Please join me in prayer, and let us pray in such a way that His angels sing in heaven for what they have heard today!"

The sermon that followed had not been written, but it would be carved in the hearts of so many there for years to come, because the Word of the Lord had come upon the people, and His joy filled the sanctuary.

Ezra Johnson sat in the same seat in the same row where he sat each Sunday, but today was no ordinary day. The great piece of ice that occupied the center of his chest, where his heart should have been, had been melted. *Lord of the Dance* was his father's favorite song. Ezra had not heard it for far too many years to count. Tears ran down his face. He was in danger of losing every bit of control he had. He felt a hand on his shoulder, he looked up and Charlie Higgins, Simon's friend said, "Are you all right, Mr. Johnson? Can I get you something?"

Johnson was embarrassed. "No, I'm all right, Mr. Higgins. It's, it's just that I haven't heard that song in years. It was my father's favorite song. I, I…"

"It's all right, Mr. Johnson. It moved me, too. That Simon, he sure is something else, isn't he? You think you know what he's going to do, and then he does this! I had no idea he could direct a choir like this. And that sermon, it was powerful! I'm coming back here next Sunday, I can tell you that! This place is so crowded, you folks are going to have to build a bigger church!"

Through his tears, Ezra managed a smile for Mr. Higgins. "You know, it's time we got to know each other, Mr. Higgins. I understand you used to be a police officer—"

"Please, call me Charlie, Mr. Johnson."

"Then you had better call me Ezra."

"Ezra. Yes, I was on the force in Philly until I retired. I moved to West Chester for a time to live near my brother, but he passed away two years ago. That's when I moved here …"

Thus began the first extended conversation that Director Johnson had ever had with a resident of Madison Acres, but it would not be his last.

As 263 people left the church that morning they were greeted by Pastor Sam on their way to the parking lot. The new members of the choir and the other residents of Madison Acres were warmly thanked for their attendance. At the end of the line was the big man.

The pastor reached out and took Simon's huge right hand in both of his own. "I'm not sure what happened today, but it was something I will never forget. I have no idea where all these people came from, or how they knew to come here today, or how you got all these good people to come to choir practice. This was some sort of miracle. I don't know how else to explain it. As for you, I hope you will be here next Sunday!"

"I wouldn't miss it for the world," Simon said, smiling his great smile. "See you Thursday night," he said.

"What song will you do next Sunday?" the pastor asked.

"I don't know yet, but the Master will guide us."

"Yes, I'm sure He will do just that!" Pastor Sam said. "See you Thursday!"

In the next moment a young woman with red hair and the prettiest blue eyes he had ever seen was standing in front of him. She reached out and took his hand in hers. "I really enjoyed your message today," she said.

"I'm so glad you were here, Ms. ...?"

"Carol Williams. I just moved here from Ohio. I'm a new second grade teacher at the local elementary school. This is such a beautiful area of the country. I'm glad I came this morning. Our choir used to sing that song when I was growing up. It's one of my favorites."

"I hope you'll come back next Sunday," Sam said.

"I'll be here," she said. With this promise, she nodded and started walking towards the parking lot.

He called out to her, "Are you doing anything this afternoon, Carol Williams?"

She turned around, smiling. "No, I hadn't planned anything but a meal in my apartment. Why do you ask?"

"I could show you around the area," the pastor said. "Give you the tour, so to speak."

"Sounds like fun," Carol said. "Yes, that would be a good idea. I know very few people except for the couple who rent the apartment to me, and I don't know them all that well. They were friends of my parents years ago. I guess I would be safe with a pastor at my side."

He stepped towards her, handing her a bulletin. "The number and email address are there. I live in alone in the parsonage. Let's say 2:00

o'clock. Call me and tell me where to pick you up. There is a lot to
see in this area. We'll make an afternoon of it. Dinner will be on me. I
know quite a few places to eat, and all of them are really good!"

Carol smiled. "It's a date … uh, rather, a good way …"

He finished her sentence, "to see the Amish country. I can teach
you the safe way to drive around the buggies."

"Oh, I know how to do that. We have Amish in Ohio, too."

"Great!" Sam laughed. "It's a beautiful day. See you soon!" he said.

"I'll call you with my address," Carol said. "Bye."

"Goodbye, Ms. Williams," Sam said, smiling.

Sam Blankenship had just met the person he would spend the rest
of his life with, and the future looked wonderful.

Chapter Six

Months slipped by. Simon continued as choir director, and
attendance at John Wesley Methodist Church was full to capacity.
The people returned each Sunday. A second contemporary service
was added at 9:30 Sunday mornings, and a whole group of musicians
came together for that service. Many of the younger families chose
to attend at that time, but the attendance at the second traditional
service at 11:00 a.m. remained just as full and joyful. Things were
happening.

As Christmas approached, Ezra Johnson received a phone call
that he had not expected. It came at 3:00 a.m. His mother had been
rushed to the hospital, and she had passed away.

The drive from Madison Acres to Philipsburg was a lonely one.
He met his sisters, their husbands and children at the funeral home.
Snow was falling.

When they went to the graveside, a tent had been set up to help
protect the family from the elements. It helped keep the wind out.

Ezra was stoic. Though the crowd was small, they all did their best
to fit beneath the tent. The pastor gave his message, and those present
were given flowers to place upon the casket. When the service was

over, his sisters wanted him to return home with them, but he begged off, telling them that he wanted to get back before the snow got too deep.

He had left his car at the funeral home to ride in the limo with the family, and he had asked the driver to take him back so he could get his car.

When they got to the funeral home, he walked to his car, opened the door, and got in. He sat there for a moment, shivering from the cold, and then put the key in the ignition and started the car. It was a large Buick. He was about to put it in gear when a voice spoke from behind him!

Ezra yelled and whipped around. Someone was in the backseat. It was Simon.

"How did you—?"

"I'm sorry, Ezra. I didn't mean to startle you! I'm back here because there is more room for me. I wanted to be here for you. I thought someone should be," Simon said.

"You scared the—" Ezra said.

"I know! I'm really sorry!"

"Simon, how did you get here? Did someone give you a ride?"

"It's not important how I got here, Ezra. Your mother is gone. I wanted to be here, in case you wanted to talk to me. We all need a friend, especially at a time like this," Simon said.

"O.K., but we had better start back now. The snow is piling up, and it gets really deep in these mountains. We have to get passed State College and over Seven Mountains to a lower elevation. I, I do appreciate that you made the effort for me. I really am glad to have someone to talk to. My mom and I were not that close. It was my fault. She tried her best, but I did something that drove us apart. I feel guilty, now. I can't talk about it with my sisters. They don't know about it. No one does."

Ezra spoke as he drove, and he was a skillful driver, used to the winter snows of central Pennsylvania.

"What you've done at the church, and at Madison Acres ..." Ezra began.

"I haven't done anything,"Simon said, "it's the Master's work."

"I know, I know, you never take credit for anything. You always give the Master the credit. I wish I could be like you, have your faith. I've never known anyone like you, Simon, and I do need a friend right now. I really do."

Ezra's voice broke with these words. Simon reached over the seat and gently placed his massive hand on Ezra's shoulder.

"You have a friend ... the Great Friend, Ezra. He's here in the car with us. He promised that He would always be where two or more come together in His name."

"But, that's just it, Simon! No one could forgive what I've done! No one! I've lived in hell for 20 years because of what I did. I can't be forgiven! I've made my life a prison without emotion, and I never let others get close. I don't dare!" Ezra said.

"That's not true. When He hung on the cross, He called upon His Father to forgive everyone there,  and they were putting Him to death in the most horrible way possible. Do you think His father did not honor his request?"

"I don't know. It's a story—a story in an old book. How do you know it's true? How can anyone know the truth?"

"Let me assure you, Ezra, I know the truth. When I speak, it is His truth, not my own. I am but one of His children and I love Him with all my heart. I travel about the world doing His will. I seek those who are poor, hurt, lost, afraid, and tormented. I show them His love, and He sustains me in this work," the big man said.

"I believe you are my friend," Ezra said. "I have watched you since you came to us. It's true that you care about everyone, and that I am afraid to care about anyone. You reach out, and I shrink away from others. You are not afraid of even making a fool of yourself, and I am terrified of what others would think of me if they knew the truth.

"If you would hear my story, then I will tell it to you. I must tell someone before I die. Perhaps you can give me absolution?"

"Only the Master can do that," Simon said softly. "Tell me. I told you I would listen, and I will not judge you because I am commanded not to judge anyone."

"My father loved his work. He was a loyal employee, the most loyal of all. When necessary, he gave his weekends to the company, and he did so more often than not. My sisters were not as close to him as I was. He was a good father, or, as good as he could be, given the circumstances of his work. The company demanded, and he performed." Ezra's hands gripped the steering wheel.

"Then, they fired him. Just like that. It was over. They stripped away the meaning of his life … ripped it from him. He was a broken man. He had gone to church and enjoyed it greatly, but he stopped going. He quit everything that had interested him.

"He started drinking secretly. He would go to the garage behind our house and drink. When he was gone, I found all the bottles hidden away in the walls and under the floor.

"I tried to reason with him, but he would not listen to me. I tried to get him to come to church, and he would not go. I urged him to look for another job, one suited to his years of experience, and he said that he would not allow anyone to ever hurt him again.

"Soon after, he had the stroke. In the hospital, the doctor told us that he might not recover because it was a bad stroke, and there was a lot of damage. He was all wired up with tubes and machines and needles sticking in him. It made me want to scream.

"What happened next was terrible. I can't accept it to this day. The very man who fired my father walked into his hospital room. I was alone with my father at that moment. I knew who he was. He had been my father's boss for 12 years. He looked at me and said how sorry he was. My father was lying there, comatose. He couldn't respond to me, let alone anyone else.

"I screamed at the man. I said, 'What the hell are you doing here? You have no right to be here! You killed him! You killed my father!

You put him in this room, in this bed! Have you come to give him back his job? It's too damn late for that!'

"The man started to cry! I didn't care. His remorse meant nothing to me. I screamed at him, 'Get the hell away from him! Go! Get out! I hope you burn in hell for what you've done to my father. If I ever see your face again I will go to prison because of what I will do to you!'

"He stepped towards me—I know now that he wanted me to forgive him, but I did not know it at the time. I am not a big man, Simon, but I hit him in the face and knocked him down, and then I kicked him.

"My mother came into the room at that moment, and she yelled at me to stop. The man got to his feet, rubbing his face, blood streaming from his nose. Again, he said he was sorry. Then he turned and left.

"I was ready to run after him when my mother grabbed me by the arm and held on. I almost dragged her out of the room in my rage, but she would not let go, pleading with me, 'Don't, don't! No more! Stop!'

"Finally, I did stop. I sat down in a chair and cried. She tried to comfort me, but I pushed her away. I could not understand the unfairness of what had been done to my father, and I could not accept the man's plea for forgiveness!

"My mother stood over me for a long time, and then she left the room. It felt like hours had passed.

She came back into the room, and I was still there. Visting hours were over and it was time to go home. Niether of us had any intention of leaving, so she went down the hall to the waiting room where she would spend the night in a chair.

"My father died that night while I slept in the chair in his room. I woke up to warning bells going off and the room filling with doctors, and nurses, and my mother.

"I jumped up from the chair, not knowing what to do, and I was pushed out of the way. I left the room and stood in the hall because there was no room for me. I was crying. He had died and I had not known it. My whole world was crashing down around me!

"Two weeks later my father's boss—his name was Harry Simpson, put a bullet through his head, killing himself. I was glad he did it. I was glad he was dead, just like my father! It made me feel better! I laughed when I heard about it. I even went to the funeral home and sat in the back so I could watch his family in their grief. We had buried my father eight days before.

"But there was something I didn't know about Harry Simpson, something about him that I would learn soon enough.

"I was in the kitchen with my mother a week after Simpson's funeral. No one else was at home. I said to her, 'I'm glad that s.o.b. is dead! He killed Dad! He took him away from us, from me!'

"My mother looked at me, and the look on her face was terrible. She said, 'Ezra, how dare you! You don't even know who Harry Simpson was! He and your Dad were in the Army together. They fought side-by-side. He saved your father's life! Your Dad never told you, because he didn't talk about the war! Harry got your Dad his job in the first place! He didn't fire your father. Yes, he was his boss at work, but another man fired your father, not Harry! Harry Simpson went to work and confronted the man who fired your father. He stood up to him. It didn't do any good. They fired Harry, too!

'He came to the hospital that day to explain all of this to me, but you drove him away. He called me the next day and told me what had happened. I was too upset to tell you. He was totally broken by the fact that the son of his great friend—your father—hated him so much! You judged him without knowing the truth. He was going through the same things your father was dealing with. He was out of a job! He was trying to find work. He was just as angry, and desperate, and disillusioned as your Dad!

'Tell me, Ezra, please tell me that you can forgive Harry Simpson. He loved your Dad! The only reason he did not come to see him was because he was going through the same things!'

"So, you see, Simon, I killed a man, my father's friend. I killed him just as if I had taken the gun, pointed it at his head, and pulled the trigger. I took him from his wife and his children because of my emotions, because I lashed out in my rage and lost all control … because I allowed myself to judge someone who was innocent!"

The tears were pouring down Ezra's face as he made his confession. He just managed to pull the car to the side of the road.

"A man died because of my anger, an anger that should not have been directed at him. I drove him to his death, pushed him over the edge, and killed him. I took Harry Simpson from his wife and children. He saved my father in war. He stood up for my Dad when they fired him. He lost his own job because of his loyalty and friendship with my Dad, and I killed him! This is why I don't believe. This is why I don't get close to people or allow them to get close to me. This is why I observe the rules and regulations, why I keep to myself!

"If there is a God, what would He want with the likes of me? I was Judas to Harry Simpson. He came to me seeking solace because of his love for my Dad, and I rejected him! He took his own life because of me! That's a sin, isn't it? I drove him to it! How can anyone forgive such a terrible thing?"

Ezra wept, and Simon remained silent. Finally, when his tears began to slow, Ezra turned onto the highway and began their journey once again.

The big man did not speak for a long time after that. They had passed State College, descended from Seven Mountains, and were going by the city of Lewistown, Pennsylvania when Simon broke his silence.

"You have lived within your torment for far too long, Ezra," he said. "It is time you lived again in freedom from this pain. You could not possibly know what Harry Simpson was to your Dad because your father had never explained his relationship with the man, and there was no possible way you could have known it. No one told you. You were ignorant of the truth.

"You did not kill Harry Simpson. He took his own life. You are not to blame. It's not for either of us to judge another. We have been explicitly told never to judge others by the Master Himself. It is a command, not a suggestion. I am older than you, Ezra, far older.

"I don't expect you to understand or accept everything I tell you immediately, but I will tell you this: You will soon know the answers to your questions. As I often say to you: all in due time, my friend. I will tell you this much. I go where I am sent. I was sent to Madison Acres because of you. Now, I will be silent. You can keep your own thoughts for the remainder of our journey. Be at peace."

Ezra was lost in his own pain. He had told his story. It was hard to accept that he was not at fault. Mr. Simpson had died and he was his father's friend. His guilt was not assuaged.

He drove his Buick in the snow that had tapered off to flurries. He wanted to get both of them home safely. That was his goal. He would achieve it. All he had to do was be careful. He was very good at being careful. He had a lifetime of doing so.

*Chapter Seven*

Another Christmas came and went. The services at John Wesley Methodist Church had been wonderful, and the New Year held great promise. Winter passed and spring arrived. As the months slipped away, Ezra Johnson had settled into a routine again. He was more open and gregarious with staff members and residents. He had even joined the choir at church, at the urging of Simon. As it turned out, he had a fine tenor voice, and he was a welcome addition to the group.

Toward early summer, the folks at Madison Acres began preparing for a craft festival. Simon had been organizing the event with the help of a newly appointed Social Director, Helen Jennings. Helen was a recent college graduate and very eager to make her mark in her first paid position.

Ezra arrived at work on a Thursday morning and had been in his office only a few moments when Anne Compton, one of the house-keeping employees, came rushing into his room.

"He's gone, Mr. Johnson!" she eclaimed. "He's gone!"

Ezra jumped up from behind his desk. "Who's gone? Did someone die?"

"No, he's gone," Anne said, breathless. "His room is empty!"

"For heaven's sake, Anne! Who is gone?"

"Simon! Simon is gone!" She appeared to be close to tears.

"Simon? I don't believe that! Why would he leave here? He's the one who holds the place together! How could he leave without saying goodbye?" Ezra demanded.

Anne said, "All of his things are gone. His bed is made. His closet is empty. This is all that's left." She handed Ezra a business-sized envelope.

He looked at it. His name was written in Simon's flowing script on the envelope.

Ezra sat down heavily in his chair. He looked at Anne. "Don't say anything to anyone until I have time to read this—"

"But I already told several people—"

"That's not good. Don't tell anyone else. They'll all know soon enough. Now, give me a few minutes to read this. I will find you and we'll decide what we need to do, O.K.?"

Ezra saw the tears on Anne's face. "Now, don't start crying—"

"But he's gone. Simon's gone! I don't know what …"

Ezra put the envelope on his desk, came around and put his hands gently on Anne's shoulders. "Anne, I need you to be strong and not start blubbering. You'll have me crying if you keep it up, and that would be unseemly for the Director to start bawling, wouldn't it?"

Director Johnson had never spoken so gently to Anne before, and he had never touched her to comfort her. Her eyes grew big.

"Yes, Mr. Johnson. I'll do my best not to cry."

"It's Ezra."

"What's Ezra?"

"My name, Anne, it's Ezra. You can call me Ezra. I knew this day might come, but let me figure out what to do about it. That's why I am here, to figure things out. Go to the cafeteria, sit down, have a cup of coffee or tea, and remain silent. I will come and find you, and then you and I can decide how to tell the people here that he has gone. All right? Can you do this for me?"

"Yes, Ezra …"

"Good, now please let me alone for a few minutes. I need to see what he wrote. Thank you, Anne. We can handle this together."

Anne left his office, and Ezra closed his door. He sat down behind his desk. He sat for a long moment. He was almost afraid to open the letter. He was frightened of what it would say. Then, he realized that this letter was from Simon! There was nothing to be afraid of. He opened the letter and began to read:

*My dear Ezra,*

*I paid for two years, they are gone, and now I am called elsewhere. I did not come here for the others, but I did come here for you. There is great goodness and ability in you, my friend. It was my job to help you find that goodness. You are ready to do great good for the Master. I take no credit for serving Him. He is due all glory because glory comes from Him.*

*Many will wonder what happened to me. I have left a stack of letters for them in my nightstand. Please distribute them for me. I don't like painful goodbyes anymore than most people.*

*Finally, you've wondered about me for these two years. It is time you knew my truth. As to my whole name, read Matthew 27:32. As to how long I have been on this journey, read Luke 9:27.*

*His peace is with you, and my love remains.*

*Your true friend,*
*Simon*

*P.S. We will see each other again. This is a promise that will be kept.*

There was a Bible on the credenza behind Ezra's desk. He reached for it and opened it. He looked up the two verses that Ezra listed. When he had read them, he sat, overwhelmed and in silence for a long, long time.

He had been healed of his guilt. He had been touched by the eternal.

Ezra stood up. It was time to find Anne. They would break the news to everyone. He had much to do. Things were going to change for the better at Madison Acres. He would see to it.

# The Sweet Ride

# THE SWEET RIDE

Tommy Burke celebrated his 13 birthday on the day they held
the memorial service for his father. His dad, Sergeant Thomas A.
Burke, Sr., was killed by a car bomb in Afghanistan along with three
other men. His Mom, Helen, could not stop crying. There were 250
people at the service, half of them in uniforms. When the bugler blew
Taps, there was not a dry eye in the group, except for Tommy's. His
father's ashes would be taken to Pennsylvania for burial in the family
cemetery.

Tommy sat stone-faced by his mother, holding her hand. Even
when they gave his Mom the flag he did not move, cry, or utter a
sound. His father's parents were dead, his maternal grandparents sat
to the right of his mother, and his father's younger brother, Uncle
Eddie, sat with his Aunt Sally on Tommy's left. Their children,
Bobby, aged 7 and Abigail, aged 4, had not come to the funeral. They
were at home in Clear Haven, Pennsylvania, being taken care of by
neighbors.

A reception was held after the service at the military base.
Mourners gathered in a hall in the building where visitors normally
met their service members. Conversation was subdued. Tommy's
mother was distraught with grief, and family members and friends
were doing their best to comfort her.

Several people, including the base commander, tried to engage
Tommy in conversation, but he would not respond to anyone. Mid-
way through the reception, he disappeared. He had been gone for at
least half an hour before anyone noticed, and when they did, everyone was concerned.

A search began, but Tommy was nowhere to be found, until one
of the officers who had been at the memorial service discovered the
boy sitting in the bleachers at the parade ground. He was watching
recruits practicing marching under the direction of their drill
instructors.

When he returned to the hall everyone was relieved, but everyone seemed to understand why he had disappeared. Tommy was grieving in his own way, and no one took him to task for wandering off. It was, after all, his birthday, and having to attend a memorial service for your father on your birthday was unthinkable.

Fortunately, school was not in session. It was mid-July and hot. the heat and humidity made it very uncomfortable. As the afternoon deepened, about 20 people remained at tables in the hall. Discussions about what must now be done were held, but Tommy had not been included in any conclusions being reached. He had gone out to a covered porch area to sit by himself, even though the heat was fierce.

Helen Burke would be going back to the hills of Pennsylvania with her son. They would be living with her parents, where she and Tommy would have support until she could get herself together. She and her husband had grown up there, gone to the same schools, and had been high school sweethearts. Clear Haven was a small town, but a good place to live. Returning there was for the best.

When Helen told Tommy of her intentions later that evening, he said not a word. He simply turned his back on her, went into his room, and closed his door. She cried even harder at his response, and her parents tried to comfort her in the tiny living room of their quarters.

It was mid-August when their possessions were packed up and shipped north. Helen and Tommy made a silent, painful drive to Clear Haven. Helen was lost in memories of happier times, and Tommy stared morosely out the passenger window, watching the hills of Pennsylvania roll by. Thankfully, the heat wave had relented and the temperature had fallen just below 80 degrees.

As they came down the hill from East End onto 3rd Street, Helen drove by Santinoceto's Italian Market on their right. Grice's Gun Shop was across the rear parking lot behind the market. Tommy's dad had taken him to the shop on many summer vacations. He felt hot tears on his face, and he held his breath.

His mother did not see his reaction. Her mind was flooded with memories of high school, the good times she and her future husband had, and dancing at the exhibition hall at the fairgrounds. There were tears on her face, as well.

She made the right on Market, drove through town past City Hall, the Ritz Theater, and the library. She drove over the Susquehanna River on the bridge and started up the hill to West Side.

The home of Wade and Marie Conover, Helen's parents, was a two-story brick house with a small yard in front. The front porch was deep, and there was a swing on it, plus a recliner, small wicker tables, and two wicker chairs with cushions.

Helen pulled into the driveway. The drive ended in a one-car garage, also built of matching dark-red brick. The yard behind the house was narrow, but fairly deep.

They unloaded their belongings. The movers would arrive the next day. Most of what they were bringing would be put into storage.

Tommy's grandparents appeared and helped take their suitcases and other stuff through the kitchen and up the back steps to the bedrooms they would occupy. They put Tommy in a smaller bedroom; Helen would sleep in her old childhood bedroom.

Tommy sat down in a chair and looked out the window at the backyard. The emptiness inside of him was like an enormous hole in his heart. He had never felt so alone. The unfairness of his father's terrible death was unbearable. He and his dad were the greatest father-son team in the world. His dad was deployed for long stretches of time, but when he was home, they had gone everywhere and done everything together. His father was great fun. Thomas Burke, Sr. had an incredible sense of humor. He could make Tommy laugh all day long. He was such a good man—moral, upright, and a true believer in God.

The light had gone out in Tommy's life. Never again to hear his father's voice, never again to sit on a dock with a line in his hand waiting for a fish and listening to his dad tell another story, and never again to feel his strong hands on his shoulders or see his smile.

Now, Tommy could cry. Now, he could weep and wail. Now, he could let loose the floodgates of his wounded soul … in this beloved house where he had spent so many happy weeks of his life on summer breaks, and even before that, when he had been very young.

The tears came. He cried. He got up from the chair and lay down on the bed, curling up like a child, and wept for his father. His mother came to him in that moment, took him in her arms, and they cried together. Mother and child, weeping in a universe that did not appear to care that husband and father were gone forever.

*Chapter Two*

Tommy was tall and thin with dark brown hair, and brown eyes. He laughed and smiled easily, a likable quality that drew most people to him. He had his father's height and his mother's frame. His father had been 6'3" and a solid 220 pounds; his mom was 5'3" and weighed 105 pounds. Tommy was already seven inches taller than his mother.

On their first morning in Clear Haven ,Tommy's grandmother prepared a big breakfast of eggs, bacon, toast, orange juice, coffee for the grownups, and a bowl of fresh raspberries. The berries had been picked at the rear of the Conover lawn. They were one of Tommy's favorite things in the whole world. The conversation around the table was subdued.

It was Sunday. Every Sunday his grandparents attended the Trinity Methodist Church, but not on this day.

After breakfast, Tommy went to the back porch and sat on the steps. The day was comfortable. The sun was shining, broken white fluffy clouds were high in the sky, and there was a light breeze. The August heat had dissipated for awhile because of a cooler front that had dipped down from Canada, bringing welcome relief.

Tommy and his dad had made it a practice to sit together on the back porch after breakfast to discuss important things, such as what they would do on a given day. The small town of Clear Haven did not offer as many choices as might be found in a larger community, but they always managed to find enough to occupy them. Because of his dad's military duties, their time together was precious, and they made the most of it.

As he sat there in his sadness, Tommy thought about his father. He pretended that he was sitting next to him. He closed his eyes and pretended that he could feel his shoulder against his own. He loved his dad so much, admired him, respected him, and thought he was the greatest dad in the whole world. Tears ran down Tommy's cheeks.

Helen was looking through the screen door at her son, tears also streaming down her face. She turned to find her mother there with open arms. She allowed herself to be enveloped in her mother's warm embrace.

"Mom! Oh Mom, what are we going to do? I'm so alone, so alone without Tom. How can I be mother and father to Tommy? How can I teach him the things that only a father can teach a son?"

She gave herself up to her pain, weeping for her lost husband. Her father came into the kitchen. He went to both of them and held them in his arms.

School began just after Labor Day, and Tommy took the bus to the high school. He was a freshman. He knew a few kids from his summer visits. He responded to them when they spoke to him, but the change in his demeanor was evident. His old happiness and easy smile were gone, replaced with a sadness that would not leave him. Grief had settled on him like an invisible cloak, and it colored his thoughts and words.

Perhaps because of the discipline he had always seen in his parents, or because of his generally pleasant nature, Tommy was a conscientious student. In the fall semester of the school term, he studied hard. Some of the students he knew from summer vacations did their best to draw him out and get him to smile and laugh, but his grief did not leave him in the weeks and months of that year.

Christmas came, and it was a beautiful time of year. Snow had blanketed the hills with a deep covering, and the street looked like a Christmas card. The tree in the Conover house was tall. Tommy's grandfather had picked the biggest tree that would fit into the living room. He had taken Tommy along with him, and urged him to choose just the right one. Tommy chose a blue spruce whose top almost touched the ceiling.

His grandparents had made a grand event out of decorating the tree. Helen's eyes shown with memories of her childhood in this warm house, and Tommy felt the chill of his spirit lighten because of how excited everyone was.

The New Year brought more snow, and Clear Haven schools, which never closed because of winter weather, remained open. However, sled riding down the hill above the Conover home became the main source of fun after school and on the weekend.

Winter turned to spring, and spring became summer. School closed in early June, and the rhythms of the Conover home changed. Helen had taken a secretarial job with a real estate office. She was working on her license.

Tommy wanted a way to earn money of his own, and his grandfather said he could use the lawnmower to mow neighborhood lawns if he sought the business on his own. He had grown another inch taller, and his thin frame had filled out a little.

He went door-to-door soliciting business, and his polite manner and friendly attitude led to success. After ten days he had 12 customers. His grandfather put a new blade on the mower, tuned it up, and Tommy set to work.

At the end of his first week he approached his grandfather and handed him $40.00.

His grandfather looked at the money.

"What's this for, Tom? You don't owe me anything."

Everyone was now calling him Tom. He had asked everyone to call him by his father's name. He did not want to be Tommy anymore.

Tommy sounded too juvenile.

"It's for the rental of your mower, Pop Pop. You put a new blade on it and made sure that it was running right."

"But, Tom, I didn't expect you to pay rent for it. It's yours to use."

"No, my dad wouldn't agree. He would say that a man deserves what he earns. You helped me get this business started. You supply the equipment, and the fuel to run it. Part of the profit belongs to you. You invested in the business. You're part owner of Burke's Lawn Service. That's how I see it."

Wade Conover was about to object again when he saw the earnest look on his grandson's face.

"O.K., that's fair. I accept my role in the business. I'll continue to supply the fuel, and I will also teach you how to maintain the mower. There's nothing wrong with a man knowing how to take care of his equipment. Do we have a deal?"

Tommy smiled. "Yes we do! I want to learn all you can teach me." Tommy turned and walked away. He did not see the tears in his grandfather's eyes.

Tommy celebrated his 14th birthday on the 12th July. The family gave him a party, and his uncle, aunt and cousins were there. They had a backyard barbecue, and Tommy had fun chasing the children and playing hide-and-seek with them.

Tommy's customer list had grown to 22, and he was so busy that he had little time to do anything else, but he did not complain. If anything, he had become too serious. His old smile and happy attitude had all but disappeared beneath his sense of responsibility. He had allowed his work to swallow up his sense of fun. His mother said as much to her parents, but Wade and Marie told her not to worry. He was like his father. When it came to responsibility, Thomas Burke, Sr. had been all business. Like father, like son.

The truth was that Thomas Burke, Jr. had discovered something that some people do not find out until they are much older. His work had become his life. When he returned to school in the fall he would immerse himself in his school work. Pushing a mower or studying subjects was a way to ignore the pain in his spirit.

Tommy had no time for laughter or fun. They were empty of truth. His father was gone forever, and he would never allow such easy emotions to enter his life again if he could avoid it. There was anger in him that was buried just below the surface.

As far as Tommy was concerned, the universe did not care. All a man had to depend on was his determination to do the job before him. Yard work or school work would one day lead to other types of work. Keeping busy kept you from thinking too deeply, and thinking too deeply led to immense sadness and despair.

His father had not spoken of the dangerous things he had faced. He had never come home to complain to his wife or son. He had kept the terrors of war to himself. When he was with them, he smiled, laughed, joked, and showed them nothing but love.

Thomas Burke, Sr. had been strong. His son would be strong, too. He would be like his father.

Tommy did not know that everything in his life was about to change. When he met his next customer, his ideas and convictions would be altered forever.

### Chapter Three

Apple Street was three streets up the hill from where Tommy's grandparents lived. It was a newer street extending along the middle of the hill to the left off Market Street, which ran in front of the Conover home. The house three doors up on Apple Street belonged to one of Tommy's customers, a family named Brown.

Tommy cut the yard at the house. His long legs made short work of the task. His grandfather had a golf cart, and there was a hitch to a low, light-duty trailer. Tommy used the cart and trailer to haul the mower, gas can and weed whacker from one customer to another.

He had been carefully instructed by his grandfather in the operation of everything, and because all of his customers were in a four-block area in their section of Clear Haven, it was relatively safe for him to drive the cart from one place to another, as long as he obeyed traffic laws.

Being a small town, local police tolerated such activity. After all, the boy's father was a war hero. The flag, patriotism and religious beliefs were quite real to the people of the community. The cynicism found in other parts of the country did not exist in Clear Haven.

Apple Street curved on beyond the Brown residence, and one early August afternoon after he had finished his work, Tommy decided to drive further up the road to see if there were other potential customers there. As he rounded the curve, he didn't see any houses. The pavement ended and the street continued as a dirt road into a wooded area. The weather had been dry. The dirt wasn't muddy. Nevertheless, Tommy decided not to drive the cart and trailer on the dirt. He parked just off the road in low grass so that anyone who drove down the road would not be hampered by his equipment.

Tommy had walked about a quarter mile when he rounded another curve and saw a dirt lane driveway on his right. There was a mailbox by the road, but there was no name or number on it.

On impulse, he walked back the lane. He had walked about three-tenths of a mile when the trees opened up and he saw a house in a clearing. It was a white, two-story clapboard house with a deep, wide front porch.

The drive continued by the house on the right side leading back to a one-story, two-car garage. The garage door was open, but there was no car visible.

A voice said, "Hello!" and it startled him.

There was a man sitting on the steps of the front porch. He had not been there in the first moment when Tommy saw the house, but he was there now.

Tommy walked over to the man and stopped on the sidewalk. Before he could say anything the man said, "Thomas Burke, I presume."

"Yes, sir. How do you know—"

"Your name?" the man said. He looked young. He had brown hair and eyes. He wore a blue denim shirt and bib overalls. "You look like your father."

The man reminded Tommy of someone, but he knew that he had never seen him before.

"What's your name, sir?" he asked.

"Polite? I like that. Too many young people are no longer polite these days. Good manners show good breeding. Respect grows where it's planted. As to my name, please, call me Reynolds."

Tommy thought this was a strange thing to say. The man looked like he was in his 20's.

"Is that your last name, sir?" he asked, respectfully.

"No, but that doesn't matter. May I call you Tom?"

"Yes, sir."

"This way, we can be on a first name basis," the man said.

"Sir, I was taught to address adults as Mr. or Mrs., so I feel a little funny calling you—"

"By my first name? It doesn't bother me, Tom. When you get to be a certain age, it becomes irrelevant. Besides, if we are going to be friends, we need to refer to each other as Tom and Reynolds. Now, I assume you came here to ask me a question?"

"Yes, sir. I started a lawn service this summer. I am out seeking new customers. Do you need your yard cut?" Tom asked.

"Look around you, Tom. What do you think?"

Tommy looked around. The yard in front of the house was obviously quite healthy, but it was a bit long. From where he stood, he saw that the house had a shallow back yard. The garage backed against the treeline, and the hill went steeply up from that point. The yard wasn't deep or wide, but it was in need of attention.

"I'd say that it could use a cut and a trim. I have my own equipment. It's just down the road from here. I could go get it and do the job fairly quick for you, sir."

"Then you best go get it," the man said. "I agree, that the grass is a bit long."

"Aren't you going to ask me the price, sir? I want to be sure it's all right," Tom said.

"I wish you would stop calling me 'sir,' Tom. There's no need to be formal here."

"I was taught to respect others. It's difficult for me to call you by your first name. My Dad—"

"I understand, Tom. It's O.K. Your dad is like you. He has the same way of standing and speaking, and it's not necessary to—"

Tommy blurted out, "My dad is dead, sir!" There was great pain in Tommy's face when he said this, and the man spoke softly to him.

"I know. I understand. It's O.K. I'm sorry if I said something to hurt you. Why don't you go and get your mower and cut the yard. The price doesn't matter. I'll wait right here. Go on now. Get your mower. You have a new customer!"

Tommy felt embarrassed. His face was red. "I'm sorry. I didn't mean to"

"I said it's all right. Get your mower. The yard could use a cut and trim. While you're getting your mower, I'll get us some ice tea. It's warm today, don't you think?"

"Yes, sir. I'll go get my mower and be right back."

Tommy swung around and went back down the driveway to the dirt road. He walked to his golf cart, started it up, and drove back up the road and the lane to the house. He parked in the driveway, lowered the ramp and backed the mower down onto the drive.

He started the mower and cut the yard. Then he got his weed whacker and did the trimming. The job took about 30 minutes.

When he finished, he put his mower back on the cart and fastened the weed whacker with bungee cords. He stood, wiping his brow, then turned toward the house. The man was standing on the porch.

"I've got ice tea, Tom. You look like you could use it. Can you spend a few moments before you have to go home?"

"Yes, sir," Tom said. He mounted the steps to the porch. There were two wicker chairs by a low table, and there were two glasses of ice tea on the table. He sat down in a chair, picked up a glass of tea, and took a drink.

The taste was wonderful. "This is really good! What's the flavoring?"

"Raspberries," the man said, smiling at him.

"My favorite," Tommy said, with a smile.

"I know," the man said.

"But, how could you know that?" Tommy asked.

The man's smile disappeared. He looked serious. "Your father loves raspberries, just like you do."

Tommy's mood changed instantly. "He's dead! My father is dead … gone! Why do you keep talking about him as if he was alive?"

"I'm sorry, Tom. I don't mean to upset you. It's just my way of speaking. Please, forgive me."

Tommy fought to control his emotions. "I'm sorry. You said you knew him. Do you remember what he was like?"

"Yes, I do remember. He was a lot like you are now. But, I have no desire to upset you more. I see how much pain this causes you. I won't talk about him anymore."

"It's hard, sir. It's really hard for me. I miss him so much! That's why I work so hard. I don't want to think about him. It hurts too much!"

"I understand. Now, you did a great job on the yard. What do I owe you?"

"It's not that big, sir. The whole job only took a half hour. Let's make it $12.00. If that is too much money, I can charge you less."

"That's more than fair, Tom, considering the cost of equipment and fuel. Here, I hope you don't mind being paid in coin."

The man handed him twelve silver dollars. They looked old. Tommy looked at them in wonder.

"These are silver dollars. My dad had a few of them," Tommy said.

"I've never seen so many. Would you rather pay me in cash?"

"No, I always pay smaller transactions in hard money. Now, I have some things to do. When you come this way next week, please bring your equipment again. The grass will be growing. It has a way of doing that all the time. It's good to meet you, Tom."

The man stood up and extended his hand, and Tommy reached out and took it. When he gripped the man's hand it felt familiar to him. That was a strange thought.

"Thank you for the business, sir. I'll see you next week."

"You're welcome, Tom. See you soon."

With these words the man walked to the front door, opened it, and went into the house, closing the door behind him.

Tommy went to the golf cart, got in and turned it around. He drove down the lane. When he got home, he plugged the cart into the outlet in the garage and went in the house.

He went to his room and took the silver dollars out of his pocket. He spread them on his bed. They were old. The dates on them were from the 1930's and 1940's. He gathered them up and put them in a shoebox in his closet. He wanted to keep them instead of spending them.

It was supper time. Tom went down the stairs. The fact that he had met someone who had known his father was both interesting and painful. He did not want to think about it, and he resolved to keep it to himself. He was afraid that if he mentioned it to his mother, or grandparents, they would start talking about his dad.

He would see the man again in a week. Perhaps he would find the courage to ask him more questions then.

*Chapter Four*

The days slipped by until the weekend, and he went to church with his family on Sunday. Trinity Methodist Church was a beautiful building.  His grandmother, Marie, was the vice president of the women's group in the church, and his grandfather served as an usher.

His mother had grown up in the congregation, attended Sunday school, and sang in the children's and adult choirs.

They had wanted Tommy to go to Sunday school, but he said that he had no desire to do so. They had to be content with the fact that he was at least attending the 11:00 a.m. service with them. His mother and grandmother had discussed ordering him to attend Sunday school because they thought that it might help him work through his anger at losing his dad, but his grandfather had stepped in.

"Absolutely not!" Wade Conover had said. "When the boy is ready, he will make that decision for himself!"

The pastor of the church was Mason Cambridge. He was in his early 40's, and his wife Jocelyn was the choir director. They did not have children, but both of them were also active in Sunday school. Jocelyn taught the middle school kids, and Pastor Cambridge led the high school group. The church's assistant pastor, Mark Owens, led the adult Sunday school. The elementary school children were taught by Marge Hendricks, who was also a 5th grade teacher in the local school system.

Marie Conover had discussed her grandson with the pastor. She had asked what could be done to help Tommy open up and talk about the loss of his father. Pastor Cambridge had gained a depth of knowledge about such things when he had served as chaplain in the U.S. Army. His response had surprised Marie.

"Marie, you need to go slow here. Healing takes time. Tom is obviously hurting gravely, but if I press him too soon, he will reject me and the church, and he might stop coming altogether."

"Are you sure about this?" Marie asked.

"Trust me. Losing the whole center of your life is devastating. Tom needs time. He should not be pushed. He has a strong mind, but even the strongest person can be broken when they lose someone they love. His dad was extraordinary. No man ever loved his family more than Tom Burke. He loved his country, too. I was trained in psychology, and I've dealt with the family members of soldiers many times. Everyone is unique. I know Tommy well enough to know that he's like his dad in many ways."

"Yes, he looks like him, and he even stands like him, but he's only 14 years old. His silence is the loudest thing in our house. He's hurting, and I want to make the hurt go away," Marie said with tears in her eyes.

Pastor Cambridge reached out and gently took her hand in his. "The Tom Burke I knew was a warrior. All of the people who go over there are warriors. If they're not totally warriors when they first get there, when they come home they are people who have witnessed things that most people never see. Some of them are terribly hurt physically, and others are hurt mentally. PTSD can be overwhelming. The suicide rate among these brave souls is awful. We are only beginning to learn how to deal with it effectively in this country. They love their country, but the cost of their service can be incredible in pain and suffering. Tom Burke had seen more than enough to be at peace with who he was. He was able to separate good and evil. He understood both. His love for God and Jesus was unshakable. His son is like him.

"In time, Tommy will mend. I've watched him since he was a little child. He works things out on his own. It's not pride. It's simply the way he processes stuff. He's angry at God. He doesn't yet understand why his father had to die. I know. Years ago I was so angry at God that I didn't speak with Him for three years. I left the Army because of an incident. Two of my best friends had been killed right next to me. I couldn't accept it.

"For three years all I did was feel sorry for my pitiful self. I took a job as a laborer with a construction firm. The work was back-breaking, but I did it well. I was filled with rage. Nobody knew that I had been a member of the clergy. I certainly didn't act like it. Men who work in construction have a very colorful vocabulary. I cursed and swore with the best of them.

"We were building a new library in a small town in Florida. I'm a reader, so I would often go to the old library on Saturdays to spend time. I lived alone in a rented room in the home of an older couple, and I had time on my hands when I wasn't at work. My idea of a good time was to get away from everybody and read for a couple of hours.

"One Saturday, I looked up and saw Jocelyn across the table. She was reading a children's novel that I had read the month before about four children who go into another world and meet incredible characters. I had liked it a lot. By the end of it, I realized that the author had played a trick on me. The story is called *The Forest at the End of the World*, and the trick is that the real message of the book is hidden within a riddle, and the meaning of the riddle is that things are not always as they appear to be.

"On impulse, I asked her what she thought of the book. We introduced ourselves, and I left the library with her so we wouldn't bother the other patrons. We went to a little park next to the library, found a bench, and discussed the book for an hour. It turned out that she had read the book before, and that she was reading it again. She told me that it was part of a trilogy. I hadn't known about the other two books.

"Jocelyn invited me to church on Sunday. She attended a Christian and Missionary Alliance church at the edge of town. I had been wandering in the wilderness of my life for over three years. I had not been inside a church in all that time. I sat for a long moment. She was beautiful and fun to talk to.

"She had no idea that she was sitting with a man who had become a roaring monster who had walked away from God.

"I didn't know how to respond to her. I had no intention of going to church. My anger had not left me in three years. My friends had died needlessly, to my mind, and I wanted nothing to do with Him.

"She must have seen the pain in my face and sensed my agony. This woman, who was a stranger, placed her hand on mine and said,

'It's time to come home, Mason. He sent me to you today. He has never made a mistake. You belong to Him. He purchased you with the greatest price anyone has ever paid: His Son. Tell me your story. Share your life with me, and I will share mine, as well. He is no stranger to pain, for His was the greatest pain anyone could feel.'

"I consider myself a strong man, Marie, but I cried like a child in front of this woman. I wept for all the hurts, the rage, the lonely hours, all the lost time of those years. She sat patiently and heard my story. Then she asked me again to come to her church on Sunday.

"We met at the door that day, and the pastor said something from the pulpit that I have carried with me ever since that morning. He said that when we pray for something that we do not receive, it is sometimes because He has something far better for us that He wants to give to us.

"I went to the library and got the other two books in the trilogy, The Ocean at the Edge of Forever, and The Mountain of the King. When I finished reading the last chapter of the third book, I knew what had happened to my friends, and I understood fully what happens to those who love God.

"Jocelyn and I were married six months later, and I returned to the ministry. I'm here in this church today because a stranger reached out to me, took my hand in hers, and showed me the love of God. I understand where Tommy is, because I've been there. I've never shared any of this with anyone here, but now I've shared it with you. Sometimes, we need to be broken before we can be mended properly."

Marie Conover's eyes were shining as her pastor finished his story.

"Now I understand why you don't want to push Tommy. He is like his father—strong, quiet, steady, and fragile, too. A boy who has lost such a father is in a terribly vulnerable place."

She patted Pastor Cambridge's hand. "Thank you for telling me your story. Each person, each family, has its own triumphs and failures. I am Tommy's grandmother, but I am not his mother. I want the best for him, and I know God has him in His hands. You're telling me to trust the Lord. I'll do just that."

"Thank you for listening to me, Marie. It means he world to me to be able to share my life with you. Rest assured that no one can better understand a boy who has lost his father than a Father who has lost His Son. Our Lord did just that so that we could be healed of all the ills of the earth. He knows your heart, and Tommy's, too. When the time is right, I will speak to Tommy. Remember, God's ways are not our ways, and His thoughts are not our thoughts. He sees things we don't see, and when we become aware of Him, everything in life changes for the better."

Marie smiled. "When you get to be my age, you're supposed to have more patience and wisdom. In my case, that's not true. I just worry about him and my daughter. I want both of them to be all right. They've given more to this country than the vast majority of our people will ever know. We take our freedom for granted. If it wasn't for men like my son-in-law, our freedom would have disappeared long ago."

Pastor Cambridge said, "If we don't figure out how to teach our young people the value of sacrifice, respect and love for our nation, we won't have much of a future. Tom Burke knew it. He gave his life for it. The selfishness of today's youth is frightening. However, Tommy isn't like others. He knows what his father did. He understands far more than so many his age. To quote someone far wiser than I will ever be, 'This too shall pass.' Give him time. He will heal."

## Chapter Five

The first four days of the week slipped by quickly. It had rained over the weekend, and Tommy was working hard cutting grass. Thursday came and went, and it was not until Friday that he made his way to the Brown's on Apple Street. When he finished there, he drove around the curve and made his way to his newest customer's house.

When he got to the point where he could see the house from the driveway, he didn't see anyone on the front porch. The door was open again on the two-door garage, as it had been the first time he was there. Still, no car was visible. He drove the golf cart to the point on the driveway where he could lower the ramp and get the mower off the small trailer.

The grass had grown tall because of the recent rain, and he decided to start working immediately. He had finished mowing and was using the weed whacker when he heard a voice calling, "Tom, there's ice tea on the porch when you finish."

He looked up and saw the man sitting in one of the wicker chairs. He waved and went on with his work. When he was done, he pushed the riding mower up the ramp onto the trailer, secured the weed whacker, and made his way to the porch steps. He mounted the steps, went to the empty chair and sat down. He wiped his brow on his sleeve.

"It's really warm today," he said. "Thanks for the tea. I can really use it!" He took a drink of the cold brew and sighed happily.

'Raspberry ice tea is the best thing on a warm day. How was your week, Tom?" the man asked.

"It's been very busy, sir."

"I thought we agreed that you would call me Reynolds, and I would call you Tom?"

"I still have a problem with that. My dad and mom taught me to treat others with respect. The military works because respect underlies all that they do. That's what my dad used to say."

"Your dad is right about that, but friends can use each other's names, and I think we can be friends if we share a little bit about ourselves. What do you think?"

Tommy thought this was a strange thing to say.

"I suppose so," he said. "You said you knew my dad. I guess I'm wondering how that's possible. You look young, hardly old enough to have known him."

"Looks can be deceiving, Tom. I'm older than I look. Much older, in fact," the man said.

"How old are you?" Tom asked.

"Let's just say that people in my family age gracefully. The number's not important. How old are you?"

"I was 14 not long ago. My dad was killed two weeks before my 13th birthday, a little over a year ago. I, I have trouble talking about him."

"Believe me when I say I understand, Tom. Your dad is a hero. The other men who died with him are heroes, too. You have every right to proud of your dad!"

Tears came quickly to Tommy's eyes. "I don't know about heroes, but I know that I wish he was here. He was the greatest dad in the whole world. We used to talk for hours about everything. He taught me so much. We went fishing together as often as we could. He showed me how to play basketball, baseball, football and so many other things. He liked doing stuff outside, and I have no time for video games or staying inside when I can be out having fun. Heck, I don't even have a cell phone, and I don't want one, either. I want to work and make money. He always told me to save for the future. That's what I'm doing. One day when I'm old enough, I want to serve in the military. I want to be like him!"

The man named Reynolds said, "You are like him. You look so much like him, it's incredible. You even smile like he does."

"You keep talking about him like he's alive! Why do you do that?" Tom said, suddenly angry.

"He is alive, Tom, he's just in a different place now," the man said.

"Do you really believe that?" Tom blurted out, ready to stand up and leave.

"Don't you go to church, Tom? Don't you believe he's in a far better place?"

"Why did God take him from me? What kind of God would do that?" Tommy fought back tears.

"Go on! Tell me why I should believe in anything like that! My dad is dead! Dead! That's all I know. He's dead!"

Tommy was ready to stand up and leave the porch when the man said, "I'm sorry. I've gone and upset you again. No one can force you to believe in anything, but you're wrong when you say you don't believe in God. That's not the truth. Your dad was a believer. If you're going to be like him, then you will be a believer, too. His faith was as strong as a mountain. You know he shared his faith with everyone who would listen to him. He was like that. He wasn't ashamed of his faith. I know he talked to you about what he believed. You are his son. He loved you and your mom more than life itself."

"How do you know that?" Tom demanded.

"He told me, Tom!"

"Told you? When did he tell you? When?"

"Before I answer your question, there's something I have to do," the man said.

"What?" Tom asked, standing up, ready to walk away.

The man handed him 12 silver dollars. "I didn't pay you for your work. I always pay. We pay for many things in life, both the good and the bad, but there is one thing we didn't pay for. God's Son paid for us. He paid it in full. Your dad knew this. He was certain beyond doubt that what he believed was real. You asked me when your dad said that he loves you? If I simply told you the answer you would not believe me, and it's important to me that you do. I want to show you something." The man stood up.

Tom had become suspicious. "What are you going to—?"

He did not finish his sentence.

"I want to show you something in the garage. If you like what you see, I think I can answer your question in a way that you won't doubt or question. Will you come with me to the garage, out back?"

Instead of waiting for a response, the man walked by Tom and went down the steps. He started towards the driveway.

Uncertain about what he should do, Tom hesitated for a moment.

The man named Reynolds turned back and asked, "Well, are you going to come and see my pride and joy? There's not another one like it, as far as I know."

"What is it?" Tom asked.

"Come and see." The man turned and walked to the driveway, turned left and disappeared behind the house.

Tom walked to the driveway in time to see him heading towards the garage. Curiosity overcame his fear, and he started for the garage when the man emerged pushing something covered by a gray tarp.

"What's that?" Tom asked.

"Like I said, it's my pride and joy," Reynolds said.

Curiosity had gotten the better of Tom. "Can I see it?"

"Of course. That's why I got it out of the garage." The man lifted the tarp and let it slide to the ground. When he did so ,Tom thought he heard the sound of distant thunder. It was a bicycle, but not like any bicycle Tom had ever seen. It gleamed in the afternoon sun.

"What kind of bike is it?"

"This is a 1952 Schwinn Panther Model D-27. The bikes of today are phenomenal with all their gears, bells, and whistles, but this is The Sweet Ride. It will take you places no other bike can take you, and show you things you can only dream about," Reynolds said.

It was truly a magnificent piece of work. And the amazing thing to Tommy was that it looked positively brand new. There was not a speck of dust or dirt on it. No sign of rust or decay could be seen. The seat was wide and comfortable-looking. It was a shining purple, or perhaps a rich burgundy color. Tom did not know what color to call it. The light seemed to shift about its structure; one moment it looked to be one color, and in the next it appeared to be a different shade.

Tom said, "Where's your car?"

"I don't need one, Tom, not when I have this. Would you like to take a ride? I adjusted the seat before you got here. You have long legs, but this is a man-sized bike, so it should fit you well."

Tom stepped closer. "You don't mind if I take a ride?"

"What if I said that you were meant to take The Sweet Ride? What would you say to that?" Reynolds asked.

"I don't understand," Tom said.

"Tell you what, just get on the bike, take it down the driveway, turn left, and see where she takes you. When you're done, bring her back to me. I'll be here when you finish finding what you need."

Tom swung his leg up and over and sat on the seat, gripping the handlebars. For a reason he did not understand, it felt as though he and the bike were one. He pushed off and placed his feet on the pedals. The driveway had a slight slope, and he descended to the dirt road and turned left out of the driveway.

He rode around one curve and then another to the short straight-away where the dirt road met the asphalt. When he left the dirt and hit the hard surface, he looked around. There should have been more houses to his left and right, but none were there. The Brown house was on his left, but it looked brand new. There was a car in the driveway. He wasn't sure of the make or model. It also looked brand new, but it resembled a car that he had once seen in an old book. This made no sense.

As he rode along, he saw other differences in the neighborhood, but Clear Haven was not that familiar to him in every detail. He had only been living here for a year, and being lost in his grief, he had paid little attention to his surroundings. There were cars on the street, but they looked new—and old—at the same time.

He turned right on Market Street and started down the hill towards the center of town. He passed his grandparents house and looked at it as he rode by. There was different furniture on the porch, and he was tempted to pull in the driveway, but something urged him to keep moving.

He got to where several streets came together and he passed over the railroad tracks. There were automobiles here and there going up and down the streets, and so he stayed to the right. The cars were new, but he knew that they were very old, too.

Tom pedaled over the bridge and noticed a large building on his right that should not be there. He read the name on the building: Clear Haven High School. What was happening to him? Had he slipped through time and somehow gone into another dimension?

For some reason, this strange revelation did not bother him. He was on the bike, and he and the bike were one.

He saw another place on his right that had not been there before. It was a restaurant called the Ritz Grill, next to the Ritz Theater. There were kids standing in front of the place on the sidewalk, and they were dressed in old fashioned clothes. He waved, and they waved back. Then he realized that he must look strange to them. He had been dressed in his Levi's, an Army t-shirt that had belonged to his dad, and his Nike's. He looked down at his shoes on the pedals, but they were no longer Nike's. They had become a pair of black and white sneakers. His jeans looked different, and the cuffs were rolled up. He saw that his Army t-shirt had been replaced with a plain white one. *What was happening to him?*

He kept going. More cars were on both sides of the street, and they, too, were old and new at the same time. When he got to Second Street, he made a left turn. He passed the courthouse on the corner, a bank on his right, and then the YMCA. He saw stores on his left that were not familiar to him. One was a Singer store, and there was a drugstore further on with the name of Quigley.

It was like riding in a dream. He stayed to the right. Traffic was not heavy, but he was careful. He saw the post office on his left, and that was somewhat familiar. Then he went by the old jail on his left. He had come to the bridge on Nichol's Street, and he crossed it, passing over the Susquehanna River. He continued his ride. The bike really was a sweet ride, its big tires rolling smoothly over the pavement.

Somehow, he knew where it was taking him, and he did not understand why. There was something waiting for him at the end of this journey, something important. His path led him to the Clear Haven Fairgrounds.

Each year the Clear Haven Fair came to town for a week at the end of July and the beginning of August. It was a county fair, and it was the biggest event of the year. His parents had taken him to the fair as long as he could remember. Now, the grounds were empty. The beginning of September was not far off. He rode by the exhibition hall that faced the back of the old football grandstand. On fair week it was packed with people there to see the various shows and entertainers who came to town.

The sun was high in the sky. When he rounded the side of the grandstand he saw the track and the football field. Clear Haven had a new high school in the world Tommy lived in, but this was not his time or place, but he was not afraid.

There were benches for the players aligned along the sides the field. Someone was sitting on a bench at mid-field on the side next to the track in front of the grandstand. No one else was about.

Tommy stopped the bike. He sensed that what was about to happen was important. He got off the bike and pushed it along to an opening in the chain link fence separating him from the track. Tommy walked the bike over the track and towards the person sitting on bench.

The boy sat with his back to Tommy. He did not turn around. He moved forward, and the boy turned around at the sound.

He jumped up and said, "Hey, that's my bike! Where did you get it?"

Tommy said, "I borrowed it from someone to take a ride."

The boy had medium brown hair, brown eyes, and looked to be about 10 years old.

"I had it at the playground last week and someone took it," the boy said. "I have been looking everywhere for it. That looks exactly like my bike. I don't think there's another one like it in town."

He paused, eyeing Tommy. "I haven't seen you before. Do you live in town? What's your name?" he said in a rush of words.

"I'm Tom. I live with my grandparents on the West Side, on

Market Street. I've lived here about a year," Tommy said. "What's your name, and how do you know it's your bike?" he asked.

"My friends call me Ray," the boy said. "Look under the seat. You'll see the letter "R" printed under it. My dad wrote it there."

Tommy bent down and looked under the seat. As Ray had said there was the letter "R" neatly printed in black ink.

"This makes no sense," Tommy said. "A man gave me this bike to ride, but it's there, all right. I don't know why he said it was his bike."

"It belongs to me. It's my bike! Dad and Mom gave it to me for Christmas. My dad's not home. He's a Marine. I really miss him!"

The boy looked very sad. Tommy felt for him.

"I understand you really miss your dad and why you would want to get your bike back. You can have it," Tommy said.

Ray stepped forward and put his hands on the handlebars. "Thanks, Tom," he said. "I've been looking everywhere for it. Are you in high school?"

"Yes, I'll be a sophomore this fall. What about you, Ray?"

"I go to Leonard Grade Elementary. I'll be in sixth grade this year. I better get home now. My mom will be worried. Thanks for bringing me my bike. Do you know how to get home from here?"

Tommy smiled and said, "Yeah, I've been coming here for the Fair since I was a little kid. It's not far away. I'm glad you have your bike. I know you're missing your dad a lot. I miss mine, too! Where is your dad?

"In Korea in the war. I'm really scared for him," Ray said. He looked like he was ready to cry.

Tom reached out and put his hand on Ray's shoulder.

"What's your dad's name, Ray?"

"His name is James. Mom calls him Jim. She misses him a lot, too. I just want him to come home, that's all."

In that moment, Tommy saw himself in the boy. He saw the pain and tears, and the fear for his father. He realized how selfish he had been, not seeing the pain of others, and not thinking enough about his mother's pain. Here was a young boy who felt the same about his dad as Tommy felt about his. He could have said all that was in his heart about his loss, but he said, "I'll keep him in my prayers, Ray. I promise."

The tears did come to Ray's face in that moment. He did his best not to cry, but there was no way he could stop the flood. He reached out and hugged Tommy, his sobs coming hard.

Tears ran down Tommy's face. He was weeping for Ray and his dad, and for himself.

The boys held each other until Ray finally stopped crying. He looked up at Tommy.

"You really mean it, don't you? You'll pray for my dad! I pray all the time for him. I hope God hears my prayers. Do you think He does?"

Tommy did not know exactly what to say, but he wanted to reassure the boy, to comfort him.

"Yes, I think God hears you. For a long time now, I didn't think so, but coming here today and finding your bike has helped me, too. You'd better get home. Your mom will be worried. Get a lock for your bike. Keep it safe from now on."

"I don't know what that is. I've never seen one," the boy said.

"It doesn't matter. You have your bike. Maybe we'll see each other again," Tommy said.

Ray smiled. "Thanks, Tom! This is like having part of my dad back. See you later!"

The boy wiped the tears from his face, mounted his bike, and pedalled away towards an exit from the park.

Tommy Burke felt like a great weight had been lifted from his soul. His pain and loss still burned within him, but he had been ignoring those who loved him, and he had not considered their needs to be as great as his own. He would try praying for Ray's dad and hope for a good outcome, that Ray's father would return home.

He sat down on the bench and thought for a long time about what had happened. Reynolds had told him that he would be finding what he needed, and he had done just that.

Tommy stood up and started walking. As he strode through the neighborhoods he saw more new old cars in driveways and passing him on the streets. People waved at him and he waved back. He kept going. When he reached Apple Street, he walked to the Brown house. The other houses beyond it were still missing, but when he rounded the curve in the road, he saw his golf cart, trailer and mower to the on the grass. Where the dirt road had begun was now solid woods. The road had disappeared!

He got into the golf cart and sat there for a long time. Had he lost his mind? Had he been hallucinating? What had happened to the road? Had he imagined everything?

Finally, he started the cart, turned onto the pavement, and went in the direction of home. When he rounded the curve the houses that had not been there before were back in place. There was a modern car in the Brown's driveway.

Tommy made a right onto Market Street, drove to his grandparent's driveway, and pulled the car and trailer into the garage. He plugged the charger in, then went up the steps and through the backdoor into the kitchen.

His grandmother smiled at him and offered him a glass of ice tea.

"Why don't you relax a little, Tom? We'll have supper at 5:30 when your mom gets home."

"Thanks, Grandma," Tom said, forcing a smile in return. He made his way through the hallway to the front door, pushed open the screen door and went to the swing on the porch. Tommy sat down, his drink in hand, and stared out at the neighborhood. He was afraid that he was seriously ill. He didn't even know what to say about it. He didn't want anyone to become upset and rush him off to a mental hospital. How could he even talk about it?

When his Mom's car pulled into the driveway, he left the porch and went to the kitchen, placing his glass in the dishwasher.

He did his best to respond normally during supper. Each of them talked about their day, but Tom said nothing about hat had happened to him. He didn't mention meeting the boy, riding a strange bike, or going to a place from long ago. He was afraid to tell them anything. He did not know how he would even begin to describe what he had seen. He was like his father. His mind was strong. He had to figure it out on his own.

Tommy was regimented in his habits. He kept his room picked up, clothes hung in the closet, or in the hamper when they needed laundering, and he always made his bed each morning.

When he went to his room that night, he stripped off his clothes, dumped them in the hamper and put on his pajamas. He crawled into bed and lay there. It was the wee hours of the morning before he was able to fall asleep.

Before he fell asleep, he decided that he had to tell his mother what had happened. He would not tell her first thing in the morning. He would have to figure out the best way to explain it. He had no desire to upset her. His revelation about his own selfishness had resulted in the realization that his mom deserved far more consideration from him, and his grandparents did, too.

*Chapter Six*

Saturday morning, the family decided to let Tommy sleep in. He had yards to cut, but it was almost 8:30 before he came downstairs. When he did appear, the dark circles under his eyes made it clear that he had not had enough sleep. He wished that they had awakened him sooner so he could get to work on time.

Like his father, he worked on a self-imposed schedule. Responsibilities had to be met. Tommy ate a piece of toast and was ready to dash out the door when his grandmother stopped him.

"Your mom is on the front porch," she said, gently reaching for his arm. "At least say good morning to her before you leave."

Tommy went to the porch. His mom had Saturdays off and was

sitting in one of the wicker chairs on the porch. She held an old photo album in her lap. She smiled at him and he bent down to give her a kiss.

His eyes caught a photo on a page, and he almost passed out. His skin went pale.

"Tommy, sit down," his mother said. "What's the matter? Do you feel all right?"

Tommy sat down heavily in the chair opposite hers. He took a big breath to clear his head. "Can I see the album?" he asked.

"Are you sure you're O.K.? Do you want me to take you to the doctor?"

"I'm O.K. Can I look at the album?"

"Yes. Here." She handed the album to him.

"Whose is this? Where did you get it?" Tommy asked.

"It belonged to your father. It was in the attic. I haven't looked at it in years. Actually, Tom, I haven't had the heart to look at his things for quite awhile. I was in the attic this morning looking for some old things, and I found it in a chest. I'd forgotten about it," his mother said.

Tom took the album from her and looked down. At the bottom of the page on the right, there was a photo of a boy astride a bicycle. It was the boy he'd met at the football field; the boy who owned the bike. He was stunned.

He pointed at the picture. "Who is this?"

His mother looked at the picture. "That's one of the few pictures we have of him. That's Reynolds Burke."

She slipped the photo out of its sleeve and looked on the back.

"It was taken in 1952. That was the year his father was killed in Korea."

Tommy's voice was hoarse when he asked, "Who is Reynolds Burke? Is he a relative?"

"He was your grandfather's older brother. His father, Matthew Burke, did not come home from the Korean War. He was your great-grandfather."

"Why didn't Dad ever show this to me before?"

"He didn't like to talk about painful things, Tom. You should know something else. Reynolds, they called him Ray, he was a Marine, like his father. He died in Vietnam. It seems that Burke men give everything for their country. Your dad's family has given far more than most."

Tears were running down his mother's face at this point.

Tommy leaned over to put his arms around his mom.

"I love you, Mom. I'm so sorry that I have been pushing everyone away. I didn't know anything about this! Please forgive me!"

"Oh, Tommy ... I don't know how—"

"You don't need to know. You're the best, most loving mom in the whole world! I'm so sorry that I haven't been talking to you. I didn't know what to believe. I've been angry at God. Something happened to me. It was strange. I think it was a dream. That's it! I had a dream. Maybe it was a dream, or a vision, or something.

"It was yesterday. I met the kid in that picture. I think it must have been God trying to tell me something. It couldn't have been real, but it felt real. He told me his dad was in Korea! I ended up trying to comfort him! I realized how selfish I've been.

"He had a bike—that bike, the one in the picture. I know that sounds absolutely crazy, and I was afraid I was losing my mind. I was afraid to tell you!

"It couldn't have happened. It's impossible! Whatever it was, it couldn't have been real, but that doesn't matter! What really matters is you, and Granddad and Grandma, and everybody else in our family, and me! We matter!

"I need to figure this all out. Whatever it was, I know I met that kid—my, my great uncle. See how crazy that sounds! Do you believe me, or do you think I'm crazy?"

The look on his mother's face was one of wonder and concern. "Do you want to talk to someone about this, maybe a doctor?" she asked.

Tommy hesitated for a moment. He didn't know what to say. His grandmother came out onto the porch.

"Tom, I'm doing the laundry. I thought you might want these. I'd hate to put them in the washer." She handed him twelve silver dollars.

It took the better part of half an hour for Thomas Burke, Jr. to stop crying. Marie Conover called her pastor, who agreed to come to the house. When he arrived, everyone had assembled in the living room.

Tommy felt shy. He was not sure how to begin. His mother, grandparents and Pastor Cambridge were waiting.

Finally, he said, "I guess I'd better tell you how it began …" When Tommy finished all of them were crying, openly. It had been a sweet ride, indeed!

The Picture

# THE PICTURE

When Johanna Godin was born, her family lived by the sea. Well, not exactly by the sea, but just a block from it. Her earliest memory was from the time she was four and her father built a sand castle for her on the beach. It was an elaborate structure with walls, towers, turrets, and a moat that they filled with sea water that kept disappearing into the sand.

Jim, her father, had worked for hours on the castle, and Diven, her mother, had recorded his progress using a polaroid camera. It had been a wonderful day together, and Johanna vividly recalled it to mind. The vast ocean and the sound of its waves, the cry of gulls, the immensity of the blue sky overhead, and her parents—young, handsome and beautiful!

Now, the pictures were ancient and yellowed in a worn album that she kept in the nightstand by her bed.

Johanna's younger sister, Ellen, arrived when she was five. When Ellen was old enough to enjoy the beach, their dad continued to exercise his architectural abilities, and Johanna helped him build sand castles for Ellen, delighting in her sister's happy laughter.

Margate was their home. They lived in a white bungalow on Gladstone. Their father worked on the mainland as an assistant manager at a supermarket. Johanna's mother taught second grade at the local elementary school. The family attended Community Church, and Johanna went to a small class with children her age while the adults were having the morning worship service.

Margate was a magical place to live. A shore town is filled with people in the summer, but her favorite times of year were fall and spring when the crowds had not yet arrived, or after Labor Day when the town was quiet once again.

She loved to stroll along the beach after school and on weekends when she was in junior high, with the permission of her parents, of course. Johanna would walk for miles along the sand, accompanied by Trixy, the family mutt. The dog would run before her chasing the waves. When they were ready to leave the beach, she would attach Trixy's leash to walk the streets of the town.

Johanna loved the ocean and its many moods. Sometimes it was quiet, almost like a vast lake. At other times it stormed, and wild waves and roaring surf filled the world with sound. The sea was ever-changing.

She would stand before the ocean with her feet in the water, shoes in hand, and stare with joy at the magnificence of it, feeling tiny and insignificant.

High school came and went. Johanna went off to college at West Chester to major in elementary education. She planned to follow her mother's path, choosing a career in the classroom. While at college, she met Bill Spencer, who was going to be an English teacher. They were destined to be married.

Upon graduation, a wedding was held that July at the Community Church in Margate, and the reception took place in the community room. Ellen, who was Johanna's maid-of-honor, took control of the festivities at one point, leading the younger people to the beach for photos. Some of the participants plunged into the water, laughing and shouting.

Bill and Johanna had secured teaching positions in Bill's home area in the Poconos, where they would be teaching in the Stroudsburg, Pennsylvania school system. Johanna had left the sea behind for the high hills of Pennsylvania.

To Johanna's mind, nothing compared to the ocean, but she had to be content with streams, ponds, rivers and lakes in the mountains as the years passed. Baby Michael arrived three years after she and Bill were married, and Louise showed up two years later.

Trixy had become very old by this time, and Bill and Johanna cried the day they laid her to rest beneath a pine tree in the backyard behind their home. They'd purchased a modest, two-story, 3-bedroom house on an acre of ground in the town of Mountain Home.

The 50-year-old house needed minor work, but it was well-built, and exhibited excellent craftsmanship. Its charm lay in its design, setting, flower beds, hedges, well-established trees and expansive yard. The house faced the road that led down the hill to the town of Canadensis. Bill had fenced the yard in their second year, anticipating the arrival of children.

Life slipped by, and the children grew. Bill and Johanna and their little family made regular trips to see Bill's parents, who lived in a neighborhood that bordered Stroudsburg.

They also did their best to go to Margate and see Johanna's parents once each quarter of the year. During the summers, they would spend a week in Margate, enjoying the beach and taking Michael and Louise to see Lucy the Elephant. They enjoyed visiting with friends and with Johanna's sister's family in Cape May, where Ellen had chosen to move after marrying Bob Fisher, one of her classmates. Ellen worked at the local library, and her husband was a rookie policeman with the city police department.

Johanna's mother, Diven, described Margate as "The town that reinvents itself on a daily basis!" There were many bungalows throughout the 1.6 square miles of the community, but one-by-one, they were purchased, torn down, and replaced with two-story, five-bedroom, five-and-a-half bath houses each year. The character of the town was changing, and as the fixed population dwindled, and schools were closed because of fewer children, more of the older homes disappeared in the march of progress. Homes that had been occupied by families familiar to Johanna and her family were now owned by people who lived somewhere else, and only showed up during the summer season.

The mountains of Pennsylvania were beautiful, but the sea called to Johanna, and she was often quiet when they had ended their visits and they drove back to the mountains.

Bill knew leaving the shore made Johanna sad, and he would keep silent as the children chattered about the beach and the fun they had, especially when their grandfather built a castle for them. Bill could take or leave the shore because he loved the mountains best of all, but he respected his wife's history, knowing that she felt as strongly about her home as he did his.

When their son Michael went off to college at Penn State, the trips to Margate had become less frequent. When Louise left home two years later to go to Drexel University in Philadelphia, Bill and Johanna resumed their quarterly trips to the shore to see her parents.

Johanna's parents were aging, as were Bill's parents. Bill and Johanna were experiencing the same thing that many families face: the empty-nest time when the children are gone and the days must be filled with other things. They had gotten a rescue dog that was a two-year-old golden retriever named Rascal. He could roam the yard safely at their home inside the fence, and he traveled with them to see Bill's parents.

Johanna's parents welcomed Rascal, too. Dogs were not allowed on the beach in the summer season, but during their trips to Margate in the fall and spring, Johanna would take him to the beach.

Years slipped by. College graduations were held, and Michael and Louise were off building their careers. Michael headed to California, where he was going to work in information technology, and Louise went to Boston to complete a Master's degree in biology at Boston College.

Bill's father, Bill Sr., developed Alzheimer's. His mother, Diane, took care of him until she could no longer handle the task herself. Bill spent as much time as he possibly could helping his mother with the overwhelming task of dealing with his dad. Johanna was there, as well, doing all she could to help.

When the end came, Diane Spencer needed a long rest, and she came to live with Bill and Johanna at their home. A few months later, Bill's mother sold her home, and the money was placed in an account to be used for her future care. She had wanted to give the money to Bill and Johanna, but they refused to accept it, saying that the money belonged to her, and that she would keep it for her own needs.

A year later, Johanna was in her classroom on an October day when the principal called her to his office. There was a phone call for her.

When she picked up the phone, her father was on the line. Her father's voice was hoarse. He had been crying.

"What's wrong, Daddy? What happened?" Johanna said, suddenly frightened.

"She, she's gone, Jo. Your mother's gone. Gone."

"Oh, Daddy! Tell me! How…?"

"Her heart … stopped. We were in the kitchen, and she just fell on the floor. I called 911. I'm at Shore Memorial in the emergency room. It's too late. They can't do anything. She's gone!"

Her father started to cry.

The days that followed were a blur. The service was held at the Community Church, and all of the family members and friends were there. The motorcade was long, and the graveside interment service was painful. Bill held onto Johanna through the whole thing.

When they returned to her parent's house, Johanna took the dog and headed for the beach, saying that she wanted to be alone. Bill let her go, knowing that she needed to be by the sea in her grief.

Six months later, they discovered Bill's mother on a Tuesday morning when she had failed to respond to their morning invitation to breakfast. She had passed away in her sleep. Another funeral and more grief followed.

Now, only Johanna's father, Jim Godin was left.

They asked him to leave Margate and come to Mountain Home to live with them. He refused, saying that Margate was his home, and that Margate was where he would stay until the Lord took him.

Bill and Johanna argued and pleaded with him, but he was adamant. Nothing would persuade him to leave the place he loved.

Three years passed. Johanna's dad had fallen four times and had a knee replaced. He used a walker, and a home health nurse came to see him twice a week. When summer arrived and Johanna was out of school, she discussed the situation with Bill at length, knowing how stubborn her father was.

"Why can't we bring him here, Jo?"

"You know how he is! We couldn't get him to leave there unless we immobilized him and brought him here in chains! Then, we would have no peace! He's bound and determined to die in that house, and if he has his way, he'll do it! If I can't get him to leave, no one can!" Johanna said.

"Then, what can we do, Jo?" Bill asked.

"If you will allow me, I want to go there and stay for a while. Rascal can stay with you. He's my dad, and he needs my help. We have the summer, but someone should stay here and take care of our home. Would it be OK if I go and stay there? I promise—"

Bill did not let her finish her sentence, "Allow you? What kind of question is this? You don't need my permission to go and be with your dad! For heaven's sake, he's the only one we have left! Rascal and I will be fine. I've got stuff to do around here. The yard needs attention. I've got to trim the dead branches from that maple. The living room needs painting, and—"

Johanna was in his arms, crying. "When, when he's gone, we'll be orphans, Bill ..."

They both cried in that moment, wondering at the swift passage of years, the deaths of their beloved parents, the hole in their hearts because their children and young grandchildren were far away, and a universe that did not seem to care about how much pain humans had to bear.

*Chapter Two*

Johanna was amazed and fearful at her father's appearance. She remembered the handsome man who had built sandcastles and given her away on her wedding day. This was her dad, who believed in the beauty of God's world, who had read wonderful stories to her as a little girl and tucked her in at night.

This frail man did not resemble her father, and yet the blue eyes that crinkled at the corners and the sound of his voice told her that it was, indeed, her dad.

She hugged him hard and then drew back, afraid that she might harm him by holding him too tightly.

The day had been hot, but a cool front had arrived, and a sea breeze made the small back patio comfortable. The houses are close together in Margate and little space is generally devoted to yards, front or back. In most shore towns, land is at a premium, and nearly every inch is filled with houses.

They were sitting on two deck chairs facing the rear of the house. A white vinyl fence about four feet high separated the properties.

"Dad, how have you been?"

"For an old guy, OK—"

"Oh, you're not old!" Johanna said. "You've lost so much weight."

"Your mother would be happy about that. I could stand to lose some—"

"But you're really thin, Daddy! Aren't you eating?"

"I don't have much of an appetite lately, Jo."

"You need to get Meals on Wheels, or whatever they call it—"

"I can get my own food out of the refrigerator—"

"Well, I'm going to make dinner! When was the last time you had a cooked meal?"

"I don't remember. It was maybe a week ago …"

"That's terrible! When was Ellen here last?"

"Your sister doesn't have summers off, Jo. She comes almost every weekend."

"She's only 30 miles away, Daddy!"

"Jo, she works! Sometimes she works on Saturday, too. It's not her fault!

"Besides, I know the two of you talk all the time, and you always talk about me coming to live with you! Ellie doesn't have the room you do, but there's no way I'm leaving this place until they carry me out! This is my home. It's where I'm going to be, until the end!"

"Why are you so damn stubborn, Daddy?"

"You don't have to swear, young lady!" her Dad exclaimed.

"I wasn't swearing. Damn isn't swearing. It's in the Bible. You know that!"

"I don't care. Your mother wouldn't like it!"

"*My mother isn't here!*" Johanna shouted in frustration. Then, she stopped, feeling awful at the look on her father's face.

"I know she's not here, Jo," her father said. "Do you think I don't know it? I know it every moment of every day. I know it each second of each and every hour. I miss her so bad, Jo. The silence in this house is endless. I miss the sound of her voice, the touch of her hand, and the songs she would hum to herself when she thought she was alone. I miss the shadow of her presence when she came into a room. I miss our walks on the beach.

"I miss you and Ellie, when I would build you sand castles and she would take our pictures. I miss buying her flowers and the way she arranged them in the vase in the kitchen window. I miss playing the radio and us dancing together in the living room. I miss the sound of her breathing next to me in the night. I miss everything about her…"

The tears were streaming down her father's face.

"Oh, Daddy! Oh, sweet Daddy!" Johanna was in his arms. "I'm so sorry!"

They held each other in their shared pain, missing the woman they called wife and mother.

That night, Johanna made meatloaf using her mother's recipe. It was the first cooked meal her father had eaten in two weeks.

She stayed with her father for 10 days, and Ellen and her husband Bob came for the weekend. The four of them went to dinner Saturday night at Steve and Cookies, and they had a great time at the beach on Sunday. Ellie and Johanna built a sandcastle, while Bob and Jim talked about the Phillies and their prospects for the season.

Bob and Ellie left for Cape May after dinner on Sunday evening.

When 10 days were gone, Johanna announced that it was time for her to leave.

"Bill has been great about this, Dad, but I need to get back. I'll come again as soon as I can. I've made you a week's worth of meals. Two are in the fridge, and the others are in the freezer. You've got to promise me that you'll take better care of yourself! Will you do that for me?"

"Yes, yes. I promise, Jo. Don't you worry! It's time you got home to Bill and to that dog, too! Next time, bring Bill and Rascal with you. Come and stay with me! The beach is waiting!"

As Johanna drove north, she said a silent prayer that her father would be all right.

When she got home she discovered that Bill had been keeping something from her.

The furnace in their home was dead and had to be replaced. Bill had decided to turn it on to see if it was operating. It was a good thing he had tried to get it to work in the summer and not waited until the cold temperatures of fall had arrived. He had not bothered her with the details, not wanting her to worry about something else. Initially, he had thought that it might be repairable, but this proved to be not the case. Its age was too great. It was time for a whole new system, which meant big bucks! Their hot water system used old style radiators.

Bill and Johanna talked about the alternatives, and they decided to replace everything, choosing a system that incorporated new baseboard units and a separate on-demand hot water system.  It would take time to do the job. There would not be a quick return to Margate.

Simply removing the old furnace and water heater, along with the old radiators and pipes required over a week. Because of the way the house had been built, installing the new system required another week. There was painting and other cosmetic work to do as well.

In the middle of the second week, the phone rang. Johanna picked it up.

Ellen was on the other end. She was crying. "Jo, Daddy's gone."

*Chapter Three*

Six months had passed. Neither Ellen and her husband Bob, nor Johanna and Bill, had the money to buy out the others from their joint ownership of their parents' house in Margate.

Bob and Ellen lived three blocks from the beach in Cape May, so they did not need a second home in another beach town. Bill and Johanna simply did not have the extra income to devote to the upkeep and taxes on the Margate property. The only thing to do was sell it. A bungalow a block from the beach in Margate was worth a lot of money. Bungalows on all sides of it had been torn down through the years and converted to larger two-story, multi-bed and bath homes. This would probably be the fate of Johanna and Ellen's childhood home, as well.

Their father had wanted them to keep the home and had said as much on numerous occasions. But wishes rarely give way to practicality, no matter how hard people want something. One thing was certain: the government would swallow a big piece of their profit, thanks to capital gains on a vacation home. The government, of course, did not deserve the windfall, but it always won in such cases.

They listed the house with the best realtor in Margate, who was a friend of the family. The sign went up in the small front yard on the April 1st.

Two weeks later, a bidding war between two buyers drove the sale price up considerably. One of the potential buyers relented, but their elation over the sale was short-lived. A home inspection revealed repairs that had to be made, causing the inflated price to dissipate. The buyer wanted to repair the home instead of tearing it down.

To their credit, Johanna and Ellen would not go below their asking price, so the repairs would have to come out of the extra money the buyer had originally bid. The buyer balked, but they stuck to their guns, and the buyer finally agreed. The house would not be razed following the sale, which was a small comfort to the sisters. Johanna and Ellen were happy that their childhood home would continue to exist! The buyers loved their house just the way it was!

The time came to clean out the house. Johanna was required to be in her classroom until mid-June, so they hired an estate-sale company to sell off many items before donating whatever was not sold. Ellen and Johanna had gone to the house prior to the sale to divide up sentimental items they wanted to keep for themselves.

They had donated a number of items to ARC, the Salvation Army and the Vietnam Vets, including all of the clothing in the house. Furniture and kitchen items were also given to charity.

Going through her father's stuff, Johanna found a 9x12 sealed envelope. Her dad had written on the front of it.

*Dear Jo,*

*If you have found this, I am gone. I saw this a few years ago and it made me think of you. I know how much you love the ocean. Please don't open it now. Wait for a day when you really need to remember the good times. We certainly have had our share of them! I will be building sandcastles for you and Ellie on another beach now. The nice part is that our day at the beach then will never have to end.*

*Love you always,*
*Dad*

Johanna began to cry. Ellie heard her and went to her, wrapping her arms around her big sister. They wept like children. They missed their parents in that moment, and their sense of loss was overwhelming. First Mom, then Dad, and now their home. The hole in their lives would not be filled by anything else.

The day of the closing arrived. The couple that was buying their house had two girls, ages 7 and 4. Somehow, this made the event bittersweet.

They went to Steve & Cookies for lunch. When they said their goodbyes, Ellen and Bob made their way to Somers Point and got onto the Garden State Parkway, heading south and home to Cape May.

Johanna told Bill she wanted to walk on the beach one final time. He offered to go with her. She kissed him.

"If you don't mind, I want to do this alone. Please don't be angry with me. You're a mountain man, I am a beach woman, and we have the best of both worlds. Please, humor me."

Bill smiled at her. "I'll wait for you by Lucy the Elephant. Take as long as you like. If you don't see me, check the gift shop."

Bill had driven to the Margate library, and Johanna left the car and made her way to the beach. She took off her shoes and stepped onto the sand.

It was a beautiful day, but the beach wasn't crowded. She walked towards the water and stepped into it, turning south away from the direction of Atlantic City, walking towards Longport.

She took her time, going slowly, lost in memories of days long ago.

Her eyes swept the horizon, gazing far out to sea, counting the boats she saw. She always did this. Her dad had told her as a little girl that the more boats she saw, the nicer the day was out on the open water. She believed him. She would always believe him. She did not feel the tears on her face.

How does one say goodbye to a lifetime of wonderful memories made by the sea? The only choice is to store them away in one's heart. Once there, they can be brought to mind when thoughts of warm sand, the sound of waves, and light, cool breezes ignite the spark that fires the mind to recall such things.

Johanna had come farther than she had thought. She saw Bill waiting for her atop the ramp that led from the beach to Lucy the

Elephant, the most famous landmark in Margate since 1881. She smiled and waved at him. It was time to go home to the mountains.

*Chapter Four*

Sometimes, it seems like the only thing faster than the speed of light is the speed of life. Bill and Johanna visited with Bob and Ellen in Cape May, and Bob and Ellen visited with them in Mountain Home, but Johanna did not return to Margate.

Johanna retired after 30 years in the classroom. She had spent all of her time in second grade. Bill always told the same tired, old joke.

"If Jo had just worked a little harder, she could have advanced to third!"

The truth was that Johanna loved second grade. She thought it was the perfect age for students to be, although, in her last decade of teaching, she did not care for the new curriculums and idiocy that was being forced upon teachers and children by people who had never served in a classroom. The American educational system was broken, but what needed fixing wasn't in the schools; it was in the homes where the children came from.

Bill taught 12th grade English for an extra five years, and they celebrated his retirement with a trip to England, Wales, Scotland and Ireland. He greatly enjoyed being where the language had begun, and visiting Stratford-on-Avon and the Globe Theater were two of the highlights of the trip that he would treasure forever.

More years passed, and Bill and Jo got into quiet hobbies they enjoyed. She had become a potter, spending time at a studio in Canadensis, learning the artistry and craft. Her plates, bowls and cups adorned their home.

Bill had decided to try his hand at writing fiction. He had written a novel and 12 short stories, and he was searching for an agent to represent him. It wasn't easy to break into a field crammed with books about vampires, alternative history, science fiction and fantasy.

He kept submitting and being rejected.

One day, Johanna said, "What's wrong?"

"Not enough sex and violence, Jo."

"Seriously, Bill, there is *no* sex and violence in your work! Your stories are wonderful! They're wholesome! Your characters seem so real. You make me cry and laugh."

"That's just because I'm losing my hair at an alarming rate, and I look funny. At least God doesn't have to keep track of as many hairs as He once did."

"Oh, your jokes are awful!" Jo said.

"Yeah,but I still make you laugh, don't I?"

Their lives had become predictable. Life was comfortable and unruffled. They were at peace.

Their children and grandchildren came to visit once a year since Michael and his family lived in California, and Louise and her family lived in Texas. Bill and Jo spent the Thanksgiving holiday in San Diego, California with Michael, his wife, son and daughter. They spent Christmas in Austin, Texas with their daughter, her husband and two sons.

Living at such distances from those one loves was not easy, but one took opportunity where one found it. Michael and Louise were living very happy and successful lives, and this fact contributed to the family's general state of mind, given the level of unhappiness of so many families in America.

Bill finally found an agent who liked the way he wrote. The man said that he wanted to shop the novel first. He told Bill that it was best to market short story collections after an author had achieved recognition. He also asked if Bill was writing a sequel to his first book. That was enough to set a fire under Bill. He had been feeling like he should give up, when he received a call from his agent. He'd finally discovered someone who could help him.

Johanna awoke in the wee small hours of the next morning to find that Bill was not next to her. She put on her robe and went downstairs.

She heard the sound of typing in his office. The kitchen clock read 6:15.

"What in heaven's name are you doing? We're retired! You don't have to go to work!" she said.

"I have an idea for a new novel," Bill said. "My characters can go on living. I've been awake half the night thinking about it, Jo. I just gave up trying to sleep. It was no good. Can you make coffee? I want to get this into a new file."

"Dr. Fletcher said you should cut back on the coffee. Have you been taking your pills?"

"Yes, I'm taking my pills, and one cup won't hurt me."

"Then, why is it that one cup turns into three, four or more, Mr. Spencer?"

"Then, make a small pot."

"You didn't answer my question," Jo said.

"Well, at least I'm not addicted to drugs. Use the Keurig. Make one cup, that's all. I've got to get this on paper—"

"There is no paper. It's a laptop and a keyboard," Johanna said.

She turned and went into the kitchen.

Bill did not see the smile, and the relief, on her face. Her Bill had become a believer in his own ability again. She knew how disheartened he'd become, and she had been worried about him.

When the coffee was ready, she poured it into his favorite mug, adding his true addiction, the French vanilla creamer he loved. She was a tea drinker. She stirred the coffee and went back to his office.

She screamed and rushed forward, dropping the mug to the floor.

Bill was sprawled on the rug. Her eyes took in the laptop's screen. She read,

*"Jo, love yo—"*

*Chapter Five*

It had been necessary to wait several days for the kids and grandkids to get to Mountain Home for the funeral. Ellie and Bob had rushed from Cape May, and the sisters handled the arrangements together. The service would be held in the Methodist Church in Canadensis, where Bill had been baptized. The family plot in the cemetery was about two miles from the church. After the interment service everyone returned to the family home.

As the afternoon wore on, almost everyone had left. Finally, only Johanna, Michael, Louise, and their spouses and children remained.

When twilight arrived, Michael and Louise sat in the kitchen with Johanna.

"Mom," Michael said, "I want you to come to San Diego. We have plenty of room. You can go to the ocean. There's lots to do. You can—"

He didn't get to finished his sentence.

"This is home! It's where you lived. It's where you grew up. It's my home. It's where I will stay!"

"But, Mom," Louise said, "you can't live by yourself! If you don't want to go to Michael's, come home with me. I have the room, too."

"I'm staying right here! My friends are here. I will get along just fine. If I need your help I will ask you for it. Your dad …" Johanna started to cry.

Louise went to her and hugged her close.

Michael stood up, feeling helpless.

When Johanna regained control, she gently separated herself from her daughter's embrace, stood up, and faced her children.

"Yes, there may come a time when I have to take one of you up on your offer," she said. "And I love you for wanting to take care of me, but I intend, the Good Lord willing, to live my life in my home, in the place where I have been for many decades.

"My church is just down the road. My friends are nearby. I still have all my faculties, and the doctor says I am in excellent health for my age. I don't have to take any medications, I'm neither over or under-weight, and I eat better than both of you do.

"And the last thing I want is to be a burden to my children!"

"But Mom—" Michael began.

"It is my decision to make, Michael. I am of sound mind and body. Besides, guilt should not be used to motivate any of us. Both of you have huge obligations to your families, just as we did to you when you were growing up. I don't know anyone in Texas or California. Your dad and I talked about this time in our lives, should something happen to one of us, and we both agreed that the one that remained would stay right here.

"I promise you both this: when I need you, I will call you, because I am not stupid. When the time comes that I can't handle this house and property, I will make the right decision. That decision may involve going into assisted living somewhere in this area, as well. I have no desire to end my life in a place where I am uncomfortable, and your homes might as well be in another universe."

"But, Mother—"

"Louise, no guilt! I won't hear it! You have made your lives where you both belong; this is where I belong. Be thankful that I am well enough to make such a decision on my own. I do have a companion—"

"Mom!" Michael said, "Do you mean there's someone else in your life? How could you—?"

Johanna started to laugh hysterically.

Her children were thunderstruck, and their faces showed it.

When she finally managed to stop laughing she said, "I'm talking about Shakespeare! He's a very good dog, and when I speak to him he listens, silently! He doesn't argue with me; he loves me, and he's much younger than I am. He has a lot of good years left in him. Besides, walking with him is great exercise. He will also help protect me, should the need arise. You two need to get back home. Your lives are waiting. It's time for a family hug. I love you both with all my heart!"

When Michael and Louise had been little, their dad had started the practice of the "family hug" each night before they went to bed. They gathered in a circle and hugged each other as a group.

When they hit their teen years, the kids decided that they did not want to do it anymore, thinking it was corny. Their dad would not relent.

"I don't care if we're a hundred and you're eighty, our family hug does not depend on age! It's about loving each other; not about a mere tradition!"

The tears were running down Johanna's face as she held out her arms, and Michael and Louise were crying just as hard. They embraced each other. Their beloved husband and father was missing from the circle for the first time in their lives. They were crying for him and for the overwhelming grief they felt in that moment.

The children and their children were gone. The house was quiet—too quiet. Johanna was sitting on the sofa in the living room, looking out the window. She had broken the rule and allowed Shakespeare to climb up onto the sofa with her. As if he sensed her sadness, he had laid his head on her lap to comfort her. Her right hand was on his head, and her left hand was on his back.

"Oh, Shakespeare, what are we going to do? You miss him, too!"

Shakespeare raised his nose and licked her hand. Johanna felt tears on her face.

"My Bill is gone to another shore, and I must wait until I join him. I miss the ocean, Shakespeare. I wish I could close my eyes and wish us there. You could run on the beach. It would be fun!"

She had been going through Bill's things. Many people hung onto many items that belonged to loved ones who were gone, but Johanna had a house full of pictures and memories. Clothes and other things should be given to someone who could use them. She had asked Michael and Louise to take what they wanted that had belonged to their father. Michael had taken a coffee mug, and Louise had selected a print out of one of his short stories. They told Johanna that was all they wanted for now, saying that their dad's things belonged in dad's house. They should remain there until a time in the future.

Johanna had understood. She had separated out the things that would go to the Salvation Army and the Vietnam Vets. She was also going to send a check to Samaritan's Purse in memory of Bill.

While going through the secretary, she had discovered the envelope that she had found among her father's things when they were cleaning out her parents' Margate home. She had forgotten all about it. She read the words he had written on the outside of the envelope.

*"Wait for a day when you really need to remember the good times."*

Today was such a day. Bill was gone. She opened the envelope. There were two items in it. A note read,

*"Jo, these make me think of you. All my love, Daddy"*

Her tears became a flood. When she regained control of herself, she read the first item. It was a poem.

*Solitary Searcher*

*Somewhere between the rising and the setting of the sun there is a lonely beach occupied by one*
*She seeks a quiet solace in lonesome reverie as she paces on the sand beside the flowing sea*
*Her vision is turned inward to other times and days*
*She sees her Mother's face dancing on the waves*
*She is her Father's daughter and she knows this to be true*
*She is made from earth and water renewed by morning's dew*
*She will walk here all her life of this she is quite sure*
*There is healing in these waters and a love that will endure.*

When she finished reading it, she sat for a long time gently stroking Shakespeare's head, as her tears began again. She realized in that moment that there were far greater depths to her father than she had ever imagined. It was clear that he had understood her in ways she had not even guessed, and she felt humbled by the realization.

A quiet amazement swept over her. How deep was the human soul, and what treasures—and torments—could be found there?

Now, she missed them all terribly, and realized how much she wanted to speak to her dad, her mom, and Bill, about what they knew of life that she had not yet learned.

Her eyes turned to the second item from the envelope. It was a page clipped from a magazine. It contained a picture of a painting. Her father had attached a note to it with a paper clip.

*Jo, clipped this from a magazine. Like the poem, it's a picture of where you live in your dreams. I can see you sitting in the chair, smiling at me.*

*Love, Dad*

The painting was of a room with three windows facing onto the sea. There was a wicker chair to the left of center, and a straw beach hat rested on the seat. A large book lay on the floor by the chair, opened to its middle. Two other books were upright and leaning against the chair.  A cup and saucer were perched on the left arm of the chair, and sunlight coming through the window reflected its panes on the floor. Best of all, white curtains billowed softly in an ocean breeze. She thought it looked as if someone had been sitting in the chair, and that person had gotten up and left the scene for a moment, perhaps to go and bring more tea or to fetch a cookie from the kitchen.

There was a warmness to the scene that was cozy. The ocean seen through the windows invited a viewer to come outside and walk along the beach.

Whoever had painted the picture understood the human spirit. There was a special kindness in the scene, an evocation of security and serenity. It was incredibly appealing to Johanna. She was amazed even more that her father understood her so well.

Johanna loved the sea, and she loved good books. She had always been a reader. This painting spoke to both of these desires. She wished she could go to that room, sit in that chair, pick up the open book and read it with the soft ocean breeze blowing through the windows.

There was caption below the painting: *Gentle Reader by Karen Hollingsworth.*

Johanna loved art of all kinds. She frequented stores like Michaels and A.C. Moore. She did not consider herself an accomplished potter, but she loved working at the studio. Painting and drawing were not her strong suits, but her home was filled with pictures of ocean scenes. Bill had encouraged her to find what she truly liked as the years had passed, and every room had framed prints, or inexpensive paintings that had reached out and touched her in some emotional way.

These two things, the poem and the painting, would now be her favorites. She had seen a double mat with 8 x 10 openings that could be displayed in a frame, vertically or horizontally. She decided to track down a print of the painting in that size, if she could find it. If not, she would make copies of both, and size them to fit.

Even purpose and movement could not assuage her grief, but now she had a goal, and searching to find the components to create the picture in her mind gave her a reason leave the house.

She stroked Shakespeare, smiling.

"Would you like to go for a car ride? Let's go see what we can find."

Shakespeare licked her hand and his tail wagged tentatively.

She was glad the dog was with her. Otherwise, the silence in her house would have been complete and devastating.

*Chapter Six*

There is something greatly wrong when one outlives a child, and Johanna had done so. Michael was gone. Louise remained, but she was in Texas.

Johanna had continued on and on, outliving family and friends.

Her 90th birthday had come and gone, and now, as she

approached her 100th birthday, the staff at Marion Manor was planning a special birthday party in her honor. She was the oldest resident in the home, which made her a celebrity, of sorts.

Age had taken its toll. She needed a wheelchair, and arthritis had twisted her joints and hands, but her mind was intact. Her sister, Ellie, and Ellen's husband, Bob, were also gone.

She had not been to the sea for fifteen years. Television programming was terrible, as far as Johanna was concerned, and she refused to watch it, preferring instead to read.

Marion Manor had a room they used as a library, and they also had a relationship with a small library in Cresco, where the home was located. One of the nurses made it possible for Johanna to use a computer to select and order books from the library, and she did so almost daily. She could, thankfully, still manage to hold a book and turn the pages. It had been suggested that she try using a Nook, Kindle, or other device to read, but she wanted nothing to do with them. For her, nothing would ever replace a book that she could touch.

Johanna was lucky enough to have a small, single bedroom. There was room for a bed, nightstand, a chair for visitors, space for her wheelchair, and a small wooden bookcase that one of her great grand-children had made for her.

The nightstand contained two photo albums. Her home and its contents had been sold when she had turned 93. She had come to Marion Manor with few possessions, but there was one treasure that she was able to bring. The framed poem and painting hung on the wall opposite her bed. She awoke each day to see it, and fell asleep each night looking at it.

Alice Hopkins, the day nurse on duty in her wing during the week made it possible for Johanna to get books from the town library. She remembered Mrs. Spencer from her childhood. Her family had lived in Canadensis and gone to the same church.

She had a fondness for the old woman, and she spent time with her, sitting in her room and talking to her, either before she went on duty, or after her shift was over. They spoke of many things. At 52, Alice was young enough to be Johanna's daughter, and Johanna had a great fondness for the younger woman, as well.

Alice loved the painting in Johanna's room. She found another poem by the same author entitled *To the Manor Borne*. She kept it at home as a perpetual reminder to always take time to show genuine interest in the people she served and often rehearsed it in her mind as she went about her nursing duties.

*The quiet lethargy of death falls soft as April snow*
*She sits – hand pressed to her brow, immersed in private woe*
*Eyes shut against the glare of light, lips frowning in regret*
*Life stolen by the many years, but she is living yet*
*Around the others sit at rest bodies in decay*
*Minds grasping at remembered youth, another endless day*
*Warehoused within the Manor—old women and old men—*
*consigned to utter uselessness, waiting for the end*
*The Master stands outside the door His hand pressed to its frame*
*He waits for each—one by one, to make them young again*

Johanna spoke of missing the sea, but Alice had never been to an ocean. In truth, she had never been far from her home area in the Pocono mountains. Johanna's descriptions of the ocean made her want to go there and walk along the sand.

Alice had gotten pregnant when she was a sophomore in high school, and her son had far too many birth defects to make travel possible. The father wanted nothing to do with her or the boy, and she had raised him with the help of her family.

She had gotten her G.E.D., and an uncle agreed to pay for college if she would do her best. She became a nurse because she wanted to know everything she could about how to take care of her son. Sadly, Jonathan had died shortly after his 13th birthday.

Alice decided to help older people, which led her to work in nursing homes. If anyone understood pain and suffering, it was Alice Hopkins. She made it her life's mission to alleviate as much of it as possible. This was why she talked to old people and listened to them. This was why she befriended them. For her, those who had no one to visit them should be treated with respect, concern, compassion and love. They needed someone who was willing to spend time with them.

Johanna had become one of her favorites. Alice had met Mrs. Spencer at church when Alice was in elementary school, and the fact that Johanna had outlived all of her friends made it doubly important to be with her. No one came to see her any longer, and her family members were too far away to come by.

The old woman's birthday was October 16th. Plans were in place for the party. She didn't know it, but some of her family was coming from California and Texas to celebrate. Everyone wanted it to be a big surprise.

On the morning of September 30th, Alice arrived at Marion Manor at 6:30 in the morning. She knew that Johanna awoke early. Her shift started at 7:00 a.m., and she wanted to sit and talk with her until she began work.

When she walked through the front door and heard the bells, she rushed down the hall. Doctor Wilson and three nurses were in Johanna's room, but there was nothing they could do. The old woman was gone. She would never celebrate her 100th birthday!

Alice started to cry. She had discovered a complete book of the poems by Johanna's favorite poet in a used bookstore, and looked forward to giving it to Johanna on her birthday. Now, her gift would never be given.

The funeral was held at the church in Canadensis. A handful of Johanna's relatives were there, and her photo albums were given to them. There had been a note in an envelope in the old woman's nightstand.

Alice took the painting home and put it on the wall in her bedroom, opposite her bed—the same place that Johanna had it in her room at Marion Manor. It would be the first thing she would see in the morning and the last thing she would see at night.

On the morning of October 16th, which would have been Johanna's 100th birthday, Alice awoke from a dream of the sea. She was walking along the beach, and she saw a huge elephant standing by the water, waiting for her. She was not afraid. She smiled and began to run towards the elephant.

Then, she woke up. She was wondering why there would be an elephant next to the ocean when her eyes took in Johanna's framed poem and painting on the wall. She sat up, rubbing the sleep from her eyes.

There was something different about the painting. What was it? Alice got out of bed and stepped closer to the painting to have a better look.

When her mind finally grasped what she was seeing, she stepped backward toward the bed and sat down on its edge, suddenly breathless. Her heart was racing. What she saw was impossible!

The painting had been different last night when she had gone to bed.

The wicker chair was no longer empty! A girl was sitting on it, and the book that had been lying open on the floor now rested on her lap. She wore a blue dress, and looked to be about 14 years old. She was smiling. A black and white dog lay the floor next to the chair, its muzzle resting on its paws.

Alice sat staring at the picture for what seemed an eternity. Finally, she was able to breathe normally, and her heart slowed its rapid pace. She felt tears on her face, and she reached up to wipe them off.

Alice Hopkins made a resolution in that moment. When summer came again, she knew where she would go on her vacation. It was time.

Johanna had done what she had always dreamed of doing. She had returned to the sea.

# The Man Who

# Runs The World

# THE MAN WHO RUNS THE WORLD

"Information Technology Runs the World!" proclaimed the sign on the wall above the desk of John Smith. John Smith was not his real name. There were five other men with the same name within the massive Business Systems company. The six men worked in a room, several hundred feet below ground, in the depths of the huge headquarters of Business Systems in Omaha, Nebraska.

Each man worked an eight-hour shift; three of them Monday through Friday, and the other three on weekends. No one knew their real names. They had been hired for the job after an extensive battery of psychological tests that determined they were best suited to the position.

The overwhelming criteria for having been chosen was that the John Smiths, 1 through 6, were impervious to boredom. There were a small desk and a comfortable chair behind it in the room in which they worked. An old-fashioned black telephone sat on the desk. It was a landline phone, but it also had a bit of electronic wizardry within it that allowed the phone to function regardless of any circumstances that might arise, such as a massive electronic pulse that would knock out the country's electricity, or perhaps a full-scale nuclear war.

The desk was made of wood. In fact, everything in the construction of the desk was made of wood. It would not conduct electricity.

On the surface of the desktop, there was a single red button. It was THE BUTTON; the most important button in the world.

Business Systems, or B.S.—some people used the term in a flippant or offensive manner—had more than a hundred thousand employees in 135 countries all over the world. They managed all the financial transactions, data gathering, accounting, credit card, and computer systems for nearly everything any company or organization did business-wise in the known world. They also controlled the computer grids that ran transportation systems, military backup systems, airline systems, trains systems, traffic lights, bridges that opened and closed, and access to thousands of civilian and military sites where security was essential.

If the black phone should ever ring, it was a John Smith's job to push the red button, the most important button in the history of the human race.

The reason that the six Johns had to be able to resist boredom was that during their respective eight-hour shift they were not allowed to do anything except sit and wait for the possibility that the phone might ring. They could not read a book, listen to music, watch TV, draw in a coloring book, write a letter, play solitaire, cut their nails, comb their hair, or do anything that could possibly keep them from staring at the phone and waiting.

The rules were simple. They wore a simple white coverall without pockets over underwear and white socks. They wore white slippers on their feet. They could not bring anything into the room with them, or take anything out. The last rule was actually silly because the only thing they might have been able to remove from the room was the chair they sat in; two armed guards were stationed just outside the door to the room. They were tasked with searching a John Smith prior to and after each shift.

The button itself was built into the desk, and the black phone would have to have been ripped away from its cord that extended into the floor. The penalty for any aberration on the part of a John was execution on the spot: hence, the armed guards. An execution was only to be held outside the room so that cleaning up the mess would be easier.

There were two different armed guards on duty for each Mr. Smith, but the guards' schedule was staggered by 10 minutes so that they changed their shifts before a new Smith arrived.

The Smith Brothers, or so they thought of themselves, were not related in any way. Obviously, each knew what the others looked like because they met in passing while changing shifts. They were also familiar with the guards for the same reason. The process of the shift change was as close to perfect as possible. One Smith would slide to the left, and the new Smith would slide onto the chair so that no more than a second or two elapsed as they changed places. The Smiths were not allowed to speak to each other, or to the guards.

The guards, in turn, could not communicate with the Johns. No one was to know anything about any of the others. To ensure that mistakes were not made, the whole process was on camera at all times. Someone in the vast underground B.S. kingdom was always observing the hall where the guards stood, and the room where the Smiths patiently sat and waited. The hallway outside the room was accessed by a secured elevator.

All of this was made necessary because THE BUTTON was, in fact, a doomsday button. Pressing it would literally end civilization as man knew it. The task of determining when to push it was not to be treated lightly. Therefore, the Johns were not hired for their sense of humor, for daydreaming, for using their individual imaginations, and they could exhibit no nervousness or anxiety. Each man sat quietly and steadily for eight hours at a time, waiting to end the world if necessary.

B.S. had such a vast proprietary hold on its systems that they were determined never to allow anyone to take over their networks. They would rather destroy them simultaneously than have them hacked. The Johns were like placid, unruffled reference librarians in demeanor. They were possibly the most boring people in the world.

Mathematical geniuses had devised the access code for the phone. Using a series of tones that corresponded to a number sequence that could not possibly be used except by direct order from the CEO of B.S., and then only with the joint approval of two designated vice presidents of B.S., the phone was fail-safe. Nothing could go wrong.

It had been over a decade since THE BUTTON had been in operation, and the Smiths had been flawless in their attention to their duty.

On the morning of September 16th at 10:07 a.m., the phone rang.

The John Smith on duty reacted instantly and pushed the button.

Planes fell from the sky, missiles shot upward from silos and submarines, trains collided, tens of thousands of stoplights stopped working, resulting in myriad accidents all over the earth. Electric grids crashed, financial systems crashed, nuclear weapons exploded, chaos erupted. Armageddon began.

A four-year-old boy in Cincinnati had taken the cell phone out of his mother's purse and accidentally dialed the wrong number.

So much for B.S.